LIFE IS A HELP YOURSELF BUFFET

LIFE
IS A
HELP
YOURSELF
BUFFET

FERN J FRANKS

First paperback edition 2024

Book design by Publishing Push

ISBN 978-1-80541-673-9 (paperback)
ISBN 978-1-80541-674-6 (ebook)

Preface

After years of caring for elderly parents, Marcie finds herself alone for the first time at the age of 50. She jumps into marriage with the first man to show her kindness, oblivious to his controlling nature and his preoccupation with money. She lives to regret this hasty decision, realising too late that Adrian is not the man she thought he was. In fact she did not really know him at all.

Adrian is very clever according to all who know him and having had the childhood most boys would be envious of, doting parents, private schooling, expensive presents at Christmas and just about everything money can afford, it was surprising then to witness his erratic behaviour which often left a lot to be desired, frequently making rash decisions and losing a lot of money. Not the sort of behaviour you would expect of someone privately educated who ought to know better than to keep falling down pot holes. Of course, his parents bailed him out every time by downsizing to smaller properties, reducing them to their current circumstances of a small rented flat on a rather downtrodden estate. This was now a bone of contention with Adrian's father who was humiliated by his current reduced circumstances, all caused by his prodigal son. The heated arguments between father and son became an everyday occurrence. It was obvious to his father that Adrian had little control over his finances and his boss seemed to be controlling his entire life. Adrian said he was only acting on his boss's instructions and people took advantage of him, forcing him into bad investments.

His mother however, thought that helping him out financially was the only right and proper thing to do. After all, he was their only son.

After the marriage, Adrian became increasingly agitated about the fact that Marcie did not appear to have any money at all, merely a current account with very little funds in it. How she had managed to survive all these years on so little he was at a loss to understand. He knew the family home had been sold and he had it on good authority (by someone he knew at the bank) that the money from the sale had been processed through Marcie's account. So where was the money? If indeed she did have money, she certainly kept it well hidden. But for all this, Marcie never for one moment envisaged being used by her husband as a foil for his own misdemeanours and inadequacies. With alarming speed she was arrested and taken into police custody and was now awaiting trial with the possibility of a custodial sentence hanging over her. Whatever Adrian had done, he had been very clever in laying all the blame at her door and exonerating himself.

Chapter One

If there was one thing Marcie couldn't stand, it was people shouting in her face. The junior barrister in front of her seemed to be working up a bit of a temper. There was spittle flying everywhere and his cold, steely eyes seemed to bear into her soul.

She was at a loss to know how she could have offended him so much. It wasn't as though she was being deliberately obtuse. She couldn't answer his questions because, quite simply, she genuinely had no idea what he was talking about, but if he thought for one minute that by raising his voice in order to intimidate her, she would become submissive and make a full confession, then he was very much mistaken. She wasn't about to confess to the crime she was accused of having committed.

"There's no need to shout. I'm not deaf and kindly conduct yourself in a manner befitting a court of law!" she admonished, momentarily feeling the shift of power. The words had tumbled out of her mouth before she could stop them.

It was after this exchange that the judge intervened and before she knew it she was being ushered into a side room awaiting the jury's verdict. She asked the court usher to fetch a glass of water as she had a bad headache and was starting to feel sick. Digging her fingernails into the glass of her watch face, she prized it open and removed the little blue tablet which nestled within it. She placed the tablet under her tongue and quickly replaced the glass as she knew she only had a few seconds before the usher returned. Leaning back in her chair, she rested her head against the wall, feeling the coldness penetrate her scalp, she closed her eyes. How on earth had it come this, she asked herself? Her solicitor had advised her that she could be looking at a custodial sentence of around five years. During the preceding months leading up to the trial she racked her brains to try to make sense of everything. A huge sum of money had gone missing from the company funds and the police were laying everything at her door.

The jury appeared to be remarkably quick at reaching their decision. She didn't know if this was a good sign or a bad one. She asked the usher what he thought about it but he said you could never tell which way a verdict would go. Back in the dock she stared at the sea of faces before her. The feeling of nausea was getting worse and her head was now pounding. Rivers of sweat were coursing down her spine, drenching her whole body from the roots of her hair to the tips of her toes. The judge was now addressing the jury but she could only see their lips moving and couldn't hear what they were saying. It was as though she was watching a movie with the sound turned off. She really felt as though she was going to be sick at any minute and was starting to panic when all of a sudden her forehead hit the floor with a loud bang. She opened her eyes momentarily and saw rivers of blood all around her; then everything went black.

Chapter Two

Leander swung his car into the parking lot and was just getting out when he spotted Jasmine. She was carrying a large suitcase and two black plastic bin bags. He watched her as she struggled down the steps from the railway station and it was only when she lifted her head that he noticed the black eye and bruising down one side of her face.

"What on earth happened to you?" he shouted. He had a good idea who was responsible even before she answered. Her brother Dean was handy with his fists, especially when he couldn't get his own way. He could feel his anger mounting. Her face looked a mess. His drug habit was getting out of control and Jasmine had threatened to shop him on more than one occasion if he didn't sort himself out, although knowing Jasmine as he did, this was unlikely to happen. He was her brother.

"I've had enough. I've moved out," she said, avoiding eye contact. He could see the tears forming in her eyes and immediately felt sorry for her. He opened the boot of the car and took the suitcase and bin bags from her.

"We'll put your stuff in here for now. Have you got anywhere to go?"

"No not yet sir."

He opened the glove compartment and took out a pair of Ray Bans and handed them to her.

"Here, put these on. If Huxley sees that black eye he's likely to start asking questions."

She eagerly put them on.

"Wait in the car. I'll go and speak to him. He's put me on the Green case for the next few weeks to see what we can come up with. I will need assistance, so you and Chris can help me." "Not sure he'll agree to that sir" she said, at once feeling despondent again. She felt as though her whole life was falling apart around her at the moment.

"Oh yes he will. He owes me a few favours. I could rake up lots of muck on him, the things that have gone on over the years, and he knows it." He then disappeared into the building and Jasmine jumped into the passenger seat, a feeling of relief washing over her. She'd always liked Lee; he was not only a good policeman but a thoroughly decent human being. Chris was the new boy. He'd only joined the force six months ago and had already got himself into hot water with the Super. Jasmine wasn't sure of all the details but she knew that it was Lee that saved the day and prevented him from getting his marching orders, stating the fact that if he'd been briefed properly and given the correct instructions the incident wouldn't have occurred. On returning to the car he gave her an update on where they were at with the case.

"Chris is down at the courts this morning. He'll ring me later with the verdict," he said, inserting the key in the ignition.

"That would be the trial of Mrs Green, his wife?"

"Yes. They've not been married very long. The tax office opened a file on her husband for tax evasion. He's appeared in court on several occasions over the past ten years, but he's walked free on every occasion."

"Due to lack of evidence?"

"Exactly, and he's good at covering his tracks so that nothing is ever down to him. They call him Houdini."

"I heard about the incident regarding the burnt out car. All the company's tax records just happened to be in the boot."

"That's happened on two occasions. Once, you can believe. Twice seems like carelessness. Who would risk it a second time?"

"We must have missed something sir. There has to be some minor detail that's been overlooked. Most liars make a mistake sooner or later."

"We've got to go over every detail of this case, and I mean everything."

"Did you ever interview him?"

"Yes, on a couple of occasions. I found him arrogant and uncooperative. He says very little and what he does say is vague and elusive. Answers every question with a question of his own, some little nugget for you to take home and think about."

"I know the type" she laughed.

"He's slipped off the hook too many times for my liking, but not this time. I'm determined to nail this joker even if it's the last case I ever work on." His mobile rang and he snatched it up off the dashboard.

"Yes Chris, how did it go? What? Alright, get down to the hospital and keep me posted."

"What's happened sir?"

"Mrs Green collapsed in court, sustaining a head injury. Chris ran over to her and couldn't find a pulse. They've carted her off to the hospital."

Chapter Three

"You can bunk up with me for now if you like Jasmine" said Leander, at the end of their shift. It had been a tedious day, examining files and reading through endless reports.

"Thanks very much sir."

"Call me Lee from now on. Can you rustle up some supper whilst I take a shower?"

"I can. I love cooking!"

They spent a lovely evening chatting over their meal with a glass of wine. Lee told her about his ex wife and how she'd left him for a much younger man. He'd heard rumours that he knocked her about a bit, but he didn't say any of this to Jasmine. If she wanted to live her life like that then more fool her. Who was he to interfere? Jasmine thought his wife must have been half mad to give up a good bloke like Lee. He may be nearly fifty years old but he didn't look it and he certainly didn't act it. She, in turn, told him about her brother Dean and how he came to be involved in the drugs scene. It had started during his last year at school, smoking the odd tab of Cannabis but over a short space of time it had escalated to the hard stuff. He then started nicking things to sell, anything he could lay his hands on, to help fund his habit. She did manage to get him into rehab once but after being discharged he lapsed back into his old habits.

"He always did have an addictive personality, even as a child. He could never do things by halves. He always went over the top."

Lee emptied the last of the wine into her glass. He'd seen this happen many times over the years, sometimes with tragic consequences and he resolved to try to help Dean get back on the road to normality before it was too late.

"I'm not sure that Dean even wants to be helped anymore. He's given up on himself" she said.

Lee washed the dishes whilst Jasmine had a shower. When she emerged from the bathroom, she wasn't sure what to do as she had no idea where she was going to sleep.

"There's only one double bed" said Lee, on sensing her nervousness. "But it's a king size and I promise to keep to my own side of the bed. I'm too old for sleeping on couches, those days are long gone! Hop in."

Jasmine was secretly delighted and wouldn't have minded if he didn't keep to his own side of the bed. Climbing between the sheets, a feeling of contentment washed over her. She hadn't felt this good about life in a long time and fell into a peaceful sleep.

The following morning, Jasmine fired up her laptop. Lee had asked her to look at all Adrian's company employee records. Huxley was given a tip off that Adrian had paid one of his employees over £100,000. All he'd been given was the name Reg. Huxley failed to find anyone on the books with that name. Rumour had it that this employee had kicked up a fuss and was demanding the return of his investment, plus interest. Having consulted a good solicitor, the case was heard in court and Adrian had to pay up. Lee knew it was a long shot but if they could find out who this person was, he might then be willing to talk. It would be a starting point. Lee had then departed for the station for the usual morning briefing with Superintendent Huxley.

Chapter Four

Marcie opened her eyes, briefly scanning the room. She was in a side ward. Good. That meant that she wouldn't have to face questions from other people. On her left sat a young police constable who hadn't noticed her open her eyes as he had his head down studying what looked like a diary of some sort. She supposed that he'd come to escort her to the prison. She quickly closed her eyes again, basking in the glory of the chance to remain in bed a little while longer and the solitude to gather her wits. Her head still ached but all she could think about now was lying still so that the constable wouldn't realise she'd woken up and start firing questions at her. She'd had enough of answering questions during the trial. How on earth had she got herself into this terrible mess? Having made a pact with herself before leaving home earlier, she resolved not to shed any tears. It would serve no purpose. She'd got herself into this mess and she would just have to get on with it. What on earth had possessed her to marry someone like Adrian in the first place? Her best friend Candice had warned her that he wasn't the right man for her and that she'd live to regret it. How she wished now that she'd paid more attention to her at the time. Candice had knocked around a bit and had a few unsavoury relationships herself, so she knew what she was talking about. Her last boyfriend had been deported after smashing the flat to bits and hurling the bed through a plate glass window, frightening all the neighbours. Candice said it wasn't as bad as it seemed. He was just angry. Although their relationship was a volatile one, it didn't appear to bother Candice. She loved him for the colourful character that he was. Someone had 'grassed him up' she said. He'd been dealing in drugs and was 'nicked' for money laundering. It didn't bother her either that he had a wife and three children somewhere or other, whom he'd abandoned leaving no forwarding address. Candice said she was a 'stroppy bitch' prone to violent outbursts and he'd left because she was making his life a misery. Marcie knew that Candice was a free spirit and lived her life on a knife edge most of the time but despite everything she was very loyal, loving, made her laugh and proved to be a good friend over the years. She also knew that Candy would have no qualms about visiting her in prison. She just didn't care what other people thought. It was none of their business. Feeling the tears welling up under her closed eyelids she fought them down, casting her mind back to the day of her wedding. The bride was supposed to be the centre of attention but she had been largely ignored by Adrian and most of his relatives, especially his mother who hadn't spoken a single word to her throughout the whole day. She knew instinctively that something wasn't quite right about the whole affair but she chose to ignore it, telling herself not to be so paranoid. She was imagining things. But she hadn't been imagining things for as soon as they arrived back home Adrian started. Firstly he demanded to see all her bank books and statements. When she told him that she only had her current account which held £32 and a few pence, he flew into a rage and demanded to know where the rest of her money was. Convincing him that there wasn't any proved to be an impossibility. He'd had it on good authority he said, that the money from the sale of the family home had gone through her account together with a deposit of one million pounds from the sale of some antique or other. When she asked him where he'd got the information from he refused to enlighten her. Feeling her scalp start to tingle, she realised that the information must have come from one of the bank employees. Someone had been feeding Adrian information regarding her account. She'd told nobody about the antique deal, absolutely nobody. The following morning her car disappeared off the driveway. Adrian had sold it and pocketed the cash. The fact that the car wasn't his to sell didn't bother him. 'You don't own anything now, it's all mine' he'd said. He'd only married her for her money. Adrian honestly thought she had money. He'd been given reassurance of the fact by someone at the bank and he positively refused to believe otherwise. He stormed out of the house and drowned his sorrows in the pub, arriving home so drunk he could hardly stand. After being sick all over the lounge carpet he passed out on the sofa. Marcie went upstairs, packed all her possessions, which were few, then left.

Chapter Five

"Lee there's a lady waiting to speak to you. She asked to speak to whoever was in charge of the Green case, would that be you sir?"

"Yes. Thanks Daniel. Where is she?"

"Interview room one. She declined a coffee."

Lee made his way down the corridor with a feeling of optimism. Mrs Green's trial had obviously brought people out of the woodwork. If people were volunteering to speak to him, so much the better as they had no new leads as yet.

"Good morning. I'm Detective Inspector Purslow." He seated himself opposite a tall slim lady with wild curly hair and bright green eyes. Before he had a chance to say anything more she launched into her tirade.

"That Adrian Green's a monster! He's used Marcie....."

"And you are?" interrupted Lee

"Oh, sorry, I'm Candice, Marcie's best friend. We were at school together."

"How long have you known Marcie?"

"Oh practically all our lives. We're the same age. As I said, we were at school together. Look officer, I know Marcie. She's hasn't got a dishonest bone in her body. Whatever happened to that money that went missing, it had nothing to do with Marcie. Believe me, I know! The fact that he's managed to lay the blame at her door just proves how clever and manipulative he is, and how stupid you lot are for believing him. Whatever nonsense he's come out with, well I can tell you now, it's all nonsense. The man's a first class chump!"

Lee couldn't help but agree with her on that last point. It was obvious to him that there was no hard evidence and he expressed his surprise at the time when he heard the court date was fixed and Marcie was to stand trial.

"Did she give you any information regarding her role within the company, by any chance? Anything at all that you think may be useful to us?"

"When she first went there she said it was all a bit peculiar."

"Peculiar? In what way?"

"Well, she was expected to keep the books and that, but Adrian wouldn't give her any of the passwords to access the necessary spreadsheets, or whatever. He used to turn the screen round so that she couldn't see, type the password in himself then turn the screen round again so that she could get on with her work. She had to keep asking, 'Can you log me into the sales ledger? Can you log me into the purchase ledger? I need to get into the nominal ledger, can you log me in?' It got on her nerves. He didn't trust her. I mean, honestly, what did he think she was going to do? She was hopeless with computers anyway. She only had a very basic knowledge. I often had to show her how to do things, very basic things actually. She could no more mastermind embezzling funds than a five year old could."

"I see, and did he eventually begin to trust her when she'd been there a while?"

"No never. Another funny thing happened too. Listen to this and make of it what you will" she gushed, eyes sparkling like diamonds. Lee thought there was something very engaging about this lady. She was smart witted and full of energy. He liked her. "Well, one day, Adrian crashed all the computer system. Don't ask me what he was doing. Heaven only knows. They lost a full day's work because of it. All the office staff complained that they'd have to re-enter all their invoices or whatever. They hadn't backed up their files or anything, so it was all lost. At four thirty every afternoon they used to do – what did Marcie call it? 'A System Save,' or something like that. It's done daily for that very reason, so that you don't lose all your work if the system goes down. Well, at four twenty two exactly, on this particular day, it all crashed. Adrian sent everyone home early, which Marcie thought was a bit strange. He made no attempt to retrieve the work. Marcie stayed in the office all night and worked on the system, with the help of Stuart. Stuart was a computer programmer. Between them they got everything back on the system and by seven o'clock the following morning, the system was up and running again. Marcie wasn't expecting a pat on the back or anything, but Adrian was furious when he found out what they'd done! It was almost as though he'd planned the whole thing."

Lee had a very good idea why Adrian would be annoyed that his little plan had been foiled. He was up to no good.

"Right, well thank you very much for coming to see us Candice, you've been most helpful. Is there a number we can contact you on, in case we need to talk to you again?"

"Sure. Call me Candy." She scribbled away on the notepad which Lee put in front of her.

Christopher waited until the coast was clear then crept quietly into the ward. Marcie was sound asleep. He opened the bedside locker and retrieving the diary out of his pocket, he placed it back into her handbag. He made his way back out into the corridor to find a lady hovering near the nurses' station. He sat himself down in one of the plastic chairs outside the ward doorway. The lady made her way over to him and sat herself down beside him.

"Are you Constable Potter by any chance?"

"Yes" said Christopher, noting that the lady seemed a little out of breath as though she'd been running but judging by her bulky frame, he doubted it.

"I'm Margaret Wilkinson. Peggy. I was Marcie's next door neighbour for years. I've known her since she was a young girl."

Chris's ears picked up immediately. Here was his chance to

gain background information. "I see. You'll know Marcie quite well then?" he ventured. She was nicely spoken and seemed openly friendly, although he knew from past experience that this was no criteria in which to judge a person's character.

"Oh yes indeed. We became great friends, despite the age difference between us. She had a terrible time of it to be honest with you. I felt desperately sorry for her. She's such a kind, generous spirited girl you see. I always think that people take advantage of someone like that, but you don't expect it from the parents do you?"

"Are you saying they ill treated her in some way?"

"To some tune! They made her life a misery. The mother was only interested in her elder sister Deidre. She had no time for Marcie. As for the father, well his temper was legendary. It didn't take much to set him off either. The poor girl could do nothing to please either of them. She, being the youngest and unmarried was responsible for looking after them both. She worked full-time too. She never stopped. Cooking, cleaning, washing, ironing and shopping. Of course nothing was ever done right. She never complained though. I never once heard her say a bad word about either of them, even though she had just cause on numerous occasions. I'm happy to say that she did eventually move out. After what happened, she couldn't go back. She didn't feel safe. She didn't know what he was going to do next."

"Did something happen to bring about the move?"

"It was scandalous! Her father's lucky he didn't end up in prison. When Marcie moved out, Deidre was furious. She called Marcie every name under the sun. Deidre married young and moved away, which only left Marcie and her brother Peter. Peter was an alcoholic. He was such a nice natured boy, just like Marcie in many ways but he started drinking at an early age and couldn't seem to stop. Marcie tried to help him as best she could. He got ill eventually and was taken into hospital. He turned yellow. When they opened him up, there was nothing they could do for him. His liver and spleen were too far gone for them to do anything poor boy. Marcie contacted the council and social services and managed to secure him a nice little flat but he died before he got to move into it. Marcie was heartbroken. They were very close although, due to his constant state of inebriation he was of no help to her regarding the situation with the parents. It was after Peter's death that Marcie started going out in the evenings. That didn't go down well with the parents. I mean, honestly constable, she wasn't a teenager. She was in her forties! The poor girl was entitled to a social life. She worked hard enough. She deserved some kind of life. Let's face it she didn't have much of a life stuck at home all the time with that miserable pair."

"What happened to make her move out then?"

"She'd been out somewhere and came back around midnight. Her father was waiting for her in the kitchen. He was livid."

"Why?"

"That's the whole point constable. They didn't like her going out in the evenings. I think they were frightened of her meeting some nice young man and marrying him. There'd be nobody to look after them then. Deidre made it quite clear that she had no intention of having them stay with her, although her house is enormous according to Marcie, so it's not as though she didn't have the space. As soon as she entered the kitchen he walloped her around the head with the poker. It was cast iron! The awful thing is constable... and this is what upset me the most..." At this point she started to weep and fumbled about in her handbag for a handkerchief, then mopped her eyes. "I'm sorry officer..."

"That's quite alright Mrs Wilkinson. In your own time..."

"He went to bed and left her there. Flat out on the kitchen floor she was, in a pool of blood. When he came downstairs the following morning, she was still lying there. She'd been there all night. Well, he panicked then didn't he? He thought he'd killed her. It was the mother who telephoned for the ambulance. He busied himself burying the poker in the back garden. I watched him digging a big hole near the oak tree. One of the neighbours on the other side witnessed it too. Fortunately she was still alive, just. After that little episode she never went back. The social services came to speak to her in hospital but she wouldn't press charges. She never went back home though. In fact she never saw either of them again. Deidre got them both into a nursing home and sold the house. She then sold all the furniture and pocketed the lot. A more selfish girl I never did meet! Poor Marcie got nothing, although the sale of the house did go through Marcie's bank account initially as Deidre only had a joint account with her husband and she wanted to keep it separate. She had her eye on a much larger house you see, much to her husband's annoyance, there's only the two of them. They have no children." She paused for breath, dabbing her eyes again.

"Let me get us both a nice cup of tea Mrs Wilkinson. Marcie may be awake by then."

"That's very kind, thank you. Call me Peggy."

Chapter Six

Jasmine parked the car on a bit of waste land opposite a row of neat little cottages. She checked her notebook to make sure she had the right house number, then made her way up the driveway to the door and rang the bell. A young boy answered the door. He was dressed in his football kit and due to the fact that he looked very clean and smart, Jasmine assumed he was just on his way out to the field.

"Hello, I'm looking for Gina. Is she in?"

"Yes she is." He shouted over his shoulder, "Mum there's a lady constable here to speak to you. I'm off now. See you later." Turning towards her he said, "Go on through, she's in the kitchen." She heard the door slam shut behind her as she made her way along the hallway. The kitchen was surprisingly large for such a small cottage and she found Gina preparing the evening meal.

"I'm sorry to disturb you Gina. I'd just like a quick word, if you can spare me a few minutes of your time," she said, noting the large casserole dish, which appeared to be full of chicken drumsticks and vegetables.

"You must be Sergeant Simmonds? This is about that rogue Adrian Green, I presume? I'll just get this in the oven. Sit yourself down and I'll be with you in a couple of minutes." Jasmine sat down at the kitchen table and watched Gina as she chopped some herbs and fresh lemons, then added them to the dish. She placed the lid on top and took it over to the oven. Washing her hands at the sink, she tossed aside her apron and offered to make some coffee, which Jasmine declined.

"He's still under investigation then?" she said, sitting herself down on the opposite side of the table.

"I'm afraid so. There are one or two things which have come to our attention that we'd like some clarification on. Adrian isn't saying much."

"There's no change there then."

"It makes our life very difficult. He won't clarify even the basic questions. Did you by any chance invest money with Adrian's company?"

"Yes quite a bit actually. A lump sum of £25,000, but shortly afterwards my circumstances changed and I needed the money, so I asked for it to be refunded. That's when all the trouble started."

"He wouldn't pay up?"

"Correct." She shifted nervously in her seat before continuing, "My husband left me you see. I'd just given birth to twins, two boys. He couldn't handle it. Just packed his bags and cleared off. I never saw him again."

"Goodness. I'm sorry to hear that. How sad. Has he been in touch since?"

"No. It's been hard, I don't mind telling you, but I'm surviving. I wasn't the only one wanting to cash in my investment either. There were eight of us but I was the only one that received a payout."

"Oh?"

"I went to a different solicitor than the others. The courts threw their case out. My uncle's a barrister, which helped. He got me a solicitor who could handle this sort of thing. I not only got my investment back but received compensation for unfair dismissal and being wrongly advised regarding the investment in the first place. Adrian had to pay all the court costs. He was fuming."

"But you did get your money back?"

"Oh yes, I got £100,000 in the end. The trial went on for a long time and it was very stressful. I've only worked part-time since. My nerves were shot to pieces. I've invested half of it for the boys, for when they're older. It'll give them a bit of a start in life. The rest went on this place."

"When you approached Adrian and asked for the return of your investment, what was his response?"

"He said it wasn't possible. I'd signed the paperwork. End of story. He refused to discuss it further, but I was desperate you see."

"Can you give me the names of the other seven people involved?" she asked, taking out her notebook and pen. "Are any of them still employed there, or have they all left?"

"I've no idea. I left some time ago. I can give you five names but the other two were outsiders. The others will probably know. Adrian and Roger are not to be trusted. They've been robbing people blind for years! If Adrian's past is finally catching up with him, then I'm glad. It's not before time. Robbing people of their life savings! It's obscene the way he's been allowed to get away with it!"

"What was your position within the company?"

"I was Roger Moorcroft's secretary, that's Adrian's partner. He started the company and ran it single handed for some years before bringing Adrian in. I never trusted either of them to be honest. They were a shifty pair. There was something very odd about the way they operated. Within a month of working there I sensed instinctively that things weren't right. Not only that, Roger could be very abrupt and rude when the mood took him."

"When you say something was amiss, could you be more specific? In what way were things 'not right' exactly?"

"Well, at the end of the first financial year, the shareholders were expecting their dividends but nothing was paid out. There was an almighty rumpus with investors wanting to pull out."

"Was the issue resolved eventually?"

"That's the mystery. I don't think it ever was, not to my knowledge anyway. Then there was that awful incident with Harriet Barry."

"Was she an employee?"

"Yes, a typist. Adrian befriended her in the same way that he did with Marcie, but she made a fatal mistake."

"A mistake in what way?"

"She inherited quite a large sum of money. It was bequeathed to her from her uncle who left it to her in his will, as the only girl in the family at the time. Adrian can smell money a mile off. He promised to marry her and she was persuaded to part with the money by way of investing it in the company. He spun her some nonsense about being able to double it in five years or whatever, but as soon as he got his hands on the money he dumped her. She committed suicide."

Jasmine felt her heart sink to her boots. 'The poor deluded creature' she thought. "How did Adrian react to this?"

"He carried on as normal, as thought it had never happened. Harriet's parents had quite a lot to say on the matter, but as far as I'm aware, nothing came of it."

Chapter Seven

When Marcie next opened her eyes, there was no sign of the policeman. Glancing through the window, she noticed that it was dark, so she assumed he must have gone home, perhaps to return in the morning. The ward seemed deathly quiet compared to the hustle and bustle of the day shifts and she could just make out the light over the nurse's station through the open doorway. Basking in the luxury of the solitude to collect her thoughts, her mind began to wander back to her younger years when life was still full of promise and hope for the future. She suddenly remembered a party held by her school friend Juliet. It was her tenth birthday and there were six pupils from their class plus one best friend. There was much hilarity when the desserts were served because Juliet had hidden a blue thimble in one of the puddings, the recipient being the old maid. Of course it was only an old wives' tale but Marcie was mortified all the same to discover it in her own dish. The way everyone stared at her then laughed had quite ruined her evening. She never saw any of them again after that evening as they all passed for the grammar school, whist she was relegated to the secondary modern, much to her mother's disgust. 'If you'd worked harder you wouldn't be in this position' she admonished. Looking back now she realised that her mother was probably right. She'd just coasted along, although she always tried her best in everything she did but it just never seemed good enough. Perhaps if she'd been smarter she wouldn't have found herself in this dreadful position in the first place. Most of her friends seemed to have married men with good prospects and there was no doubt that some of them had done rather well for themselves, despite the fact that in Marcie's view they had what she would term as 'very loose morals'. None of that mattered in the long run. It certainly didn't matter to the men they'd married. Trying to make sense of it all was a waste of her time, this she knew for a fact as she'd spent her entire life trying to please her parents, to no avail. Her sister Deidre on the other hand, could do no wrong. At eighteen, Deidre had met and married a lovely man called Dennis Fordham. Marcie always thought he was far too good for the likes of her sister, who could be extremely demanding if she didn't get her own way. But he clearly adored her and Marcie got along very well with him. Not that she saw much of them, as having moved a good distance away after their marriage due to his job being relocated in the South, it was usually a flying visit at Christmas. Even this was sometimes too much for Marcie as she often overheard Deidre and her mother discussing her behind her back. 'There are winners and losers in this life mum' said Deidre, 'and I'm afraid our Marcie's one of the losers.' As she lay in her hospital bed, she turned the phrase over in her mind 'one of life's losers.' She'd certainly made a mistake in marrying Adrian, but did that really make her a loser in life? Right at this very moment, it certainly seemed like it.

When Lee reached the flat, there was no sign of Jasmine. He felt his heart give a jolt. Had she moved out already? He certainly hoped not as he was enjoying having company again after all the lonely years since his divorce. Jasmine was certainly good company and they laughed a lot when they were together. He checked the kitchen table to see if she'd left him a note but as there was no sign of one he went in to the bedroom and checked the wardrobe and the bathroom to see if her things were still there. To his great relief, they were. Half an hour later she returned. He greeted her at the door.

"Your eye's looking better" he said.

"I've camouflaged it with a bit of make-up. I found the mysterious Reg that the Super failed to spot."

"You're joking? He went through those files with a fine tooth comb, or so he said at the time."

"Well he can't have given it his full attention! Reg is the nickname of a lady called Regina, known as Gina to all her workmates and affectionately known as Reg to close family and friends."

"So you've been to see her?"

"I certainly have. I'll tell you all after supper. Chris is coming round at seven o'clock so he can eat with us. We'll confer notes and decide what to do next," she smiled at him, rolling up her sleeves. "What's in the freezer?"

Peggy was enjoying the young Constable Potter's company. She lived alone and her only son, having married a Scottish girl, moved to Perth after the marriage and she rarely saw them these days, even at Christmas. She offered to pay for the tea but he told her the ward sister had brewed it fresh for them from her own kettle.

"They do seem a very pleasant lot here don't they?" she mused, sipping her tea.

"I've encountered much worse in my time."

"Yes, I'm sure."

"Can you think of anything else that might help us with our enquiries Peggy? The more information we can gather the better chance we have of putting together the whole picture of what actually occurred."

"Well," she hesitated, looking over her shoulder to make sure that they were alone and that nobody was listening in to their conversation before continuing, "I shouldn't really say this, it not being common knowledge. Marcie never told anyone about it but I found out by accident through a friend of a friend if you get my drift."

Chris's ears picked up again and he leaned forward across the table so that he could hear, as Peggy's voice had dropped to a whisper.

"Marcie always had a thing about rummaging around in antiques markets. It was one of her favourite hobbies. One day, about a year ago, she purchased a piece of artwork, a painting. She only paid about £20 for it. The stall holder was a little old lady, who was oblivious to the true value of it. Where the painting originally came from I've no idea, a house clearance probably. Well, now here's the thing officer, and you wouldn't believe what happened next but it's true I tell you. When Marcie got the painting home, after studying it for quite some time, she had it valued. It was a Rembrandt. Not a copy either, it was the original! What are the chances of that happening? It's something you read about in works of fiction! I only got to hear about it because one of our ladies at the Women's Institute has a market stall opposite this lady in question. I've no idea what she sells. I think someone said she manned it with her husband. Something to do with war memorabilia I think. Anyway, once Marcie realised its true value, she returned the money to this Irish lady with the valuation note Sotheby's had given her. She wouldn't keep it herself. She said she couldn't have lived with her conscience, knowing that she'd done a little old lady out of that sort of money."

"How much was it worth?"

"I'm not sure, but it was an awful lot of money, as you can imagine. I mean, a Rembrandt!" She paused again momentarily to sip her tea then continued "Of course, word got around amongst all the stall holders. The Irish lady upped sticks after that and bought a huge property in Ireland."

"Do you happen to know this Irish lady's name?"

"Mrs Liversedge I think, or Livesey, something like that. The house was near Donegal. She grew up there as a girl. No one saw her again after she left."

"Does your friend from the WI still run this stall?"

"Oh yes, I think so, at weekends. Her husband works at the local school; he's a history teacher there. That's where they met. Marjorie was the school secretary for a good number of years until she had the children, then she developed health problems. She helps out in the local charity shop on Friday mornings now. She's one of these busy little bees, always got to be on the go doing something or other. I don't have that problem myself," she chuckled.

"Neither do I Peggy!" he laughed, getting out his notebook.

Chapter Eight

Leander parked his car in the supermarket car park then strolled across to the cabins which stood on a patch of waste ground to the rear of the unit which sold coffee and bacon sandwiches. He bought himself a coffee and strolled around the back and looked at all the cabins, six in total. One was a hive of activity with people queuing outside. They seemed to be collecting parcels. He spotted a lady carrying a laptop and watched her as she made her way into the fourth cabin, a border terrier trailing behind on a lead. He followed her in and waited until she'd spoken to the receptionist before approaching the desk. A detailed discussion was in progress, the lady with the dog was explaining that she'd just bought a new laptop and couldn't get her emails working properly. Her brother-in-law had set it all up for her she said, then after two days it all disappeared. Lee smiled to himself, remembering his own clumsy attempts at setting himself up. He waited until the receptionist had taken all her details before showing his ID. The dog suddenly started barking and shot under the counter.

"Hamish! Come here!" she shouted, cursing under her breath. "I'm so sorry," she said, trying to hold on to his lead. "He's probably spotted a spider or something. He knows I don't like them," she laughed, now on her knees crawling under the counter to rescue him.

"It'll be Benji, Stuart's rabbit. Well, it's his daughter's actually, but he comes here when there's nobody in the house. He's a house bunny. He's only a baby and his daughter collects him on her way home from school usually" said the receptionist. She lifted the counter to let the lady out, as she was carrying the dog under her arm.

"I'll call in tomorrow afternoon if that's alright?" she said, making for the door.

"Yes sir, what can we do for you?" asked the receptionist. Lee told her he'd arranged a meeting with Stuart.

"I thought that chapter had closed with the court case" Stuart said sheepishly.

Lee ignored the remark and sat himself down in the only available vacant chair before saying, "How did you come to work for Adrian Green?"

"It was Roger that employed me initially. He'd had two attempts at computerisation but it had failed on both occasions, so he'd gone back to a manual system. He brought me in to help set things up. I designed a bespoke system, based on his business needs at the time."

"How long were you in his employment for?"

"Oh about five years in total."

"And you left of your own accord?"

"Yes. I was bored. It was alright in the beginning. The first year, I spent setting everything up, then we did a parallel run alongside the manual system, just to see if it would work. When we switched over, it was just a matter of ironing out discrepancies and modifying things, but the business expanded so quickly, with the client base increasing rapidly, that we sort of out grew the system. So the next couple of years were spent trying to sort that out. It was a while before we were running smoothly again. The last year of my employment there it was just a case of keeping things ticking over. There wasn't much for me to do really. I felt like a spare part, so I decided to go back working freelance, like I used to."

"And you bought this place?"

"Lord no! I only rent it. My client base doesn't run to buying an office I'm afraid. My wife's a beautician. She bought a small salon and runs it with the help of a young apprentice. I help her out with the mortgage on that. It keeps her happy."

"I want to talk to you about that incident with the system crashing. You helped Marcie recover all the lost files I'm told. What happened exactly?"

"Oh, that! I'm not sure what went on actually. I'd left their employment by that time. Roger blamed it on Adrian. It was Marcie that rang me asking for advice. I felt sorry for her, so I stayed with her until we'd got everything back on the system."

"Did you speak to Adrian or Roger before you left?"

"No. There was nobody around. I went home to bed for a couple of hours, then I telephoned Roger, who said Adrian was dealing with it. Marcie rang me to tell me Adrian didn't react well. He was shocked to see the system back up and running when he arrived at the office and wanted to know who was responsible. "

"Why would he be annoyed?"

"That's the bit that confused us both. The poor girl wasn't expecting a gold medal or anything, but a simple 'thank you' would have been nice. She was exhausted after staying up all night to put things right. She thought he'd be so pleased. They're an ungrateful pair. Roger's the brains behind the whole outfit, but heaven knows why he employed Adrian, he's clueless."

Lee fired a few more questions at Stuart but he suddenly became guarded in his comments and wouldn't be drawn on any questions relating to the business, stating that his job was to work on the system itself. The running of the actual business wasn't down to him, he said. Lee could see that he was being cagey and probably knew more than he was prepared to say, but knew he'd have to pay him another visit somewhere down the line. He thanked him and left.

"Dr Singh has requested no visitors for the time being. The patient is concussed and needs to rest. She won't be going anywhere for the next couple of days, so if you want to call back in a day or two..." the ward sister informed them. Chris thanked her then turned to Peggy.

"It looks like we're out of luck, for today at least. Can I offer you a lift home?"

"Oh that would be grand, constable. My buses are only one an hour. I never seem to time it right!" she chuckled. She followed him out to the car park and settled herself in the passenger seat before speaking again. "That young barrister in the court was very aggressive in my opinion. Is it normal practice to intimidate people like that? He was bordering on being downright rude."

"I'm inclined to agree with you there. As for it being normal practice, I hardly think so. Lack of experience in my opinion and the judge was right to intervene."

"Marcie held her own though. I nearly cheered when she admonished him."

"Has she had these black-outs before?"

"That's the legacy her father left her when he clouted her with that poker! She gets these thunderbolt migraines. They come on very suddenly without warning, poor girl."

"Thunderbolt migraines?"

"Yes, or something like that, thunderclap or whatever. Very severe they are. They knock you for six for a few hours. My road is just on the right, after the zebra crossing."

Chris drove the car to the end of the road and swung round in the circle at the bottom to face a smart semi with a very impressive rose garden to one side.

"Will you join me in a decent cup of tea?" she asked. "That grey water they serve up in there gives tea a bad name. I'll make us a sandwich."

Chris was about to refuse until she mentioned the sandwich. He'd had nothing to eat all day and was half starved. Half an hour later he was comfortable ensconced in the lounge with sandwiches and cake. He watched Peggy as she brought in a large china teapot and two decent sized mugs.

"Did Marcie ever mention Adrian buying a boat?" he asked, fully expecting her to deny all knowledge.

"Well, it's one of the first things they argued about. They'd only been married a day when her car disappeared off the driveway. She was about to telephone the police when Adrian told her he'd sold it. He used the money for his share in this boat which Roger had purchased."

"Was there a name? I know it's an odd question but most boats have a name don't they?"

"Yes I'm sure you're right, but I don't recall her ever mentioning it. Or maybe she did and it didn't register with me at the time. If I bring anything to mind I'll let you know, more tea?"

Chapter Nine

Jasmine had difficulty finding a space to park her car and ended up half a mile up the road. She liked to leave it where she could keep an eye on it. She knew this area well and car theft was rife, especially after dark. As she walked back to number nine, she took note of all the rubbish in people's front gardens. Old mattresses, broken bits of furniture, rusted bikes and the like. 'They don't even seem to have any proper curtains up at the windows' she mused to herself, 'just bits of rags.' The whole place looked grubby. Jasmine knew that no matter how poor she was, she would strive to at least make sure the place was clean and reasonably tidy. There was no excuse for living in squalor. Surprisingly, number nine was immaculate with neatly trimmed borders and rows of bedding plants. The garden was a mass of colour. She noted the Sanderson print curtains and glass vases lining the window. The front door opened before she had chance to ring the bell.

"If it's about last night's fiasco, you'll be wanting number fourteen" she said, flicking a duster to one side.

"Actually it's you I wanted. It is Grace isn't it?" said Jasmine.

"Yes."

"You used to work as a cleaner for Roger and Adrian. Is that correct?"

"Oh that pair of jokers. You'd better come in" she said, opening the door wide.

"I take it that you are no longer in their employment then?" asked Jasmine, seating herself at the kitchen table.

"No. I was asked to leave. They said I was gossiping too much with the staff."

"And they dismissed you for that?"

"I knew too much. I'd been there since the beginning. You just wouldn't believe the things that went on. Mind you, I felt sorry for Marcie. She was a nice person and the only one in that place that I had any time for. Adrian didn't deserve her. She was way too good for him. To think that Adrian had private schooling, well if he's the product of a private education, it's doesn't say much for the system. I used to enjoy it in the beginning. Things were relaxed and friendly. We used to have a good laugh but then Adrian turned up and things soon changed."

"He wasn't popular then?"

"Nobody liked him! He had a knack off sniffing out the weak and the vulnerable. Poor Marcie didn't stand a chance. He had a warped sense of his own importance. If there were any important visitors around I used to listen to him waffling and bluffing. I've never heard such nonsense. He used to talk about 'smashing the glass ceiling by using his business acumen and commercial awareness'. He had no difficulty in putting people in their place if he thought they were getting the upper hand. He'd hit back by quoting rules and regulations, this Act, that Act, bylaws etc. But for all that he was an absolute coward."

"Why do you say that?"

"He used to stir the pot, load the gun with the bullets, so to speak, then he'd leave someone else to fire the gun so that nobody could blame him for anything. Nothing was ever his fault. But he made some serious errors. His father bailed him out on two occasions. They had a beautiful five bedroom house on Wood Lane but when Adrian got in a financial mess they sold it and downsized to a smaller property. Two years down the line it happened again and they ended up selling everything including the caravan. They're in a rented flat now. His mother dotes on him but it led to some serious rows between Adrian and his father."

"Rumour has it that Adrian's very clever."

"Well, he certainly has a knack of reading people's emotions and preying on the vulnerable. As you are probably aware yourself, there are people in this world who are manipulators. Adrian was like that, the sort of person who would withhold vital information, crucial to the matter in hand, just so that he could retain the upper hand. Power, that's what motivates him, power over other people."

"Did you ever hear either Adrian or Roger mention the purchase of a boat?"

"Roger bought a boat, I believe. It's moored somewhere in the Greek Islands I think. He was a funny bloke was Roger. Hardly spoke to the staff and when he did it was usually to tell them off for something they'd failed to do. If he ever had to attend a function that required a partner, such as a dinner dance, he used to use an agency. The same lady used to accompany him. I probably shouldn't say this but it was rumoured that he and Adrian were an item, it you get my meaning. It wouldn't surprise me, but you can't believe all that you hear, people gossip."

"What about auditors?"

"I only ever saw them on one occasion. An elderly gentleman from a company called Anderson's. It's a well known firm of accountants. They're based in the town centre. He couldn't make sense of the books. He said he'd been doing his job for over fifty years. He was very experienced but he couldn't get his head around the files. Roger passed it over to Adrian, as usual. I don't know what occurred but we didn't see him again after that. It's rumoured that he was paid off, to keep his mouth shut. It was only a rumour mind. You know what folk are like."

"Was there a company accountant?"

"Roger was the accountant. I wouldn't trust him to do my books if I ran a business! They weren't nice people to work for. I've had some dodgy bosses in my time but there was something distinctly odd about those two. Don't get me wrong when I say that, I can rub along with most people, but they were up to no good. Then there was that business with the poor lass that committed suicide. It was a terrible business. It should never have happened."

"Yes I heard about that. You've been very helpful Grace. Thank you for your time. If you happen to think of anything else that might help us with our enquiries, give me a call." Jasmine placed her card on the table then left.

Chris made his way to Lee's apartment and rang the bell. He'd taken to having his evening meal with them in order to discuss the day's events and monitor their progress with the Green case. He looked forward to this part of the day as his own bedsit only had a small galley kitchen with a rickety cooker that took ages to get going these days. Jasmine had cooked Moroccan Lamb. The aroma of exotic spices hit his nostrils as Lee opened the door.

"Wow, something smells good," he said, following him through the hallway into the kitchen. Jasmine ladled the food out into bowls and Lee poured them all a glass of wine.

"Are we celebrating?"

"Hardly, Huxley was on my back again this morning. I'd nothing new to tell him."

"No new leads then?"

"No, they're all being cagey and saying very little. How did you get on today?"

"Well, I need to talk to you about something I did which wasn't strictly on the level if you know what I mean, but I thought it might help us."

"Shoot."

"When I went to the hospital, the nurse disappeared for a few seconds to get me a cup of tea and whilst she was gone, I looked in the bedside locker. Marcie's handbag was open and I could see a diary, so I removed it and started reading through some of the entries. Not that there was an awful lot in it, but what was there might be of use to us, so I took it to the office and photocopied the whole thing. I've got a record of all the entries but whether any of it will be of significance, only time will tell." He paused momentarily, checking Lee's face for clues, but when he didn't speak, decided to continue. "There's mention of this boat. I've been on to the Greek authorities. It's moored somewhere in Rhodes. Our contact is a guy named Mantos. He speaks very good English. I got on famously with him. They're going to check all the ports."

Jasmine was failing to see the significance of this piece of information but remained silent. Lee continued eating for a few minutes before making any comment.

"Don't worry about procedures in cases like this, it's not important. What is important is what they're using the boat for. If it's just for their own pleasure, all well and good. If it's for any other purpose, we could be in business. That's providing they find it of course. Rhodes is an island which makes it easier to pass the drugs on to the dealers."

Jasmine silently admonished herself for not seeing the obvious. She put it down to tiredness. It had been a long day.

Chapter Ten

Gerald dumped his bags in the hallway and made his way into the kitchen where his wife was waiting for him. She smiled at him and gushed "Welcome back darling!. I've missed you." She busied herself filling the kettle and asked him if he wanted tea or coffee. Something about her whole countenance instinctively told him that he'd made a huge mistake in coming back into the marital home. They'd been separated for 8 months when she suddenly decided she wanted to give the marriage another try, citing the fact that she'd made a terrible mistake in wanting to end the marriage and the affair with her significant other was at an end. Gerald wasn't at all sure that he believed her but gave her the benefit of the doubt after her tearful pleading and begging. The smile she'd just given him didn't carry any warmth. It was more the smile of an assassin who'd finally got their own way. Her eyes told a very different story to the one she was striving to portray.

"Where's Beth?" he asked, looking around him, then directly at her.

"She's....well, she's...gone."

"Gone? Gone where exactly?"

"She's left home. She wanted to be with her boyfriend."

"She's far too young to be leaving home to set up with a boyfriend. She's only sixteen!"

"Good heavens Gerald, we're not living in the dark ages! She's old enough to know her own mind!"

"Not at sixteen, she isn't. Have you two had a row?"

She ignored his question and turned her back, fussing with the coffee beans and delving into the cupboard looking for cups and saucers. He couldn't bear the thought of his darling Beth at the mercy of some young scoundrel who'd take advantage of her generous nature. The house just wouldn't be the same without her. She was part of the reason he'd decided to come back home. He knew that he'd have to find her. He'd make it his business to find her.

Beth was starting to feel the cold. She'd been sat on the wall opposite the bus station for over an hour and there was no sign of Ashley. He never was one for punctuality but he'd never been this late before and she was starting to feel tearful after the terrible row she'd had with her mother. Ashley had promised her that he'd look after her and take care of her but there was no sign of him. He lived on the other side of town and she didn't want to confront his mother because Beth wasn't flavour of the month, she not being good enough for her darling boy Ashley. She couldn't face the humiliation of going back home either. Picking up her suitcase, she headed towards the pub which was about a mile up the road. She hadn't enough money for a taxi but she could just about manage a drink at the bar. Her suitcase seemed to get heavier with every step and by the time she reached the pub she was about ready to drop and her feet were pinching in her best shoes. She was just about to cross the road when she spotted Ashley sat at one of the outside tables. He had his arm around a girl with long blonde hair and he was whispering something into her ear which made them both laugh. Suddenly they were kissing. Beth hid behind a tree, feeling hurt and confused. Could this girl be his cousin or something? It certainly wasn't his sister for he only had two brothers. From her hiding place she watched them for a further half hour. It was obvious that he'd totally forgotten about their arrangement. The pub forecourt was packed and she couldn't face a confrontation with all these people watching. She couldn't bear the humiliation. Picking up her case, she headed off back up the road the way she'd come, with no idea what she was going to do now.

Lee decided to take Jasmine with him to speak to the auditors at Anderson's, not that he was hopeful of gleaning much information out of them, as everyone connected with Roger and Adrian seemed to clam up the minute they saw him.

"This looks a smart outfit" said Jasmine. "They're obviously a bigger company than I thought. These offices look brand new. Perhaps we'll even get a decent cup of coffee, if we're lucky."

"Don't count on it!" he laughed. "What's the betting that old Mr Anderson has retired and we get fobbed off with some junior associate?"

The concierge greeted them at the door and gave them visitor's passes before asking them to take a seat. They waited a good ten minutes before a young man emerged from the lift and showed them into a side room, which was empty except for a couple of plastic chairs and a small table. A flip chart stood in the corner. The young man introduced himself as Kevin Maitland and asked how he could help them. Lee explained about the investigation and asked if he could speak to the person or people involved in the audit.

"Right, I see. Forgive me for sounding vague, but I've only been here for a few months so I'll have to make some enquiries upstairs. Meanwhile, I'll organise some coffee for you, if you don't mind waiting."

"Thank you. We're in no hurry, we'll wait" said Lee. The coffee arrived five minutes later with a message from Kevin that the original audit was conducted by Mr Richardson and Mr Apse. He then explained that Mr Richardson had since left their employment but Mr Apse would speak to them shortly as he had a client with him at present. Twenty minutes later they were seated in Mr Apse's office.

"I'm not sure that I can be of much help to you I'm afraid" he said, shuffling a pile of files to one side of his desk. "I did give the police a statement at the time but the trouble was of course that a lot of the paper records were destroyed in a fire, so it made things difficult. I couldn't make any sense of the paperwork that remained. It was quite obvious to me that no proper records were kept. Mr Richardson did go through some current stuff with a lady called Marcie McAndrew and everything was in order, but of course she'd only been with the company a short while, about six months I think."

"Did you discuss the matter with Roger? He was the accountant I believe."

"He fobbed me off with Adrian, who was very uncooperative to say the least. He hadn't a clue what he was talking about. In the end I wrote Roger a letter to the effect that a proper audit couldn't be completed and I made out an invoice for our charges, according to the hours we'd put in. We never heard from them again after that."

"Have you any idea where Mr Richardson went when he left here?"

"Yes, he set up his own business, something to do with computer technology, IT support, that sort of thing. He has a small office."

Jasmine noted down the details and they headed back towards the lifts. Once the lift doors had closed she said, "He sounded genuine enough, didn't he?"

"I've spoken with him before. He's a very nice man actually. I don't know what I was hoping to learn by today's visit, but it was worth a try. We'll track down this Richardson and see what he's got to say."

"Dean! For god's sake are you going to lie in that bed all day? Aren't you supposed to be in work today?"

"Don't shout mum, I'm feeling rotten."

"I'm not surprised, the hours you keep. It was four o'clock in the morning before you put an appearance in. Where had you been till that time? You're up to no good! You can't carry on like this lad, it's no way to live. You'll have Jasmine after you again. She's got to do her job you know."

"Don't worry about Jaz, she'll not shop her own brother. I'm not kidding mum, I really do feel ill. Call the doctor or something. I feel as though I'm dying."

She stood looking at him rolling around on the bed. She was undecided as to whether to call the doctor or not. She didn't want him seeing Dean in this state. He'd know straight away about the drug taking and she'd be embarrassed. She could hardly hold her head up in the village as it was. 'I'll give him another half hour, if he hasn't rallied by then...' she said to herself. She was half way through the door when she heard a thud. Dean lay in a crumpled heap on the floor.

"Dean! Dean!" she yelled. "Speak to me!" He was out cold and the panic started to set in. She didn't want to be responsible for her own son's death.

Beth spent the night in the bus station, curled up on one of the benches. She freshened herself up in the ladies toilet and checked her purse. She'd just enough money for a cup of tea and a teacake. Making her way out into the High Street, she decided on the transport cafe near the market. It was cheaper there. Settling herself on the wall, she placed the polystyrene cup on a flat bit of stone and tucked into her teacake whilst she thought about her next move. Part of her desperately wanted to confront Ashley and find out why he'd decided not to turn up last night. Had he genuinely forgotten or was it deliberate? Either way, he owed her an explanation but after what she observed of his behaviour with the mystery blonde, it was pretty obvious really. He hadn't been serious about them setting up home together. After she'd finished her tea, she decided to call in at her father's office. He wouldn't refuse to speak to her, of that she was certain. He'd advise her about what to do, although she wasn't sure if her mother had already got to him with her side of the story regarding the row they'd had. She knew that her mother could be very persuasive, especially where men were concerned. There were some women that seemed to possess the ability to get anything they wanted out of a man, her mother being one of them. She only wished that she possessed some of the magic then maybe Ashley wouldn't have treated her the way he had.

"Bad news?" asked Lee, on seeing Jasmine's worried look. She switched off her mobile and tucked it back into her pocket. He'd heard her telling someone not to mess around and just call an ambulance.

"It was mum. Our Dean's collapsed unconscious. She can't rouse him. We all know why she's reluctant to do anything. Questions will no doubt be asked, but I don't want to get involved unless I have to. Believe me when I say I tried everything to get him to straighten himself out. I really did try to help him but I got a bashing for my efforts. He can sort himself out. I'm not tolerating that sort of behaviour. Mum's the one I feel sorry for. Everyone's talking behind her back."

"He might be under pressure from the drug dealers. They're thugs. Once you start working for them, there's no escape. I know this sounds a bit harsh, but maybe this incident will be the turning point for him. Bring him to his senses. It's never too late Jaz. He's still a young man. He's got his whole life ahead of him. We've got to help him."

Jasmine didn't answer but just sat staring down at her hands resting in her lap, lost in thought.

Chapter Eleven

"I've brought you a nice cup of tea Mrs Green," said Mabusi. She was the orderly that Marcie had befriended. She looked after everyone on the ward. They all loved her. Nothing was too much trouble for her and she often ran errands for people, fetching newspapers and sweets from the shop and washing people's hair when they weren't up to doing it themselves. "You had a visitor earlier this afternoon but you were fast asleep so she'll come back tomorrow," she said, straightening the bedcovers.

"Who was it?"

"Peggie. She came with that young policeman. Now don't you fret. Drink your tea."

Marcie's heart missed a beat as soon as she mentioned the policeman. Had he come to escort her to the prison? She wasn't ready to face that just yet. She wanted to be alone with her thoughts and she immediately thought of Gerald. Where was he at this moment? Having returned to his wife, she wondered if everything was going well for him. She just wanted him to be happy. They'd had the most glorious six months together, the memories of which she'd cherish for the rest of her days. As she sipped her tea she recalled the pavement cafe's they'd enjoyed on the streets of Paris, always coffee as Gerald wasn't a tea drinker. They went up the Eiffel Tower and then took a cruise on the river Seine. The next day they visited the Louvre, where they spent the whole morning before walking to the magnificent cathedral, Notre Dame. Marcie had never seen anything like it. The evenings were usually spent in the Latin Quarter where they ate and drank until bedtime, chatting with the locals before heading back to their hotel. It was the most glorious five days of her whole life. She'd never been away with a man before and although initially worried about the physical side of the relationship, she needn't have worried as Gerald was gentle and kind and she took to it like a duck to water. It all felt so right and natural. She remembered feeling incredibly hungry as Gerald didn't eat during the day, just coffee. In the evenings he ate fish and salad with a glass of wine. At first she felt as though she was going to faint through lack of nourishment but she soon got used to it and at the end of the six months she'd shed over four stones in weight, going from eleven stones five pounds to seven stone. Of course, she knew deep down that it wouldn't last. On returning home, his wife contacted him and that was the end of it for Marcie. When he rang her to tell her that his wife wanted a reconciliation she went numb and only remembered thanking him for the wonderful time they'd had together. She'd not heard from him since. The world suddenly became a duller place with no purpose or meaning to it. Gerald knew about her marriage to Adrian and of the impending court case. She wondered if he'd attended the court hearing, but she couldn't recall seeing his face amongst the attendees, and she'd had a good look around. The only people she spotted were Peggie and Candice. Their friendship had proved invaluable to her and she hoped that the prison sentence wouldn't put them off, for she couldn't bear it. The lady in the bed across the way had visitors, a gentleman whom she assumed was her husband and a young girl which reminded her of Gerald's daughter Beth. She had the same blonde hair and blue eyes and even wore similar clothes. Gerald often brought Beth with him if they were going out for a meal in the evenings as his wife wasn't one for cooking. She wondered what Beth was up to now. Not being academic, she'd failed her exams but Gerald didn't scold her, for she'd enrolled herself at cookery school. It was the one thing she loved doing. There were rows galore at home after Gerald left, which he put down to teenage strops. Beth and her mother were arguing constantly but Gerald said it would all settle down with time.

Marcie wondered if she'd be able to find work after she'd completed her prison sentence. She hoped so, for she had no way of supporting herself. She couldn't ask her sister Deidre for help, she would just refuse to give it. 'I'll think about all that when the time comes' she told herself and closed her eyes, willing herself to fall asleep.

Chris parked his car in the only available space on the busy main road. The terraced houses all opened directly on to the street. Lee had given him the task of contacting all the other employees, the details as supplied by the young lady who'd been successful in claiming all her money back plus compensation. The others all lost their cases due to the fact that they'd used a different solicitor. The other lady had gone to an independent barrister and won her case. Chris wasn't sure what kind of reception he'd receive or how much initial investment capital had been lost but he knew how he'd feel himself if someone had done him out of all that money. He wondered if they were all still active in fighting their corner. 'I wouldn't let it drop. No way,' he told himself as he rattled the letterbox. There didn't appear to be a doorbell and he noticed a child's bicycle propped against the wall. The basket on the front contained a pair of blue discarded mittens and a Peter Rabbit book. A smartly dressed gentleman opened the door. "Oh," he said, on seeing Chris. "Is it about the bins?"

"Er, no actually, I was hoping to have a word with Charles. Charles Williams?"

"Oh right. Come in. It's just that we've had all our rubbish bins pinched. The council replaced them a month ago and they've gone again. Hooligans! Come through, he's in the back yard with his daughter. "Charlie, there's a visitor for you. A policeman," he shouted through the back door.

"Have you been a naughty boy dad?"

"Don't be cheeky."

"You go into the lounge whilst we make some tea. Come on Helen help me get the cups out."

"Can we have biscuits grandpa?"

"We'll see."

"I won't keep you long Mr Williams," said Chris.

"It's to do with that Adrian Green I take it? A right pair of rogues them two! They did me out of £10,000. It was my life savings! My wife never forgave me. She left me a year ago. That's why I'm living with my father. I'd nowhere else to go."

"I'm sorry to hear that. Are you still actively seeking retribution?"

"You must be joking! I haven't got the money for that. I've just drawn a line under it all. I did go to the Citizens Advice Bureau initially to see if there was anything I could do. I thought I might be able to get legal aid or something but the solicitor there wasn't very encouraging. We were badly advised at the time and they made us sign some legal document. When it got to court the judge threw the whole case out. If we hadn't signed that piece of paper….but I have to take the blame for that myself. I should have read what I was signing. I didn't read the small print, as it were. We thought we were doing the right thing. The only people that gain in these matters are the solicitors."

"Is this solicitor still in business do you know?" asked Chris, accepting a cup of tea from the tray proffered by Charles' father.

"I've no idea to be truthful with you. We were all dismissed, all six of us."

"You didn't think to try for compensation? For unfair dismissal?"

"One of the girls tried contacting an employment tribunal but there again it came down to the fact that we'd all signed this document. No joy. The awful thing is, my best pal John, we were friends from our school days, he had six children and the stress of it all brought on a heart attack. He died instantly. It was Adrian that talked us all into investing. He promised us all sorts, how he could double our investment within two years. Looking back, I can't believe how gullible we all were. It was all nonsense of course."

Chris noted down the name of the solicitor and a few other details, then left.

"What are you rummaging around in there for? What are you look-ing for?"

"All these suits you've got in here, you never wear half of them. They would fetch a bob or two together with your car. I don't know why you insist on hanging on to things. We never go anywhere."

"Just stop right there. I've sacrificed enough for that son of yours. Look what he's reduced us to. Take a good look around you. What do you see? I've worked for over fifty years as a civil engineer with nothing to show for it and look where I've ended up. In a rented one-bedroom flat, a few bits of tatty furniture. We haven't even got a garden to sit in."

"Stop exaggerating. We've got a little balcony, we can sit out. We've got everything we need here. You're becoming too materialistic."

"Sit out? Looking out onto everyone's dustbins, I don't think so. I'd be ashamed to ask anyone back here, it's a disgrace. Adrian's had quite enough out of me. The shop is closed. If he gets into any more scrapes he's on his own. I've nothing left to give and don't you dare sell anything that belongs to me without my knowledge. I'm keeping my car and my suits. He's had just about everything else. He's not having the clothes off my back as well. You indulge him too much. It's about time he learnt to stand on his own two feet and take responsibility for his own actions and welfare. He's a grown man not a schoolboy."

"Don't keep referring to him as 'my' son. He's your flesh and blood too. Where are you going?"

"To the pub for a drink. I need one."

Beth eased off her shoes and rubbed her toes. After walking three miles to her father's office her feet were killing her. She sat in the little park just off the main road and tried to think clearly. Ap-proaching the receptionist, she was told that her father wasn't in the office this week. Disappointment overwhelmed her. Having only a few coins left in her purse, it now looked as though her only option was to go back home but she couldn't face the wrath of her mother. If only Ashley hadn't let her down, things would have been fine. She'd imagined herself to be in love but he obviously hadn't felt the same way about her. How well had she really known him? His mother had probably been instrumental in steering him in another direction. She was tired and hungry and was due back at college tomorrow. She couldn't think clearly and her thoughts became muddled and confused. She lay down on the bench, willing herself to fall asleep as the tears poured down her cheeks. 'What an utter fool I've been,' she told herself.

Chapter Twelve

Tom picked up his pint off the bar and took a long swig before deciding where to sit when he suddenly heard a voice from behind him shout, "Tom, good to see you! Shirley's let you off the leash at last has she?" Looking over his shoulder, he saw one of his old workmates, the Managing Director, Bernard Latham.

"Hello Bernard, it's good to see you. How's life treating you?"

"I'm retired now old chap, for my sins. Come and join us, I'm with a neighbour. I'll introduce you. Sally this is Tom Green, an old friend. We worked together for forty years. Tom this is Sally, my neighbour from two doors down."

Tom eyed the attractive lady sitting nursing a glass of red wine. She smiled at him and gave him a cheery 'hello' before offering him one of the sandwiches from the enormous plate in the centre of the table. "We don't normally indulge like this but these were left over from the buffet. There was a Women's Institute meeting here earlier. I'm a member. Did you say your surname is Green? Are you by any chance related to Adrian Green?"

"Sally's a freelance accountant," proffered Bernard.

"Oh, I see. Well, yes as a matter of fact, Adrian's my son. Why do you ask?" said Tom, suddenly starting to feel hot under the collar. What on earth had his son been up to now? He noted her beautifully manicured nails and the lack of a wedding ring on her left hand.

"In my line of work you hear things. The tax office...."

"Don't tell me anything more. I don't wish to know!" he admonished.

Bernard noted the tension in the air and decided to divert the conversation by asking, "I say old chap, how about you coming back to ours for a spot of supper? Miriam's a very good cook and it'll give us a chance to catch up on what's been happening."

"That would be great Bernard, thank you. Are you sure Miriam won't mind?"

"Not a bit. We do a lot of entertaining these days, especially since I retired."

"Actually there is something that I want to speak to you about," he said and downed the remains of his pint.

"Steak, on a Thursday?" laughed Chris. Lee was opening a bottle of Jasmine's favourite wine. It was a little sweet for his own taste but he could live with anything alcoholic.

"Huxley's been on at me again this morning. We're no further with the investigation. I'd nothing much to tell him. He wanted to know what we'd been doing for the past week."

"Rome wasn't built in a day. We'll get there" said Chris cheerfully. "I've just got a good feeling about this case."

"I'm glad somebody has" laughed Jasmine.

"I spoke to Mantos again yesterday. They're actively checking all the ports. It's on red alert. It would be a feather in his cap if he found it. He might even get promoted."

Jasmine couldn't help smiling to herself. The poor lad was delusional if he thought that things were that simple. Life just wasn't like that, but his optimism and enthusiasm was a plus in her book. At least he was keen and interested which was more than could be said for Huxley, whose attitude she'd never liked. He was lazy in her opinion and she wondered how on earth he'd got to be a Superintendent.

"What sort of reception did you get from these other employees? Anything new surfaced?"

"He's done a lot of people out of a lot of money. It would appear that he persuaded them to invest in companies and schemes without them knowing for certain that they actually existed. Where the money disappeared to is anybody's guess."

Lee nodded. He'd come to the same conclusion himself after speaking with the auditor. "Jasmine can go with you tomorrow. Try to speak to all of them if you can. I'd like to know their stories. I'll tackle the other auditor, Richardson. Tuck in everyone."

"Adrian and Roger's powers of persuasion must be exceptional," said Jasmine, forking some vegetables on to her plate. "I mean, how on earth do you persuade someone to invest in such a dodgy business like theirs?

"Well," said Lee, "It's possible that the investors had an inkling that things weren't quite above board, but decided to invest anyway as they thought that it might benefit them in the long run. If you look at millionaires and how they made their millions, can you say without doubt that they came about their wealth honestly and without pulling the odd 'fast one' so to speak?"

"I'm sure you're right" said Chris. "What became apparent, on speaking to these investors is that Adrian had mastered the skill in gaining people's trust but without parting with too much information regarding the exact details of the transaction. There's an art to all that. I'm sure I'd never achieve it. Perhaps that's why Roger employed Adrian in the first place."

Jasmine began to realise that perhaps she'd misjudged Chris. There was more depth to him than she first thought and he continued to surprise her with his thoughts. She felt as though they were driving up a blind alley. Every enquiry met with a dead end. "But surely, even the cleverest of people don't get away with this sort of thing indefinitely, do they? It's fraud. He's bound to make a mistake sooner or later."

"He already has. Several times, but of course the mistakes are never down to him and as he so pointedly remarked in court, he cannot be held responsible for other people's mistakes" remarked Lee. He began to think that there was something very fishy about the way Huxley was badgering him on this case. He seemed keen to wrap things up and put the case to bed, whereas what he ought to be doing is encouraging them to dig deeper and cast their net wider. Something didn't feel quite right, he wasn't sure what it was but if he allowed his instincts to guide him, Huxley wasn't as lily white as he made out, irrespective of the fact that he was head of the police force.

"Here's your tea Mrs Green." It was Mabusi. She placed the plastic cup on Marcie's bedside table. "Anything you want from the shop today my honey?" Marcie smiled and shook her head. "No thank you."

"I wish all the patients were as easily pleased as you" she laughed.

"What was all the commotion earlier? It's normally very quiet first thing. There seemed to be a lot of people in white coats milling about," she whispered.

Mabusi made her way to the side of the bed before whispering back "It's a young girl. An attempted suicide."

"Oh dear," said Marcie, "What on earth happened?"

"She threw herself in the river. Your nice policeman fished her out, probably saved her life." She leaned in further so that her face was practically touching Marcie's before adding, "A nice lady walking her dog spotted her sitting on the bridge. Next minute she tipped herself over the side. Drink you tea." She sauntered out into the corridor shouting, "Cup of tea for you today Mr Rice?" Marcie wondered what had happened in the young girl's life to make her want to commit such an act. These last few months, especially since Gerald had disappeared from her life, she'd often thought of doing something like that herself, but wasn't brave enough. She kept telling herself not to look back, only to live in the moment and move forwards, but she couldn't believe how easily fooled she'd been by Adrian's guile. He was not only a control freak but nasty with it. If only he'd shown her an inkling of compassion or kindness it would make things more bearable, but he hadn't. Looking back, the signs were all there but she'd misread them. The way he always chose which restaurants they ate in and even ordered the food for her. Cinema visits were always films that he wanted to see. He never once asked her what she'd like to do on their dates. He pre-planned them all, to his own satisfaction. Then there were comments about the way she ought to dress and behave. He didn't like her seeing her friends, even if it was just for coffee. Every hour that she wasn't in the office had to be negotiated with him, in case he'd got something planned for them, but she only saw his behaviour as kindness. How stupidly blind she'd been and now she was paying the price for it. 'What makes a person behave in such a way?' she asked herself. What had happened in Adrian's childhood to make him turn out the way he had? Children weren't born like that, it was learned behaviour. Where had he learnt it? She sipped her tea then fell into a blissful sleep dreaming of Gerald.

Chris stepped out of the shower and rubbed himself down with a towel before throwing all his uniform into the washing machine. He'd just been edging around the road block through the paddy lights approaching the bridge when he was flagged down by a lady with a dog.

"Stop! Oh, please stop!" she yelled, waving frantically at him. He braked hard and parked his bike at the side of the road before asking "What's happed madam?"

"Oh, please come quickly officer! I've just seen a young girl throw herself off the bridge!"

"Deliberately? Are you quite certain?"

"Yes, I'm sure. Hurry up or she'll drown." Chris followed her to the centre of the bridge and leaned over the side. "There she is officer" she shouted, pointing up stream to what looked like a bundle of rags. He scrambled under the bridge and scaled the rocks, flinging off his jacket and shoes as he did so. He knew that this section of the river was particularly rapid, it being a popular spot for people discarding their unwanted rubbish. One large heave and it was gone within minutes, carried upstream, never to be seen again.

Fortunately he'd always been a strong swimmer and edged himself off the rocks into the icy cold water. The fast moving current carried him backwards with every stroke until he acclimatised himself and put a spurt on. The body hit a rock, which gave him the advantage of catching it eventually by grabbing hold of what appeared to be hair. Placing his arms underneath the arms of the body, he managed to drag it to the river bank where the girl with the dog was waiting for him. She grabbed hold of an arm and with the help of the dog; they dragged the body out of the water. After laying the body flat on the ground she turned back to help Chris out of the water.

"Are you alright officer? You were magnificent!" she yelled, as though trying to make herself heard above the noise, when actually there was no need to shout because there was nobody else around. Without waiting for a reply, she turned her attention back to the body on the bank, turning it over. "It's a young girl, poor thing."

"Let me check if she's still breathing." He checked for a pulse and was relieved to find that there was a very faint one. The lady with the dog was called Linda and the dog was called Hamish. She was downstairs in his kitchen making a cup of tea. His spare uniform was still in the original packaging, so she offered to iron out the creases for him. Hamish was chomping on a digestive biscuit, his tail batting back and forth with glee.

"Will she be alright do you think?" Linda asked, handing him a mug of steaming hot tea.

"I've every reason to think so. She'd not been in the water for very long, thanks to your swift action."

"If I hadn't just happened to be passing...." she paused to sip her tea. "It was Hamish that alerted me. He suddenly started barking. I thought he'd spotted a rabbit or something. It was then that I saw her. She had a suitcase in her hand."

"Did she indeed?"

"Yes. I don't suppose we'll ever find that, with that section of the river being what it is."

"We'll check. Meanwhile, I'll have to make out a report. Would you mind accompanying me to the station to sign a statement?"

"Of course, it's the least I can do."

Chapter Thirteen

"Detective Inspector Purslow" said Leander, extending his hand.

"Oh yes, come in inspector. Take a seat if you can find one. Sorry we're in a bit of mess here. We had a leak and we had to mop the place out. These offices aren't waterproof. "

Lee found himself a chair and placed it directly in front of the desk. "I'd just like to ask you a few questions regarding the audit you did for Adrian Green and Roger Moorcroft, during your employment with Andersons."

"Gosh is that investigation still going on. I thought it was all dead and buried. Wasn't there a court case recently?"

"Yes, that's why we're continuing with our enquiries. Any information you give us will be treated in the strictest confidence of course. We need all the information we can get. I understand that you dealt with Marcie McAndrew?"

"Yes that's right. She went over all the files since the commencement of her employment there. Everything was in order. Unfortunately she'd not been there long and there didn't appear to be any records of anything prior to her arriving on the scene. Or if there were, she didn't know anything about them and we couldn't find anything in the system. When I approached Roger about it he got aggressive and told me only to deal with Adrian. Adrian advised us there'd been a fire and all the paper records had been destroyed. That still didn't explain why there was nothing on the computer system. He'd make a good politician that man. He can talk for hours without saying anything."

"What was your overall impression of Mr Green?"

"I didn't like him. He looked down his nose at everybody and the way he used to speak to his staff.... well, all I can say is that if I spoke to my staff like that, there'd be a mass walkout."

"Was Roger around much whilst you were there?"

"No, I only spoke to him on the telephone. He was on his boat, according to the gossip in the office. Somewhere in Greece, Rhodes I think they said. I can't remember the name of it now....but I think it began with an M."

"Was there any other gossip that might be of use to us?"

"Well there were rows galore between Adrian and Roger according to the staff. Roger's got a bit of a temper. He was prone to throwing tantrums if he couldn't get his own way. He threatened to sack Adrian on more than one occasion. Adrian, if rumour can be believed, was prone to making howling errors but he always managed to worm his way back into Roger's good books by throwing huge sums of money into the pot. His father helped him out of a few scrapes on more than one occasion. The staff used to call him Houdini. There's not much else I can tell you I'm afraid."

"If anything comes to mind that you think would help us with our enquiries, please contact us." He left his card and threaded his way over the rubble towards the door.

Beth woke up to find someone standing at the side of her bed, looking intensely at her. She had no idea where she was or what had happened to her. "Where am I?" she croaked.

"You're in hospital my dear. You lie still whilst I go and fetch the nurse" ordered Mabusi. There was a flurry of activity around the nurse's station before the ward sister appeared. She drew the curtain around the bed and immediately took her temperature and her blood pressure.

"Hello. I'm Sister Crowther. You've had a nasty experience. The doctor will be here shortly to speak to you and check you over. How are you feeling?"

"What happened to me? I can't remember anything."

"It sometimes happens in these cases. Don't worry. Try to rest. You were fished out of the river by a policeman. Luckily, a lady walking her dog spotted you and got help. You're a very lucky lady." She smiled at her young patient then started writing on the clipboard at the foot of the bed.

"The river? Good gracious! Oh Lord!" she whispered.

"Do you remember throwing yourself off the bridge last night?"

"No. No, I can't remember anything. Are you sure that's what happened? I'm so sorry for causing all this trouble. I can't imagine what I was thinking."

"How do you feel?"

"Very tired and my throat's sore."

"You swallowed a lot of water from the river. Drink plenty of liquids and you should be alright in a couple of days."

Doctor Singh gave her a thorough examination before declaring her unharmed from her ordeal, except for a few superficial scratches to her hands and face from the impact with the rocks. Beth was acutely embarrassed and couldn't think what on earth had possessed her to do such a stupid thing. It was a moment of madness. She remembered calling at her father's office and being told that he wasn't in that week. Her world suddenly turned black, disappointment overwhelming her. She certainly had no recollection of throwing herself off a bridge!

"We'll keep you here for a couple of days, under observation. Just in case of any after effects" said Dr Singh, pushing back the curtain. He turned his attention to the patient in the bed opposite. A young man wired up to a drip. Beth heard the doctor call him Dean.

"I've left the shopping list on the kitchen table for you. Don't be long."

Tom picked up the list and stuffed it into his jacket pocket before heading for the door. "Where are you going today? Is it your coffee morning?"

"No, that's next week at Sylvia's. I'm having lunch with the girls."

"Do you want me to drop you anywhere?"

"No, I'm being collected in about ten minutes."

"Right, I'm off then." Tom jumped into his car and wondered why she'd told him not to be long with the shopping when she herself was going out to lunch with the girls. She was a control freak, just like Adrian. She had to know his every move, every minute of the day. Well, today he decided to fit in a bit time to himself. Acting on impulse, he drove over to Sally's house and rang her doorbell. Sally was dressed in an overall and wearing rubber gloves.

"Oh, hello Tom! It's nice to see you. Sorry, it's my cleaning day. Come in."

He could smell furniture polish and disinfectant. The smells mingled together, tormenting his nostrils. "I just wondered if you fancied a spot of lunch? I've got the shopping to do, but that can wait. Shirley's out to lunch with the girls. I thought we could drive over to that nice garden centre and sit outside. They've got a lovely little cafe there. We're early enough, so we'll get the pick of the tables."

"Actually Tom that would be lovely. I'm feeling a bit down at the moment. Give me a minute to change out of my apron."

Tom was delighted. He wasn't sure how Sally would take his invitation, but he was so fed up with things at home that he decided to take a chance. After all, what had he got to lose? She was lively and good company and they got on famously together. He felt as though he'd know her all his life. She came down the stairs five minutes late wearing a pale blue summer dress and espadrilles. Her hair was brushed up into an elegant chignon, held in place with a sparkly clip. Tom ushered her into the passenger seat and they set off down the lane. "So what's eating you then, to make you miserable?" he asked.

"Oh, I'm just generally fed up. Nothing seems to be going right for me at the moment. Two years ago I had to re-mortgage the house.

I'm self employed as you know and it's difficult finding a continuous supply of work. I'm paid well when I get the jobs, but it's how to survive during the gaps. I do a bit of part-time hair dressing on the side, just family and friends mainly. That helps a bit. I've been thinking about moving away and starting again somewhere else to be honest."

"Really? Where would you go?"

"I've always fancied Australia or New Zealand. I'm sure I'd get work. I'm a fully qualified accountant."

"Have you got relatives or friends over there?"

"No, but I wouldn't let that stop me."

"I admire your drive and determination Sally. We'll talk about it over lunch."

Chapter Fourteen

"Lee there's a message here for you," said the desk sergeant. "A Mr Richardson called. He's remembered the name of that boat. Marigold. He said Roger named it after his mother, Mary. Her maiden name was Gold, Mary Gold."

"Right, I see. Good lad. Thanks. Any coffee going"

"The kettle's just died on us. We'll have to get another one."

"I'm not going all day without a brew!"

"I'll go" offered Jasmine. Lee handed her a couple of twenty pound notes from his wallet. "Marigold? What kind of a name's that for a boat? Sounds like a cow," she laughed, as she made her way out of the door, chuckling. It confirmed what they already knew from the entries in Marcie's diary. Of course it didn't necessarily mean anything. After all, it's easy enough to paint over the name and call it something else, but it was always worth investigating. Huxley was away in the Lake District this week, entertaining his in-laws, so he could breathe a little easier. Taking his desk diary out of his drawer, he planned his day. Firstly he wanted to talk to the parents of the young lady that committed suicide, Harriet Barry. Next he wanted to talk to the lady from the escort agency who'd accompanied Roger to his formal dinners and such. Tomorrow he'd tackle the lady from the WI who ran the market stall with her husband. He was beginning to feel frustrated. Normally by now he'd be well on his way to solving the case, but this particular scenario was proving beyond his comprehension. Over the years he'd developed a policeman's nose and if he listened to his own conscience and followed his intuition, Huxley had either cut a few corners or had his palms greased. Either way, it was no wonder he was pressing for a quick outcome. He'd even threatened to take all three of them off the case if they didn't come up with anything constructive during the next few days. 'Well, we'll soon see about that' Lee said to himself. He telephoned Mrs Barry, only to be told that Mr and Mrs Barry were both at work and wouldn't be home until about six o'clock. It was the housekeeper who'd answered and she said she would leave a message for them.

"I usually serve the evening meal for them around six thirty, then I go home. I'm sure they'd be willing to speak to you regarding their daughter. Shall we say around seven thirty? If you leave me your number I'll ring you back if it's not convenient." Lee thanked her and rang the escort agency. They proved to be very accommodating and he discovered that the lady he needed to speak to was called Millicent.

"Of course, she's under no obligation to speak to you" the gentleman who answered the telephone pointed out. "But I'll call her now and see if she's willing. Hang on whilst I make enquiries." Two minutes later he came back on the line with an address in the town centre, not far from the police station. Leaving the car behind, he decided to walk it. The fresh air was just what he needed and would give him time to get his thoughts in order. He was becoming more than a little fond of Jasmine. In fact he was slowly falling in love with her. He'd never felt so comfortable in a woman's company and wondered if this was because he'd known her for several years in the force. He wanted to believe that she felt the same way and sincerely hoped that she did, despite the age difference. One thing he knew for certain was that inviting her to share his flat was something he didn't regret, whatever the outcome. He assumed Millicent's address would be a flat, wrongly as it turned out. It was a very smart town house. He noted the Land Rover parked on the driveway and rang the bell. A tall slim lady answered the door.

"Ah, you must be Detective Inspector Purslow? Come in. I've made coffee."

Lee followed her into the lounge and waited for her to bring in the coffee before seating himself in one of the two armchairs. He tried to guess her age and put her at around late forties. She was dressed in a calf-length black dress with a silk scarf around her neck, held in place with a colourful clip. Her stiletto heels could be heard clip-clopping on the kitchen tiles. Her red hair was waist length and fell in soft curls. He wouldn't say that she was beautiful but she was certainly striking. A ginger cat leapt onto the sofa and settled itself on one of the cushions.

"This is Poppy. She keeps me company. I've been on my own for over a year now. My husband passed away last January" she said, handing him a bone china mug. "Do you take sugar?"

"No thank you. I'm sorry to hear about your husband. Had he been ill for a while?"

"No, it was a short illness really. He was only forty eight. It was heart failure. I'm not sure that I can be of any help to you with your enquiries inspector. I've not worked for Roger for about two years now."

"Are you still registered with the agency?"

"Yes. Although I don't do as much as I used to, not since my husband passed away."

"How long had you worked for Roger?"

"Oh, it must have been around five or six years in total. It ground to a halt when Adrian appeared on the scene."

"And you used to escort him to these black tie functions and the like?"

"Yes. Dinner dances, that sort of thing. He was batting for the other side, if you know what I mean, so there was no hanky-panky."

"Did you get on well with him?"

"Not really. I found him rather starchy. Don't get me wrong, he was pleasant enough, but he didn't go out of his way to socialise with me, if you take my meaning. He made it clear that it was a business transaction and had to be treated as such."

"How did he introduce you to his associates?"

"It was always the same. I was his 'partner' Millie. No one was fooled for a second. Everyone knew which side of the fence he was....but it's of no importance."

"What were they like, these 'associates' who attended these events?"

"I used to love going. My husband wasn't one for socialising much, so it got me out of the house. I got to know some nice people over the years. You tended to see the same faces."

"Are you still in touch with any of them?"

"Yes, with some of the wives and girlfriends. We meet for coffee and go shopping, that sort of thing."

"I'd appreciate some details of these ladies, if you don't mind. We're trying to trace the business people Roger and Adrian dealt with."

"Most of them were people he played golf with or they were members of the gentlemen's club in town, The Mayfair Rooms on Grafton Street."

"If there's anything that you can think of that would help us with our enquiries, we'd be extremely grateful. Anything you tell us will be treated in the strictest confidence of course."

"They didn't talk business in front of me. They did most of their business transactions on the golf course or at the Mayfair."

"Did you get the impression that everything was....'above board?' and within the confines of the law?"

There was a long silence whilst she lit a cigarette and offered Lee one, which he refused. She blew out a line of smoke before saying, "No, not really."

"Could you elaborate on that?"

"That's the trouble. I couldn't put my finger on anything specific, but it was just a feeling I got. Put it this way, I wouldn't trust any of them, but the ladies were a good laugh. They don't concern themselves too much about what their husbands get up to. They just enjoy the lifestyle that it affords.

"Did you ever meet Adrian?"

"I only met him on one occasion. It was a Christmas celebration, of sorts. It was when Roger first employed him. I think the idea was to introduce him to all his contacts. I found him rather irritating to be perfectly frank. He had stupid names for everyone, The Walrus, The Hippopotamus, The Rottweiler. I had no idea who he was talking about. He kept whispering in Roger's ear and giggling like a schoolgirl, such childish behaviour."

"I get the picture."

"Your Superintendent was often around on these occasions, what was his name? Huxley? I didn't take to him much either. I pride myself on being a pretty good judge of character. My husband used to say it was one of my best features." She picked up Poppy and placed her on her knee. "I do miss my Jim inspector. There isn't a single day goes by that I don't wish he was still here with me. Life can be terribly cruel at times, can't it? You must see it every day in your profession."

"Just a bit" he said, placing his empty cup and saucer on the coffee table. "Did Huxley ever interview you regarding Roger's business dealings?"

She shook her head before saying, "No, never."

Lee thought this to be rather odd as he knew he'd seen reports on file, to the contrary. He took down the names and addresses of her friends, then left. As he walked back to the station, he wondered if Millicent would telephone all her girlfriends, warning them to expect a visit and to be extra careful. He had a certain amount of sympathy for Millicent as he'd felt much the same way when his wife left him for another man. Life lost all its meaning for a while, quite a long while, if he was honest. The worst of it was that he hadn't seen it coming. They'd had their arguments over the years, but nothing major. Life as a policeman meant that he was away from home a lot, the unsociable hours, getting calls in the middle of the night to attend to some emergency, even having to cancel annual leave at the last minute, resulting in holidays being missed. It wasn't surprising that she got fed up with it all, but for all that, he loved his job and wouldn't want to do anything else. There was a nip in the air rendering it cold and he wished he'd brought his coat with him.

Marcie opened her eyes to see Mabusi topping up her water jug. "How is the young girl? The girl who threw herself in the river? What did you say her name was?"

"Her name's Beth. She's with the social worker at the moment. The doctor doesn't seem overly worried as her injuries are minor and she's doing alright. They're more concerned with the young man, Dean his name is. He's not making much progress. Beth sat at his bedside all yesterday, talking to him. He's in a bad way."

Gerald's daughter was called Beth and Marcie wondered if it was her. She didn't want him to see her in this state. She realised she was being silly, as if he'd be interested in her now. He'd gone back to his wife. She was history as far as he was concerned. The thought filled her with sadness. Mabusi interrupted her thoughts.

"They're taking you down for another x-ray today Marcie my love."

"Are they? Why?"

"You fractured your skull when you fell and you smashed your eye socket to pieces."

"Oh yes. I'd forgotten. Thank you."

"Porridge in five minutes, the breakfast trolley's doing the rounds," she wandered out into the corridor humming a Frank Sinatra tune.

Marcie sipped some water and lay back on her pillows, trying to remember the last time she'd spoken to Beth. Gerald had taken them both to a steak house to celebrate her getting on the college course. Her mother didn't approve and there had been rows. Gerald was trying to be peacemaker and telling her to follow her own path in life. He said it was important that she found something she was happy doing and Marcie agreed with him saying, 'you spend a long time at work, so it makes sense to find something that you enjoy doing.' Marcie asked her why her mother was unhappy with the idea of her doing a catering course and she said that it didn't pay enough and she'd live to regret it. Gerald said it was only natural that a mother would want the very best for her child but Beth didn't see it that way. She said her mother was just being spiteful. Marcie smiled to herself, remembering the rows she'd had with her own parents regarding her choice of career. 'The trouble with you Marcie, is that you're a plodder' said her mother. Looking back, she knew there was a grain of truth in this, for she had been quite content to just coast along instead of striving for something better. If she had worked harder, who knows what she could have achieved and now she wouldn't get the chance as she was about to start her prison sentence? A porter arrived with a wheelchair.

"Are you ready for your x-ray Mrs Green?"

"Yes," she smiled. "Let's get it over and done with." Settling herself into the wheelchair, she wondered if she would be able to see into the ward opposite to confirm her suspicions that it was Gerald's Beth who'd been brought in from the river.

"I've really enjoyed this afternoon Tom. Thank you. It's brightened up my day and my headache's gone."

"Good, I've enjoyed it too. Thank you for coming at such short notice. Are you serious about leaving the area?" said Tom, hoping that she'd change her mind.

"Yes I think so. I need a fresh start."

"Have you ever been married?"

"No but I lived with someone for four years. He left me for someone else. He was very good looking but the trouble was he knew it. Girls used to throw themselves at him."

Tom laughed and admitted, "I never had that problem myself." After driving for a few minutes he suddenly said, "Sal, will you come out with me again? It's quite made my day you agreeing to accompany me this afternoon. My wife spends a lot of time with her Women's Institute friends these days."

"Yes I'd love to come out again. How about Thursday? I've got work to hand over tomorrow but Thursday would be great for me."

"My wife goes to the hairdressers on Thursday afternoons then she has coffee with her friend who lives opposite the salon, so that would be alright. I'll give you a ring tomorrow evening." He drew up outside her house and waited until she disappeared inside the front door before waving and driving off. He pulled up in the supermarket car park and did a quick trot around the isles pulling items off the shelves before paying at the till and placing the items in the boot. Glancing at his watch, he decided to call in at the pub for a quick drink before going back to the flat. He couldn't think of it as home because it didn't feel like a home to him. The pub car park was practically full but he managed to dive into a space which had just been vacated. Making his way over to the bar, he was just about to order his pint when he spotted Shirley sat at one of the tables tucked away in a corner. She had her back to him so she wouldn't have seen him and she certainly wasn't with her WI friends. She was sat with Lionel Massey. So that was her little game was it? He wasn't aware that that scenario was still going on. Well now he knew. He made a quick exit before she had chance to spot him.

Chapter Fifteen

The Barry's house was a fairly standard semi in a quiet road which backed onto the golf course.

"Come in inspector. My wife's just making coffee, will you join us in a cup?" said Mr Barry pleasantly, shaking Lee's hand. "My son's in the lounge with his girlfriend so we'll use the dining room." He led the way through the hallway into a room just to the left. A large oval, highly polished mahogany table stood at one end of the room which overlooked the garden. There was a small patio with steps leading down to a long lawn.

"Nice garden you've got here Mr Barry" said Lee truthfully.

"My wife and I are keen gardeners. I tried to get my son interested but he's only interested in motorbikes at the moment, bikes and his girlfriend Daisy."

Lee waited until Mrs Barry appeared with the coffee tray and was seated down at the table before speaking.

"I'm making general enquiries regarding the business dealings of Roger Moorcroft and Adrian Green. I understand that your daughter Harriet was employed there?"

"Yes she was, for a short time. A few months," said Mr Barry. Lee noted that Mrs Barry had reached for her handkerchief and began dabbing at her eyes.

"I'm sorry, this must be very upsetting for you, but the investigation into their business affairs is still ongoing and any information we can get will help us with our enquiries. Anything you tell us will of course be treated in the strictest confidence."

"I wish to God that she'd never set foot in the place!" barked Mr Barry. "We knew nothing about her investing all her money in the way she did. Had we known we'd have advised her against it, but she was hopelessly in love and that rendered her blind to Adrian's scheming."

"It was her Uncle's money you see. My husband's brother passed away and he left her a substantial sum of money in his will," said Mrs Barry, suddenly finding her voice.

"Exactly how much money are we talking about?"

"He left her £50,000 in total but she spent £5,000 on a new car. Adrian persuaded her to invest the other £45,000 in his hedge fund. He told her that he loved her and they were to be married. No dates were ever mentioned and he never gave her a ring," said Mrs Barry.

"He told her he could double it in twelve months and at the end of five years she'd be looking at an investment of around £200,000. It was all nonsense of course. We knew nothing about it until we got the telephone call from the hospital. As soon as he got his hands on the money he completely blanked her. She took an overdose and never recovered," said Mr Barry.

"I'm so terribly sorry. How old was Harriet?"

"She was twenty five. She wasn't a teenager, and she wasn't without intelligence, even though I say it myself. She went to the grammar school. She got nine O Levels and four A Levels, she could have gone to university," advised Mrs Barry. "When I think of how well she could have done if only she'd been more sensible." She dabbed at her eyes again before continuing. "She never had boyfriends you see. She was a quiet girl, so we were surprised when she suddenly announced she was getting married to Adrian. I mean, she'd not been at the firm five minutes and we'd never met him."

"She was reluctant to bring him to the house for some reason" continued Mr Barry. "I think it was more likely that he refused to come, knowing full well that we'd ask too many questions. She handed over that money in good faith inspector. It's scandalous what those two have got away with. The solicitor said she'd signed some piece of paper, which basically stood up in court as a legal document. If she hadn't signed that, well we might have had a case but the court just threw it out. But I tell you inspector, she can't have known what she was doing. If only she'd used just a small part of her inheritance it wouldn't have been so bad but Adrian was very persuasive in getting her to part with the whole lot."

"Was she given any paperwork in connection to this investment?" asked Lee, knowing full well what the answer would be.

"No, nothing" said Mr Barry.

"Well, nothing that we know about anyway" offered Mrs Barry. "She became very secretive. We couldn't get anything out of her when we asked questions. Looking back I should have noticed that she wasn't happy. I can't help feeling that we failed her in some way. If only she'd talked to us about it, well I'm not sure what we could have done about it but we'd have tackled the problem together. We'd like to see justice done. I can't bear to think about them doing the same thing to some other poor soul. We understand there was a court hearing regarding his wife. Maybe that wouldn't have happened if we'd been more active in seeking some answers. If there's anything we can do to help inspector..." she dabbed at her eyes again.

"What I want to know is, what an earth has happened to all that money? What on earth have they done with it all?" Mr Barry was getting annoyed and frustrated. "We never got any answers from that Huxley fellow of yours. He was a waste of space if you ask me. He was about as much use as a chocolate teapot!"

Lee had to stifle a smile as they were his own sentiments exactly. "Can you give me the name of the solicitor you used?"

"Yes, we've got all the details here. You can read his final letter, informing us that the case is now closed" said Mrs Barry who opened the writing bureau and proceeded to rummage through the paperwork inside.

It was gone nine o'clock when Lee eventually got back to the flat. Jasmine and Chris where going over all their reports from their enquiries that day. They were eager to know how he'd fared at the Barry's.

"Your supper's in the oven. There's no wine left I'm afraid" said Jasmine, heading for the kitchen.

"That's alright I'll pour myself a whisky. How did you two get on today?"

"It's all following the same pattern," said Chris. "It's as Gina said, because they used a different solicitor, they lost their cases in court. It was thrown out. Gina was the lucky one."

"There's got to be something we've missed," said Lee, sipping his whisky.

"Would it be any use having a word with his father?" Chris asked. "He had to bail Adrian out on two occasions. Not just small amounts either. Presuming that the first payout was to pay Gina back, what was the second payout for?"

"Perhaps to pay for his half share in the boat" said Jasmine. "We called in at the offices today and were told that Adrian and Roger hadn't been seen for about three weeks. Nobody knows where they are."

"Why does that not surprise me?" said Lee sarcastically.

"If they're in Rhodes on that boat, so much the better," said Chris hopefully. "They don't muck about abroad. They chuck you in prison and ask the questions afterwards."

Beth spent most of her days at Dean's bedside. His skin was still a funny yellow colour but at least he was talking now. He told her that someone had spiked his drink on purpose. When she asked why anyone would do that he said it was because he was refusing to cooperate anymore. He didn't elaborate on the details but said he was sick and tired of his life the way it was. Always looking over his shoulder and being bullied the way he was. Beth asked him why he hadn't gone to the police and he said because he'd end up in prison himself. She knew then that whatever he'd been up to, it wasn't legal. He asked her what had happened to her to make her jump off the bridge like that, so she told him about her boyfriend letting her down. Dean said he must be mad as in his eyes she was a real bobby-dazzler. After that their friendly banter went on all day, each taking the rise out of the other. The doctors had told Dean there was liver damage and that the next forty eight hours would be critical. Beth couldn't bear the thought of anything happening to her new friend and sat holding his hand when he was too weak to talk. At night in her own bed she prayed to God asking him to save Dean and make him pull through.

"Did you have a nice time with your friends?" asked Tom. He'd put the shopping away and started the evening meal when Shirley arrived home, all smiles and full of the joys of spring, which wasn't like her normal behaviour at all.

"Yes thank you. I don't want any tea I'm still full from lunch. I'll run myself a bath" she said, hanging up her jacket in the hall. She skipped along to the bathroom without even looking at him. Tom wanted to see if she mentioned running into Lionel, but she hadn't. In a way it made him feel less guilty about taking Sally out. Deep down he knew their marriage was dead in the water. It had been ever since they sold their last home in order to bail Adrian out of another one of his 'predicaments' that he'd got himself into. Shirley had insisted that they help him. It was their rightful duty as parents, she said. The rows that followed went on for a long time. He ate his meal then poured himself a nightcap from the drinks cabinet. When he eventually made his way into the bedroom Shirley was sat up in bed reading a magazine.

"Do you want a drink or anything before I turn in?" he asked her.

"No thank you, I'll just finish this story then I'll call it a day" she said, giving him the briefest of glances before going back to her article. He made his way back onto the lounge to finish his drink. Lionel Massey was a man who'd never married but he came off good stock. His father owned a big estate in the Yorkshire Dales with several acres of land, most of which was used to grow fruit and vegetables. His stock supplied all the local hotels and B & B's. Lionel wasn't interested in working on the land with his father and therefore took a job in property management, which is where he'd worked all his life. He was a member of the golf club, which is where Tom and Shirley met him. Tom had yet to see him on the golf course but he seemed to turn up at all the Christmas parties and functions throughout the year. Tom didn't take to him, judging him to be an oily tyke but Shirley seemed quite smitten, especially as Lionel tended to throw compliments around like confetti. He wondered what Lionel's motives were. Did he intend to break up their marriage by proposing to Shirley? Tom didn't think so. Lionel just didn't seem the type to commit to anyone, let alone to a woman of Shirley's age. Thinking back to the rows he'd had with Shirley over the last few years, he wondered if she'd instigated them on purpose to get him so fired up that he'd just up sticks and leave, making the way clear for her to hook up with Lionel. Well, he wasn't going to make it that easy for her.

Chris ran into the local corner shop for some provisions. It was his day off and he'd no cereal, bread or milk for his breakfast. He'd decided to take a walk around the outskirts of the golf course as he needed to think about the Green case and go over all the information he'd gleaned so far. Sometimes important facts would jump out at you, helping to turn the case. This thinking time had proved invaluable in the past and he hoped it would again. Arriving back at his flat, he poured some milk on his cereal and placed a slice of bread in the toaster when his phone rang. It was Mantos informing him that he'd spoken to the harbour master at one of the ports and he assured him that he'd definitely seen this boat called Marigold. Chris was overjoyed and thanked his friend, as that is the way he thought of Mantos now, vowing that if he solved this case he'd come over personally and they'd have the biggest celebration ever. He threw the pots in the sink and poured himself a mug of tea from the pot, which was now stewed due to the length of time it had stood. After a quick call to Jasmine letting her know the good news, he threw on his anorak and headed out into the fresh air. There was a strong wind, rendering it rather chilly. He was glad he'd put on his scarf and wound it tighter around his neck to keep warm. Looking out onto the golf course, he was surprised to see how busy it was. No matter what time of year, you would always find someone having a round or two. Suddenly a red woolly hat blew past him. He ran after it, just managing to grab it before it made its way on to the course. In the distance he could hear a dog barking. He turned to see Linda, also straining at the end of his lead, was Hamish.

"What kind of batteries do you put in him?" he laughed.

"Oh thank you! It's my best hat, I only bought it yesterday. Hamish is such a lively dog I usually let him off the lead for a bit to let him use up all his energy. The trouble is I can't keep up with him!" she said between gasps. "How's our young friend coming along? Or shouldn't I ask?"

"She's making good progress, slowly. Fingers crossed and all that. Her name's Beth. I called in yesterday evening to see her. She's perked up a bit. Neither of her parents have been to see her yet. The father's away on business apparently but he's due back tomorrow. No sign of the mother though. Beth said they'd had a few rows about her choice of career. She's at catering college. She strikes me as being a lovely young girl. I'll never understand why some people have children if they don't want to be bothered with them. Of course, there might be a perfectly good reason why her mother's hasn't called to see her, she might be ill or something, but even so, she could have left a message. I asked the nursing sister if there had been any telephone calls and there hasn't, but she said she'd left several messages on the house 'phone. They're thinking about putting her on a cognitive behaviour course or something.

They strolled along together, chatting and laughing, talking about anything and everything. "Is it your day off too then?" he asked.

"Yes. I don't open the studio on a Monday. I'm a potter. Having the Sunday and Monday off gives me time for Hamish. Plus I have to do my books and clean the house and all that. I was just thinking about the girl, Beth did you say her name was? I could do with a little help in my studio. How about if she came in a couple of mornings a week to help out? Would that count as therapy?"

"I'll mention it to the ward staff next time I call in. Actually, thinking about it, you could come with me, if you like."

They'd reached the main road by this time and having learnt that she had no man in her life at present, Chris asked, "Have you got time for a spot of lunch? The pub's calling me. I've got a real thirst on. We can sit outside with Hamish; it's covered over so it won't be too draughty."

"I've not had any breakfast yet, I'm famished too. Yes, let's do it! Hamish!" she shouted. They both ordered the ploughman's lunch which arrived with a bowl of scraps for Hamish. Chris took a long swig of his pint and couldn't remember when he'd last felt this happy. He watched Linda as she sipped daintily at her glass of Guinness, her blonde hair falling in a tangle onto her shoulders. She seemed lost in thought for few moments before asking if there was someone called Sergeant Purslow at his branch.

"Yes," said Chris, intrigued. "He's my boss actually. Why do you ask?"

"Well, when I went to collect my laptop from Stuart, there was nobody in reception so I hung around and I could hear him speaking on the telephone to someone. He was shouting "No, no I didn't tell him anything! Purslow, yes Sergeant Purlsow. No I didn't! I said absolutely nothing!"

"Interesting. Did you hear any names mentioned, except Purslow?"

"No, but whoever it was on the other end of that line was certainly giving him a hard time. They were arguing. I waited until I heard him slam the receiver down before pressing the bell on the reception desk. When he came out of his office his face was flushed.

I asked him if everything was alright and he said, yes everything's fine."

"It might be worth me paying him a visit. It sounds to me as if he knows more than he's letting on. Withholding information is a crime in itself."

"More importantly, why is he protecting them? What is he scared of? What will happen if he tells all that he knows?"

"It's our job to find out."

"Shall we go back to mine for a coffee?" she offered.

"That sounds good to me," he smiled at her and helped her on with her coat before looking under the table to find Hamish fast asleep.

By the time Marcie got back to her bed, breakfast was over and Mabusi offered to make her a slice of toast.

"No, I'll wait for the tea trolley, but thank you for offering" she said, sliding under the covers to keep warm. The radiology department was always busy and she'd been hanging around for over an hour before being seen, then when she got to the front of the queue they'd sent her paperwork to the wrong department and she had to wait another half hour. She didn't hold out much hope of getting the results until the next day. The thought of finally being discharged and sent to the prison to start her sentence made her feel nauseous. She lay back on her pillows, determined to enjoy her last hours of freedom before being locked up in a cell. Her thoughts went back to the day of her wedding to Adrian and the conversation she'd had with one of his aunts. She made some comment about Adrian's mother being convinced that her son was being controlled by Roger. The aunt said that it was common knowledge that there was more to it than that and everyone was surprised when he suddenly announced that he was getting married. Marcie didn't make any comment and just smiled politely and steered the conversation in another direction, knowing full well what she was implying, but not wanting to believe it. Now it seemed obvious that she was right.

If Adrian's only sin was that he'd fallen in love with Roger then sure-ly that wasn't so bad was it? She could forgive him if that was all he was guilty of but it was the lack of respect he'd shown for her that she couldn't stomach. If only he'd treated her with kindness, she could have forgiven his behaviour, after all he couldn't help feeling the way he did but to deliberately leave her carrying the can for his own misdemeanours was not only cruel and heartless, but morally wrong. She'd always been a great believer in facing the truth head on and standing behind her own convictions. It was the only way. She was just about to close her eyes when she heard a voice from the doorway, calling her name.

"Marcie! Mabusi told me it was you! She said you'd missed your breakfast so I've brought you these. Mum left them in reception for me this morning. She couldn't stop as she was off to work," said Beth, sitting herself down in the chair at the side of Marcie's bed.

"Oh Beth! It's so nice to see you. How are you feeling? I heard about your accident. I'm so sorry. What on earth happened?"

"Here, have a biscuit," she said, opening the packet and offering her one. "I'd had a row with mum. A blazing row actually. We'd not been getting on since dad left but things came to a head one night and I slammed out of the house. Ashley and I went to the pub and we planned to run away together, only he let me down. On the night in question, he never turned up, so I went to the pub and there he was, with his arms around another girl. He'd obviously for-gotten all about our arrangement, either that or he hadn't meant a word of it. He promised to look after me and all that. I couldn't face going back home to mum so I went to dad's office, hoping to speak to him for advice. He'd know what to do and wouldn't turn me away, but he wasn't in the office that week, so I walked back to the bridge. I don't remember anything else. I woke up in here. Mabusi told me that a lady walking her dog spotted me hurling myself off the bridge with a suitcase in my hand. She alerted a policeman and he waded in the water and dragged me out. Mabusi said I was lucky to be alive."

Marcie's eyes filled with tears. "Oh Beth darling, nothing is ever so bad that you have to throw your life away like that. Life is a gift. All life is a gift. Whatever problems you have, there will always be help out there for you."

"Yes, I know that now. I don't know what came over me. It was a stupid thing to do. Of course my suitcase has gone. It had all my best clothes in it. I've nothing to wear. The social worker came to see me yesterday. He said it might be a good idea if I went on the recuperation programme for a short while. Whatever that is! I'd better get back, Dean might be awake. He's the young man in the bed opposite to mine. Here's the tea trolley. You will come and speak to me before you're discharged won't you?"

"Of course I will."

Chapter Sixteen

Marjorie was sorting through a box of books when Lee entered the shop. "Good morning" she shouted, jovially.

"Good morning. Would you be Marjorie?"

"Yes, that's right" she smiled, straitening up and coming towards him.

"I wonder if I might have a quick word, if it's convenient?" he said, showing her his ID card.

"Oh, nothing wrong is there Officer?" she gasped, looking alarmed.

"I just want to confirm a few details that will help us with our enquiries," he said. "I believe you run a market stall with your husband? Is there somewhere that we could talk in private? It should only take a few minutes."

Marjorie's mind went into overdrive. Had they sold something that was stolen property? Had her husband been involved in some dodgy dealings that she knew nothing about? "I'll just speak to Lillian, the manageress," she said nervously and disappeared through a curtain at the back of the shop. Lee looked around at all the piles of junk lining the shelves and tables. Did people really buy any of this stuff? He supposed that they must do otherwise the shop wouldn't be there. He immediately became ashamed of his own thoughts as he knew there people who lived on the bread line and had no choice but to do so. Fortunately he'd never had to resort to this but his mind suddenly cast back to his days as a student when he'd had to walk to college because he'd no money for his bus fare and only eating one meal a day, usually pizza which he had to share with his other flat mates.

Marjorie reappeared with another lady. "We can use the back room officer. Lillian will mind the shop for a few minutes," she said, guiding him through the curtain. There was a musty smell and the place felt damp. She led him into a small room just off to the left. She flicked on the light and moved a few boxes and bags of clothing to make room. "Sorry about the mess but it's the best we can do I'm afraid. Sit yourself down. Now how can I help?"

"It's about the lady who owned the stall opposite yours, Mrs Livesey?"

"Mrs Livesey, you say? That doesn't ring any bells. Do you mean Mrs Savage? She had the antiques stall?"

"Sorry, yes that would be her, my mistake. There was an incident regarding the sale of a painting which turned out to be extremely valuable. Do you know anything about that?"

"Oh yes, the Rembrandt! Yes, it's true officer! The poor old soul didn't know it was an original, she just thought it was a copy. Well, I mean you would wouldn't you?"

"Do you recall the lady who bought it and returned the money?"

"Yes, Marcie. She was a lovely girl. I mean, how many people would be honest enough to do a thing like that? After she had it valued, she sold it and banked the money. She came back and showed the evaluation ticket to Evelyn, that's her Christian name. Well, she was so shocked and even more shocked when Marcie insisted on returning the money. She said she couldn't live with her conscience if she didn't. She said she didn't feel as though the money was rightfully hers."

"What happened after that?"

"Evelyn sold the stall and bought a large estate in Ireland, in the Donegal region, her home town. She'd always intended to go back there. She never married you see and she never had any children of her own, so there was really nothing to keep her here. Most of her family members had long since passed away. Well, I suppose that's what you'd expect when you get to her age, she was eighty seven you know."

"Are you or any of the other stall holders still in touch with her by any chance?" he asked hopefully.

"My husband and I aren't good letter writers but I think Evelyn was very friendly with one of the cleaning ladies, Grace her name was. She was Irish too, although she came from County Mayo I believe, not Donegal."

Lee wondered if it was the same Grace that used to clean for Roger and Adrian. "Which day does Grace usually go in to clean?"

"Only once a week, on Mondays."

"Right you've been most helpful Marjorie and thank you for your time. I'll leave you to get back to your duties. I'll no doubt catch up with you and your husband next time I'm in the market hall. Goodbye."

Peggy approached the nurses' station and asked tentatively, "I've come to see Mrs Green, Marcie, she's not in her usual room."

"Yes she's gone down for an MRI scan, she'll be back shortly if you'd care to wait," said the nurse. "They're changing the sheets on her bed whilst she's out of it but you can sit outside until they've finished, you won't be in anybody's way."

"Thank you" said Peggy and she made her way back to the room. She sat down in one of the chairs in the corridor and glanced across at a lady sat opposite. "Are you waiting for Marcie too?" she asked.

"Yes, I'm Candice. We're old friends. We were at school together."

"Oh yes, Candy, I've often heard her mention you. I'm Peggy, I used to be her neighbour, when she lived at home with her parents. Didn't you go to live in Scotland at one time?"

Candice pulled a face before replying, "Yes I did. My boyfriend was Scottish. We parted company a while back. He was married actually. I know, I know, don't say it! He had two small children too, so it was difficult, but I just fell for him. I eventually returned to England and he followed me over here. He said he couldn't live without me, but it was a volatile relationship and he went back to his family. I've been on my own ever since."

"So where are you living now?" asked Peggy, glad to have some company at last. She'd hardly seen or spoken to anyone this last week or so and she was beginning to feel very isolated.

"I'm in a flat. It's a big old house that's divided up into 4 separate apartments but the landlord's just sold it to a local builder who's turning it into offices, so I've got to find somewhere else."

"I've got a spare room you could have, that is if you don't mind sharing a house with an old biddy like me. What were you paying in rent? You can pay me the same" she said, rattling on without waiting for a reply. "Get all your belongings into a taxi and make your way over to mine. I could help you. What do you say?"

"That's the best offer I'm ever likely to get!" she laughed. "Thank you Peggy, but are you sure?"

"Yes dear. I could do with some company. My son married a Scottish girl. They live in Perth and I hardly ever see him or the grandchildren. Even at Christmas they tend to go to her family in Inverness. Come on then, let's get cracking. No time like the present," she said, beaming from ear to ear.

"Where did you get to today?" asked Jasmine. "Any joy?"

"No nothing whatsoever. This case is a non-starter. We've no new leads. When Huxley returns he'll more than likely take all three of us off the case" Lee said.

"He's away for another week yet. There's time."

"Tomorrow I want you to pay another visit to their cleaner, Grace. Was she Irish by any chance?"

"Yes. Why do you ask?"

"Ask her if she cleans in the Market Hall on Mondays. If she does, I think she may have the address of the old lady who Marcie bought the painting off. She moved to Ireland and I think Grace kept in touch with her. See what you can find out. Chris, I want you to pay a visit to Stuart. Sound him out and see what you can get out of him. I'll go to the Market Hall and speak to Marjorie's husband. His wife's a very nice lady but the husband may know more."

"I know it's not strictly correct procedure but could we check Huxley's bank account? See if there are any large deposits of cash?" said Jasmine. "He may have accepted a bribe to overlook certain evidence or even to turn a blind eye.....I'm probably wrong but I can't help feeling....."

"I've got the same feeling, but it's hard evidence we need. Large deposits of cash could have come from anywhere. No, it wouldn't help us. What puzzles me is why the courts dismissed the case the way they did. It's obvious to me that Roger and Adrian are up to no good. Anyone with half a brain can see that. The trial went on for hours. Eventually the clerks became so confused. They couldn't make any sense of what was presented to them. It was a clever move on their part."

"I can't believe they were so easily fooled" said Chris. "Something's not right about this whole case. Barristers don't just give up like that."

"Tomorrow afternoon, we'll all convene back here. After lunch we'll go over all the reports again in the files. There must be something we've missed."

"This business of Adrian deliberately crashing the computer system," said Chris, "Did Marcie actually contact Stuart to help her out or did he just turn up? I mean, if he suddenly just appeared, it's a bit suspicious, don't you think? Adrian and Roger may have pre-arranged it, if you see what I mean, for him to look as though he was in fact helping Marcie to rectify things but what he may have been doing is working on their behalf to conceal something."

"The thought did cross my mind" said Lee. "We'll need to have another go at him. He was definitely concealing something, I could tell by the look he gave me as soon as I walked in, copper's nose and all that."

"There are some nasty people around," said Jasmine. "If Stuart is guilty, then how can he live with his conscience, knowing that an innocent woman has been accused and arrested for something that he's done? She's been scandalously abused by all of them if you ask me. How will the poor girl trust a man ever again after this?"

"If they are involved in drugs, I hope our Greek friends throw the book at them when they catch them, and they will. You've only got to look at what drugs are doing to young people. Look at where your brother Dean's ended up. How is he by the way?" asked Lee.

"I've not managed to get to the hospital yet. Mum's been every day and she said he's extremely poorly."

"Tomorrow morning, go and see him. You can look in on Marcie at the same time. Ask her if she actually contacted Stuart the day that the computer system crashed."

"Alright, shall I bring some fish and chips in for lunch on the way back?"

"I'll answer for all of us – yes please!" grinned Chris, who never turned down any offer of food these days. Last night he'd taken Linda to see Peggy and they'd spent the evening discussing Marcie and her brother Peter. Her older sister Deidre married young and moved to Hampshire. When Marcie left home, after the incident with the poker, Deidre placed both her parents in a nursing home. There was no question of them living with her and Dennis, even though they had the room. Dennis expressed his concern at the time and said they should do their bit, but Deidre wouldn't entertain the idea. She then sold the house and all the furniture and mercilessly pocketed the lot. He couldn't help feeling that Marcie had been much put upon by her family. Peggy said that Deidre's husband Dennis was a very nice man and thought the world of Marcie and Peter. Peggy admitted that she never took to Deidre as she tended to be rather sharp in manner. The sort of person who didn't suffer fools gladly. Dennis was far too good for her, Peggy thought. When Linda asked her what Marcie's mother and father were like, she said they hardly left the house, so nobody ever saw either of them. They were a strange pair, she said. When he took Linda home they sat on her sofa in front of the log fire drinking their cocoa. One thing led to another and they'd ended up spending their first night together. Chris couldn't remember a happier time. Things were definitely looking up for him.

84

Chapter Seventeen

Beth was determined to go back to catering college and with Mabusi's help, she'd telephoned the course tutor and explained that she'd been ill and was currently in hospital, but would soon be discharged. Mrs Bray, her tutor, had been very sympathetic and assured her that she hadn't missed too much and with a bit of work she would be able to catch up. Her father had called to see her last night, just as the visitors were all departing. Having only just arrived back in the country, he was alarmed to learn what had happened to his precious Beth and he spent a good hour talking to the doctor. She didn't get chance to ask him how things were progressing at home with her mother but as he promised to call again today, she hoped they would have more time to talk. The social worker had been talking to Dean for over two hours and the curtain was drawn around his bed. His mother appeared just as Mabusi was dishing out the morning tea, so Beth asked for an extra cup. They sat talking for a long time and Beth rather liked her. Her devotion to her son was plain for all to see but she was concerned that she'd failed him. There were strange men circling the house outside and she wondered how long it would be before they came knocking at the door. 'I don't like the look of them Beth' she said. What she didn't tell her is that she'd searched the house from top to bottom and couldn't find any drugs. She even inspected the garden. Beth asked her where Dean's father was and she was saddened to hear that he'd died young, of a rare blood disorder. 'They couldn't get his meds right' she said. 'That must have been very hard for you' Beth sympathised. 'The children were only little, so yes, it was hard. But we battled on as best we could.' She wouldn't be drawn about what had happened to her son and Beth didn't press her. Suddenly, the social worker drew back the curtain and asked Mrs Simmonds if he could have a word with her in private. When they'd gone Beth shot out of bed and made her way over to Dean's bedside.

"What did he say?" she whispered, looking over her shoulder to make sure that nobody was in earshot. Dean still looked washed out but the horrible yellow cast was definitely disappearing.

He groaned and asked her for some water before speaking. Beth filled his glass and handed it to him. "They want to put me in this drug rehabilitation centre," he said, sipping his water.

"Where is it?"

"He did tell me but I can't remember. I was only half listening. I still feel really awful."

"Will they make you go? Can't you just go home?"

"I've got no choice really. I need monitoring and these people know how to handle cases like mine, so I'm reassured." He closed his eyes and promptly fell asleep. Beth sat holding his hand for over an hour before getting back into her own bed. She was woken up by Mabusi, who was dishing out the meals. Dean's bed was empty.

"Where's Dean?" she cried, starting to panic.

"They've taken him to the rehabilitation unit. They're used to handling these cases. He'll recover better in there."

"But where is it?"

"I'm not privy to that information Beth my darling," she said, patting her hand.

Beth burst into tears, the loss of her new friend completely over-whelming her.

"Don't you go upsetting yourself all over again. They won't let you go home if they think you've relapsed. Look, I tell you what I'll do, Dean's sister is here talking to Marcie. She's a policewoman. I'll get her to come and talk to you before she leaves. How does that suit you?"

"Oh, would you? Thank you so much! You're my best friend

Mabusi. What would I do without you?"

"That's what they all say. Now you be a good girl and eat your dinner."

"So you didn't telephone Stuart on the day in question?" asked Jasmine, eyeing the meal sat on the tray. It looked better than most of her own meals these days.

"He just turned up" said Marcie.

"What was his excuse for just turning up like that? After all, he'd left Roger's employment some time since."

"He didn't give one. I thought it a bit odd at the time but I just assumed he'd spoken to Adrian or Roger. It was shortly after this incident that the police compounded my computer and I was arrested."

Jasmine sat scribbling away in her notebook before looking up to see Mabusi hovering in the doorway. She made her way over to the bedside and whispered in Jasmine's ear.

"Before you go, can I ask a favour? There's a young lady in the next ward, Beth her name is. She's become rather fond of your Dean. Would it be in order for you to speak to her? I think she'd like to keep in touch with him."

"Of course I'm just about finished here. Thank you Marcie." She thought that the bruising around her face still looked bad and couldn't help feeling sorry for her. "Good luck with the recovery."

Jasmine's visit had given Marcie food for thought. 'I've been going through certain periods of my life with my eyes shut' she thought. She could hear her mother's words to this very day 'It's about time you woke up girl! You're half asleep!' How right she'd been but Marcie refused to admonish herself too harshly for she tended to take people at face value. Surely that wasn't a sin, was it? Lying back on her pillows, she began to think of Gerald. Had he used her too? It certainly seemed like it now. She made a pact with herself that when she was eventually released from prison, she would live out the rest of her life peacefully. I'll find myself a little cottage somewhere, she thought, and depend on no-one but myself. She wondered also, if she would be able to study in prison. Perhaps she could re-train for something. You did hear about people doing degree courses whilst serving out their sentences. Perhaps she could do the same. Feeling a little more optimistic, she resolved to speak to the prison wardens as soon as she arrived and set the ball rolling. There was no time to waste and it would help pass the years nicely.

Jasmine dished out the fish and chips whilst Chris filled the kettle and set it to boil. Lee was already seated at the kitchen table, going over his notes. Chris fetched the salt and vinegar from the larder and set them down in the middle of the table next to the bread and butter.

"Just thinking," said Chris, seating himself down on a packing case piled-up with cushions, for Lee only had two chairs. "Didn't Huxley's wife work for the bank?"

"Yes she did. Still does, to my knowledge" Lee confirmed, looking up and tossing his notebook aside. "Why do you ask?"

"Well, it's just something Peggy said. That's Marcie's neighbour. She said Marcie was convinced that Adrian only married her because he thought she had a vast deal of money. When he discovered that she'd got none he went berserk. He said he'd had it on good authority that the sale of the house had gone through her bank account and also the deposit of a million pounds. Marcie never told a single soul about the sale of that painting. Peggy only found out through Marjorie, who's a member of the WI. Peggy's also a member of the WI. She eventually asked Marcie if it was true and she confirmed everything. So, if Marcie never told anyone about it, then how did Adrian get to know about it? And how did he know about the money from the sale of the house going through her bank account?"

"Well they all mix in the same circles don't they?" offered Jasmine, "The golf club and the Mayfair club. But I can't see that Marjorie and her husband would have spread the word about. Word could have spread around to the other market stall holders, but even so...."

"You don't think Huxley's wife divulged the information to Huxley, who consequently happened to let it slip in conversation?" asked Chris, looking directly at Lee.

Lee thought it was exactly the sort of thing that Huxley would do, but didn't voice his thoughts out loud.

"Huxley's a member of the Mayfair club isn't he? And the golf club," said Jasmine. "They're all a bit too chummy if you ask me. But he may have been drunk or something and let it out by accident. I imagine his wife told him in confidence. She could lose her job over this. It's confidential information."

Lee turned the information over in his mind for several minutes before attacking his meal, making no comment. He'd certainly have something to say to Huxley when he returned.

Chapter Eighteen

Shirley put on her best dress and new shoes. She'd had her hair done and was feeling joyful as Lionel was being particularly attentive to her at the moment. They'd arranged to meet at seven thirty. Fortunately she'd managed to hang on to all of her own clothes and jewellery, it being only Tom who'd sacrificed most of his possessions, at her insistence. 'My stuff's not worth anything' she'd told him at the time. 'Your things are all designer labels. People will pay good money for them.' Lionel was taking her for a drink and a meal at a new country club that had opened on the other side of town. 'No-one will know us there' he'd told her. 'We can relax and be ourselves without being noticed by anyone we know.' Having told Tom that she was seeing a girlfriend from the WI, she skipped down the lane, full of the joys of spring. Tom watched her go, not fooled for a moment about who she was actually meeting. But he didn't much care as he was going round to Sally's. She was a good cook and offered to make a special meal for just the two of them. He retrieved her favourite white wine from the back of the fridge and went into the bedroom to change. He'd only got two decent shirts and two pairs of decent trousers and one suit. Shirley had cleared the rest out. He was amazed that he'd managed to hang on to these few bits, so eager was she to strip him practically bare in order to save Adrian from dismissal, which was what he always threw at them when he was in one of his 'fixes'. 'Do you want to see me thrown out onto the streets? Your only son?' he'd shout. Tom no longer cared about Adrian's welfare. He was old enough to look after himself. He wasn't without intelligence. He'd had a good education and as far as he was concerned, it was about time he learnt to stand on his own two feet and act responsibly for a change. 'Nobody could have done more', he thought to himself. 'I've sacrificed enough. What's left of my life, I intend to enjoy, with or without Shirley. If she prefers Lionel's company to mine, then so much the better, for I actually prefer Sally's company'. Having met with Bernard, his old boss, he'd managed to cash in the policy he'd taken out at the beginning of his employment with the firm. After forty years service, it had racked up a fair bit of interest. This had given him a nice little sum, something he'd managed to keep secret form Shirley. If she got wind of it he knew exactly what would happen to it. It would go straight into Adrian's coffers. 'Well they're not getting their hands on this' he told himself.

"Peggy, look at all these unpaid bills in this drawer," shouted Candice, her face a picture of concern.

"What dear? Oh, those. Yes, well I'll get around to paying them eventually. I admit I've let things slip a little since Arthur died."

"Are things....you know, difficult financially?" asked Candice tentatively.

Peggy sank down into her favourite armchair with a sigh. "Arthur used to deal with all that sort of thing. I'll get myself sorted eventually."

"Right, well let's get them all out onto the table and sorted into date order. We need to get organised or we'll be cut off or something" she said rifling through the entire drawer. On seeing the look on Peggy's face she added, "Don't worry. We'll pay them one at a time. This one's a red letter. Telephone bill £56. Why so much? Surely that's wrong?"

"It's when my son's wife was in hospital. She had a bad time of it, but she's alright now, thank goodness. My son was very worried, naturally. I must admit I nearly had a fit when I saw how much I'd racked up."

"You do own this house though, don't you?" Candice decided it was best not to mince words.

"It's my son's actually. When Arthur died I put it in his name. He's agreed to let me live in it until my death. It'll make things a lot easier when I do eventually go to my maker."

"He doesn't charge you rent or anything does he?"

"No he's a lovely boy, even though I say so myself. That wife of his, well let's just say she's not my type, if you know what I mean."

"You're not keen on her then? Don't you get on?"

"I don't see that much of them really. I've had two visits since the children were born. I do miss them all."

"Don't they invite you to go and stay with them occasionally?"

"No, not really, although I'm sure it's Ivy's doing. They tend to go to her side at Christmas. It's not that she's unpleasant or anything, just...well...."

Candice laughed. "Well Peggy, as long as your son's happy, that's all that matters."

"Yes, he seems to be. Although heaven knows what he sees in Ivy."

"Right, I'll put the kettle on for a cup of tea then we'll sort through this lot. I'm here now, so don't you go worrying yourself about anything. We're a team, remember."

"Oh Candice, you are a breath of fresh air. I'm so glad I met you. I've just had another thought Candy. Ought we to fetch Marcie's things from her flat? I walked past the house a few days ago and there was a 'for sale' sign outside. I knocked on the door, hoping to speak to the landlady but there was no answer."

"I wonder if she's decided to sell up then. We'll go tomorrow morning and fetch her things back here. She hasn't got much in the way of possessions from what I can remember but there might be some urgent post waiting on the mat."

"She can come back here until she sorts herself out. She'll want to find another job too."

"I did ask my boss if there was anything going at our place, but there isn't unfortunately."

"Did you say you were in advertising or marketing?"

"Marketing, it's quite cut-throat but I've been there a long time so they can't bully me like they do some of the younger staff. My boss and I understand each other."

"There's no chance of romance then?"

"It's a woman actually."

"Oh, sorry, I just assumed..."

Candice laughed. "We rub along alright most of the time. I don't think either of us have the energy to argue the way we used to in the old days. She's mellowed a lot over the years, but she has to have a bit of backbone or she wouldn't survive in that role. The men would just walk all over her. What work did you do Peggy, before you were married?"

"I was a typist at the Gas Board. I started off in the typing pool then worked my way up to personal assistant to the director. I worked right up until my son was born. Twenty years in total."

"You get less for manslaughter these days don't you?" Candice laughed. Peggy laughed too.

"You're right it was pretty boring most of the time. If I had my time again I wouldn't waste it sat in an office like that."

"What would you rather have done with your life then?"

"Oh well, I don't regret meeting Arthur for one minute. He was a good man, even though I say it myself, but I've always fancied running a little boarding house, breakfasts and afternoon teas, that sort of thing, nothing too fancy, just plain fare. I think I'd have been very happy doing that."

Candice poured the tea and carried the tray into the lounge. "Shall we have some of that fruit cake that's left?" she said. "We deserve a treat."

"She's in that room across the way" said Mabusi, pointing to a side ward. She watched him as he walked towards Marcie's door. He was a tall well-built gentleman, well-dressed and quite good looking. Mabusi wondered who on earth he could be and would make it her business to find out before the day was out. Marcie was laid back on her pillows with her eyes closed. When she heard footsteps approach her bed, she opened her eyes to see Dennis, her sister Deidre's husband.

"Oh Dennis! How nice to see you. Is Deidre with you?" she asked, struggling to sit up.

"Here, let me help you" said Dennis, straightening her pillows. He pulled the door to so that it was almost closed before sitting down in the only available chair at the side of her bed.

"Have you driven all the way from Hampshire?"

"Yes."

"You look tired. You must be exhausted after such a long drive."

"Oh never mind all that" he laughed. "How are you? I heard about your accident at the trial. What happened?"

She related the details as best she could, up to the minute she passed out. After that it was all a blur. She didn't want to be reminded of it and quickly made attempts to change the subject. "Seriously Dennis, you do look tired. You're not driving back tonight are you? Stay over tonight and get some rest."

"I'm not going back actually. That's why I'm here. I've nowhere else to go Marcie. I hadn't realised you were still in hospital and called at your house, hoping to bunk up with you for a few days. There was no sign of your landlady but there was a young man with a clip board walking about. He was from the estate agents. They're selling up it seems. He wanted your room cleared out as soon as possible as they'd got a potential buyer. They did send you a letter, but of course you wouldn't have seen it, being in here. I've got all your stuff in the boot of my car, so don't worry. " He looked down at his shoes.

"Not going back? What on earth do you mean?"

"I've left Deidre. We've been on different paths since the day we married you know. Things came to a head last night and we had an almighty row. She's been seeing another man. She denied it of course but I'm not stupid. It's been going on for quite some time. He's a neighbour of ours."

"Oh Dennis, I'm so sorry."

"Don't be. It's the best thing that could have happened really. He's welcome to her. I've given her the house. We've both got savings and she's got her own car. She wanted to move to a much bigger house but I was against it from the start and told her so. The house we've got is more than big enough for the two of us, but she wanted something grand and swanky. She went to the estate agents behind my back and well...she's bought this huge mansion of a place out in the country. She completely cleaned out our entire bank account."

"That sounds typical of Deidre. What will she do now? What will you do?"

"Oh she'll move lover boy into the new place. As for me, I'm ready for a fresh start." "What about your job?"

"I was made redundant a month ago. The firm's gone into liquidation. I got a bit of redundancy money, which will tide me over for now."

"Will she file for divorce, do you think?"

"I expect so, or I will. I'm not going back and that's definite. She said some very hurtful things."

"Don't take that to heart. People say all sorts of things they don't mean when they're angry."

"Oh she meant them alright. It's been a wake-up call for me Marcie. Last night I finally saw her in her true colours. It's taken me a while to come to my senses but I now realise that I don't love her anymore. I won't bore you will all the sordid details, she is your sister after all, flesh and blood and all that."

"You don't need to say any more Dennis. I lived with Deidre for years before she married you, remember. I know exactly what she's capable of."

"I wanted to make amends somehow, for the way she treated you over the sale of your parent's house. Half of that money should have come to you and Peter. She sold all the furniture and your mother's jewellery and kept the lot. You father had some expensive camera equipment too, which fetched a fair bit. She bought herself a designer handbag and matching shoes with that."

"Don't upset yourself over that. You know me well enough by now to know that money isn't important to me. Look, I tell you what Dennis, go to Peggy's. She'll put you up for a few days. It'll give you time to get yourself sorted. Tell her I sent you, she'll understand." She wanted to add, that she would follow him there as soon as she got out of the hospital, but just managed to stop herself in time. The prison sentence had momentarily slipped her mind.

Jasmine rang Grace's bell, hoping she'd called at a convenient time, for she was one busy lady for her age, always going here and there with several part-time jobs on the go. The door opened almost immediately.

"Oh it's you Sergeant Simmonds. Come in. I've just finished my shift at the church hall. I'm half way through my porridge," she said leading her through into the kitchen. "The kettle's on. What's occurred? Have they arrested them yet, the dastardly duo?" She fetched two mugs out of the cupboard and rattled on without waiting for a reply. "It's hard work polishing all that brass and wood in the church. My bones ache something shocking when I've finished in there. That toffee-nosed piece that does the altar flowers gets right up my nose with her stuck-up attitude. One of these days I'll swing for her."

Jasmine sat down and took off her hat, placing it on the empty chair next to her. "What's she said that's upset you so much then?" she laughed.

"It's the indirect way that she ever so casually drops into the conversation that all her kids went to private school and then on to university. Her husband has private health insurance from his place of work, which includes all the family. And of course she had to mention the villa that they rent in Italy every year for the whole of August. No bucket and spade job for her thank you very much."

"Do you know Grace we never had holidays when we were kids. We were too poor but one day my mother frog-marched us up to the ferry port and we sailed to Ireland. It turned out that one of her work colleagues had bought a caravan and there was a week's gap in the bookings. She let us stay in it for free. We lived on baked beans and swam in the sea every day. We walked miles over hills and just generally enjoyed being out in the fresh air. At night we played draughts and snakes and ladders and did jigsaws. The fact that we were together was enough. It was the best holiday we ever had. I often think back to those days when life gets tough. It always warms my heart and sees me back on my feet again."

"There are some wonderful beaches on the West coast. I spent all my youth there. We lived in County Mayo. My uncle ran a small business. There were eight of us in that house. A little two up and two down it was. Some weeks when the business didn't do so well, my aunt had to take in washing and ironing just to feed us. It's a wonder we survived at all."

"Finish your porridge. I'll make the tea. I wanted to ask you about Mrs Savage in the market hall. You clean there on Monday's don't you?"

"That's right I do. I used to do Fridays as well until recently and they cut me down to just Monday. I do the library on Tuesdays and the physiotherapists on Thursdays. The library's a doddle but the physio's a terrible place. They're so strict. The rules and regulations! I sometimes wonder if it's worth it. I'll look for something else I think."

"Correct me if I'm wrong" said Jasmine, placing two mugs of tea on the table, "but you've kept in touch with Mrs Savage haven't you?"

"Yes. Evelyn writes once a month. She's very frail now of course."

Jasmine waited, knowing that there would be more to follow.

"That nephew of hers gave her a hard time of it when she first bought the property. It's a fair size you know. She runs it as a B & B for the ramblers but her health's let her down of late. I can't for the life of me remember the name of her nephew now. He was a bad lot from the sound of it. He got mixed up in drugs. Of course he came to her, cap in hand, with a sob story about him being homeless and jobless, so like a good Samaritan she took him in. Well, that was a mistake!"

"What happened?"

"As soon as he was through the door he was demanding money from her. When she refused to give him any, he cut up rough, threatening her with all sorts. He said he was going to the police and that he'd tell them the property belonged to him. He repeatedly threatened to get her arrested. She became afraid of him."

"Is he still there?"

"No, he disappeared. He came home drunk one night, boasting that he didn't need her help because he knew where he could get his hands on a decent stash of money. She tried to talk to him and did her utmost to straighten him out but he wasn't having any of it. The money was hidden in a caravan somewhere and he said he intended to have it before anyone else got their hands on it. He left after breakfast the next morning and she never saw him again. A week later there was a report in the local rag about a fire on a camp site nearby. One of the caravans had exploded. They blamed it on a faulty Calor gas bottle". Grace decided not to say any more for fear of incriminating herself. She knew the drugs barons would be on to her if she divulged any names. But for all that, she rather liked Sergeant Simmonds and wanted to tell her that the caravan belonged to Adrian and that Evelyn's nephew was somehow involved. She sipped her tea, lost in thought for a few moments and was almost lost for words when Jasmine broke her reverie by asking her if this incident had any connection with Adrian and Roger. She looked her directly in the face but said nothing. After a few seconds she nodded, then added, "But you didn't hear that form me. They'll come after me. They're a bad lot, violent."

"This nephew, he must have lived around here then?"

"Yes he did, but not with Evelyn. She lived alone."

"Well thank you Grace. I'm most grateful for your time. If I were you I'd ease up on the cleaning, but if you're serious about ditching the physiotherapist place, there are jobs going at the new supermarket. You might want to try there."

"Oh, right. I'll investigate that. Mopping a few floors would suit me better."

"You've got my card haven't you? If anything untoward occurs as a result of this meeting, please ring me."

"I will. You know, what you told me about Ireland has made me think. My sister is always asking me when I'm going to pack up here and 'come home.' She's been keen for me to go ever since my husband died."

"Have you got family over there, apart from your sister?"

"Yes lots. I usually only go over there for Christmas and the New Year. It gets harder and harder to come back here every year."

"It might be worth you giving it some serious thought. Why don't you go over for a short break and talk it over with your sister? You could pay Evelyn a visit whilst you're there."

Grace merely nodded as Jasmine made her way to the door.

Chapter Nineteen

"Right, what have we got? Huxley's due back in a couple of days. If we've nothing concrete to give him, we're off the case," said Lee, pouring out the coffee. Jasmine and Chris were going over their notes, scratching their heads.

"We know Evelyn's nephew was involved with a drugs gang. It's more than likely that he made off with a large sum of money which was hidden in the caravan. There were no human remains in the debris from the explosion, according to the police reports. So we can assume he got clean away. Adrian gave a false name when he went to inspect the site after the explosion, but from the photographs, it was definitely him. We don't know the son's name but according to Grace, Adrian and Roger were involved. We can guess at what The Marigold is being used for," said Jasmine, stirring two sugars into her cup.

"I thought you'd given up sugar," laughed Chris.

"I had, but stress has taken over. It's back on. What worries me is that somebody's lying, either that or Huxley's falsified reports."

"Something's definitely not right about this whole case. It's becoming obvious that Huxley doesn't want us delving too deep" said Chris.

"He certainly didn't go over everything in as much detail as he made out. What do we do now boss?" Jasmine was careful not to call him Lee in Chris's presence.

"What happened when you interviewed Stuart?" Lee asked, hoping Chris had more luck than he had.

"He refused to speak to me. He told his receptionist that he was far too busy and in any case he'd already told everything he knew and he'd nothing further to add."

"According to Marcie, the day the computer crashed, Stuart just appeared on the premises. She certainly didn't call him in. She was adamant about that," Jasmine confirmed. "So, either Adrian or Roger spoke to him, or more than likely it was all prearranged."

Lee sipped his coffee, deep in thought. His instincts were telling him that they'd never get to the bottom of this case. They were merely going through the motions. It was just a paper exercise. Yet, in his mind it made him even more determined to plough on until they dug up something that would turn the case in their favour. A young girl had lost her life and lots more had lost their life savings, together with their marriages and home lives. It couldn't be allowed to continue. "Right," he said at last, "This week, I suggest you two get down to the golf club and that gentleman's club in town. Find out anything you can from anyone who knows Roger or Adrian. I'll go and see the solicitor who handled Harriet's case. We also, at some stage, need to speak to the solicitor who handled the court cases of the employees who lost their cases. Regina mentioned there were eight investors. Do we know who the other two investors are? She said they were outsiders, so presumably they weren't company employees."

Chris and Jasmine shook their heads.

"Hopefully the solicitor will enlighten us," Lee closed his notebook and tossed it aside. "Anyone fancy a nightcap? I've got some good whisky."

"Could I have brandy please? I think I'm starting with a cold."

"What about you Chris?"

"Whisky for me, thanks. I spoke to Mantos again yesterday. The harbourmaster at the port said he remembered Roger because of his attitude. Why does that not surprise me? Who on earth do they think they are these two?"

"According to Marcie, Adrian does have a softer side. She said she saw it when she first met him. He can certainly turn on the charm when he wants to" said Jasmine.

"You mean when he wants something, more like" Chris mused. Turning to face Lee, he asked, "How did you get on at the Market Hall? You spoke to the WI lady's husband I take it?"

"Yes I did. He was a very pleasant fellow. He was a mine of information regarding the Second World War. I could have spent all day there with him. He said Mrs Savage was deeply embarrassed about the incident with that piece of artwork and it upset her greatly. There had been a few other incidents prior to that but nothing on the scale of the Rembrandt. It made her realise she was getting too old to continue but they all loved her and were sorry to see her go."

"It comes to us all eventually" Chris said, taking a large gulp of his whisky. "You're right, it is good boss."

"What will you say to Huxley?" Jasmine wanted to know.

"Don't worry I've got a few aces up my sleeve. He may still take us off the case of course, but I'm not going quietly."

"How would you feel about the three of setting up our own Private Investigating Business?" Chris laughed. "I've always fancied that. Let's make it Plan B if we get the sack!"

"I'll drink to that!" laughed Jasmine, clinking glasses with him. She glanced at Lee but he didn't seem to be listening. It wasn't like him to be so silent and she wondered if he'd got other things on his mind apart from the Green case. Her favourite time of day was when she could crawl into bed next to him. He'd been true to his word and kept to his own side of the bed although their discussions sometimes went on well into the night. She hoped that tonight would be one of those nights as she was getting fed up of working under Huxley. A change to private investigating, now that she came to think about it, seemed very appealing.

Beth had been back at catering college for two weeks now and she was enjoying herself. Life at home was strained between the three of them. Her mother seemed to have acquired an active social life and was out most evenings. Her father was quiet and withdrawn, clearly not happy. She wanted to talk to him about what was bothering him but knew it wasn't her place. Whatever was going on between her mother and father would have to be resolved between the two of them. Inserting her key in the lock, once again there was no aroma coming from the kitchen which meant there was no meal on the go. She was starving. Her father was sat at the kitchen table going through his appointment diary.

"Hello dad. Mum out again?"

He closed his diary and stood up to give her a kiss on the cheek. "Fancy eating out tonight? I can't see much in the fridge to be honest."

"Oh, yes please dad! It will be like old times. Remember when you were seeing Marcie and it would be just the three of us? Do you know they were the happiest of times. I spoke to Marcie before I left the hospital. She wished me luck with my studies and ....well, you don't want to hear all this really do you, having turned over a new leaf with mum. I'll just nip upstairs and change then we can go." Gerald watched her skip up the stairs two at a time. How on earth could he break it to her that he'd made a huge mistake in coming back home? He wanted desperately to make a happy home life for her but feared it would never happen whilst he remained under this roof, but to leave again would be like throwing in the towel. When he went to the hospital to collect Beth after she was discharged, he glanced into Marcie's room and saw her lying there, fast asleep. His heart had missed a beat at what he'd thrown away. He'd had a chance of happiness and he didn't grab it.

"Do you fancy Italian or Thai?" Beth asked, wriggling into her jacket. It was the new one Gerald had bought her as her suitcase of clothes had never been recovered from the river. He took her to a warehouse in town where he could use his trade card and get a good discount. She stocked up on a few staples, trousers and tops, a couple of dresses and some shoes. Gerald broke out of his reverie with a start before replying, "We'll try the Thai restaurant first, if that's full we'll go to the Italian, they're not as fussy about pre-booking." They chatted away in the car, with Beth telling him about how the course was going at college. He was pleased that she'd slotted back into her old routine with relative ease. He just hoped that she didn't run into Ashley because that would upset the applecart. He'd have something to say to that young man if he ever showed his face around these parts again. All the time Beth was languishing in that hospital bed, he'd not visited once. If he wanted to finish the relationship then he should have done the decent thing and told her to her face. After two years, he owed her that much. The lad was a cad, but he supposed that the youth of today didn't have the same old fashioned standards of yesterday. They parked the car and made their way across the town centre on foot. The restaurant was opposite the town hall and as they rounded the corner, they both stopped dead in their tracks, for there in the front window of the restaurant was Beth's mother. She was sat with a man and they were holding hands across the table, gazing into each other's eyes like long lost lovers.

"Look dad! It's mum! She's with that reprobate! I thought she said that was all finished and done with. You were supposed to be making a fresh start and everything. She was obviously lying! The two-faced cow!" spat Beth. She fished her mobile out of her bag and switching it to camera mode, took three snaps on zoom. "There! We've got proof, if she dares to deny it!"

Gerald knew in his heart that she hadn't given up on lover boy. It was obvious really, but he secretly hoped that he'd got it wrong. On seeing them together it made him realise what was missing from their relationship. She never looked at him that way and never had. This man had obviously got something that he hadn't.

"Come on, let's go to the Italian. Can I have a small glass of wine dad?"

"Yes alright but just a very small one." They linked arms as they made their way back the way they'd come.

Tom decided to leave his car in Sally's garage. He didn't trust Shirley any more. Given half the chance, she'd have it sold and pocket the money. He told her he'd lent it to one of his old colleagues who needed it for a couple of weeks. Mind you, it was a bit of a pain getting on the bus with all the shopping bags, but he considered it worth it. There had been an enormous queue at the till in the supermarket this morning and he was later than usual, arriving home at almost lunchtime. As he made his way through the front door, he was greeted by three suitcases. His first thought was, 'what on earth is she throwing out now, surely there's nothing else left to sell?' Shirley was sat at the kitchen table, dolled up to the nines, reeking of scent.

"Ah, you're back. I was going to leave you a note but I thought, 'no' that wouldn't be right. I need to speak to you in person."

"Are you going on holiday or something?" he asked, wondering where on earth she'd found the money for such extravagance.

"No, Tom. I'm leaving."

"Leaving?" he said, incredulously.

"Yes. Lionel and I want to make a life together. It's now or never."

"Oh, I see," said Tom sitting down at the table opposite her. "I've only ever wanted you to be happy Shirley, you know that and if...well if Lionel makes you happy then....well I'm pleased for you."

"You and I have been drifting apart for years Tom. We think differently, whereas Lionel and I, we're of the same mind on everything. We're a team."

"What do you want me to do about this flat? I'm not staying here without you."

"Do whatever you see fit. I'm off now." She picked up her handbag and he watched her as she made her way up the hallway to the front door, her stiletto heels clip-clopping on the linoleum.

Chris had drunk three glasses of whisky besides the two glasses of wine he'd had with his meal. Although not exactly drunk, there was no way he'd be driving home. Looking through the curtains he could see the rain lashing against the windows. He didn't fancy walking home in this weather and he didn't want to fork out for a taxi either as it would leave him short for his weekend with Linda.

"You'd better kip here on the sofa," offered Lee, on seeing the look on the lad's face.

"I'll get you a blanket" said Jasmine, collecting up the glasses.

On climbing into bed, Jasmine decided that she had to get to the bottom of what was eating her boss. He was behaving strangely. "Are you alright Lee? You've been very quiet tonight. Is the case getting to you?"

Lee was annoyed with himself for dropping his guard. The fact that he'd fallen in love with her was something he never thought would happen to him again in his lifetime. It had shaken him up. He couldn't eat, sleep or think properly and it was driving him half mad.

"I was just thinking" he said, ignoring her question. "How about the three of us taking a trip across to Ireland to visit Evelyn Savage, are you up for it? We might get some information regarding that nephew of hers. We need some names otherwise we'll never track down the ringleaders."

Jasmine couldn't believe her luck, but didn't want to show too much enthusiasm as it might look unprofessional. "It couldn't do any harm could it? According to Grace, she's a lovely person. Every-one at the Market Hall loved her."

When Lee mentioned it to Chris the following morning at breakfast, he went quiet and pulled a face. "The thing is boss...well, I sort of promised Linda...well, you know how it is. We were going to make a bit of a weekend of it. It's her birthday on Sunday. I don't want to let her down."

"Right, well that's easily solved. Go and pack and tell her to do the same. Be back here in one hour. She can come with us. The break will do us all good."

Chris couldn't believe his ears and ran through the door like grease lightening, grinning from ear to ear. Lee smiled at the essence of youth and wished that he still had it.

"So who was your handsome gentleman friend yesterday?" asked Mabusi, placing a cup of tea on Marcie's bedside unit.

"Oh, that was my sister's husband. His name's Dennis," she smiled, thinking back to the conversation she'd had with him, but decided not to say anything about him leaving Deidre. She just hoped that Peggie was able to accommodate him.

"Aw, and here's me thinking you had an admirer," she laughed, her whole body shaking as she did so.

"How on earth do you stay so cheerful Mabusi? What's your secret?"

"It's all bluff. I'm crying underneath this veneer of loveliness" she chuckled, straightening the blankets and topping up the water jug. "The doctor has the results of your brain scan" she whispered. "I heard him mention it to the Sister just now. I hope that it's good news."

"Good morning Mrs Green" said Dr Singh. He was accompanied by a young trainee doctor who looked nervous. Marcie hoped that it wasn't going to be bad news, for she didn't feel able to cope with it on top of everything else.

"Your scan results didn't show up anything severe, I'm happy to say. We wanted to make sure because of these severe headaches that you'd been getting. There is some bruising and swelling. This should dissipate with time, so the headaches will eventually cease. Now, as to your eye, how is your vision? Can you see alright?"

"Yes doctor, I can. Perfectly, thank you."

"Good" said Dr Singh. He turned to his trainee to discuss the findings from the x-ray, pointing out grey areas on the plates. Sister Matthews bustled in, closing the door behind her. Marcie's heart fell to her boots. This was the moment she'd been dreading. Were they about to discharge her? Was she about to be taken to the prison to begin her sentence? She could feel the roots of her hair tingling and the sweat forming on her brow, neck and chest. She clutched at the blankets and once again, felt the nausea rise up in her throat.

Chapter Twenty

Lee's budget didn't run to four air fares, so they'd taken the boat. They sat in plastic chairs on the upper deck, all four of them feeling queasy as the Irish sea was at its notorious best, vibrant and choppy. Chris was disappointed that he'd not felt up to the pint of Guinness he'd promised himself. Right now he couldn't even manage a sip of water. Linda seemed to be fairing a little better, having bought a bottle of juice from the bar, she swigged at it to keep herself hydrated. Jasmine had fallen asleep, her head resting against a hand rail.

"Whose mad idea was this?" Lee said, taking deep breaths.

"Yours actually boss" laughed Chris.

"Shoot me next time I get any more bright ideas like this."

"It'll get easer once we get going a bit" offered Linda, cheerfully. "The sea is always rougher near the ports. Be patient."

After about an hour, the journey did indeed get smoother and calmer. Then just as they were about to start enjoying the tranquillity, down came the rain in great torrents. Raindrops a foot long lashed against their faces, the wind whipping through their hair.

"We'd better get inside before we drown!" yelled Jasmine, struggling to stand.

Once inside the lounge Linda chuckled, "Thank goodness for that! For a minute I thought we were going to be washed over the side!"

The rest of the journey passed amicably enough, the four of them reminiscing about past holidays over cups of tea and sandwiches. As they docked, they made their way out of the port towards the tourist information office to enquire about accommodation. The lady behind the desk was extremely helpful, offering them rooms at her sister-in-laws boarding house, which had just closed as it was the end of the season but a quick telephone call remedied that and two minutes later they were in a taxi.

"You're from Manchester then?" said the taxi driver. "I recognised the accent. I go over for the football every season" he said jovially, then proceeded to give them all chapter and verse of every match he'd attended since his boyhood, not once pausing for breath until they pulled up outside a neat little bay windowed house, fronted by a beautiful garden. "Here we are. You'll find your host most accommodating. She's a nice lady." Lee paid the fare, giving him a generous tip. They marched up the driveway and rang the bell.

"My goodness, look at the state of you all! You're soaked to the skin. It'll be hot baths you'll be wanting before your dinner." A grey haired lady in an overall stood before them, smiling from ear to ear at the prospect of a little extra income to see her employer through the winter months, which she knew could be bleak at the best of times. "I've put clean towels in your rooms and all the beds are made up with clean linen" she said, bustling them into a room just off to the right of the hallway, which she called 'the boot room.'

Their rooms were enormous and nicely furnished with king sized beds. There was a generous tea tray with sachets of tea, coffee and hot chocolate together with a selection of shortbreads. On the dresser stood a bottle of water and a carafe of sherry with two glasses. The bathroom was fitted with a power shower, a roll-top bath and a heated towel rail. A selection of complementary toiletries stood at the side of the wash basin together with a box of tissues. Two fluffy white bath robes hung on the back of the door.

"She's thought of everything" said Jasmine. "This is absolute luxury. I'm determined to enjoy this!"

"Look at the size of this bed. Now that's what I call a bed" said Lee, bouncing up and down on the mattress. His stomach still hadn't returned to normal after the boat trip but he didn't want to spoil things for Jasmine, so he made an effort to be cheerful.

"I hope we get something useful out of this trip" Jasmine called from the bathroom as she unpacked her bag. Lee didn't care much whether they gleaned any new leads or not, he was feeling jaded and tired. His head ached and he felt feverish.

"I think I'll have to turn in early tonight, I feel lousy."

"We'll make a night of it!" she called, hoping that tonight would be the night he reneged on his promise to keep to his own side of the bed.

Chris and Linda had stripped off their clothes and jumped straight onto the bed, determined to make the most of their time together. They didn't care if anyone could hear them or not. Enjoyment was the name of the game. An hour later, Linda sat up in bed and announced, "We'd better get washed and dressed. Dinner's at seven o'clock. Chris, there's something I should have told you." Chris sat up, suddenly all ears.

"What?" he said. He'd no idea what she was going to say.

"When I told you I was single...well, it's not strictly true. I'm married. My husband and I parted company eight years ago, but we never divorced. So, technically speaking, we're still married," she said, sheepishly. When Chris made no reply, she continued. "I thought it best to be honest, especially now that....well, I'm excessively fond of you. You do know that don't you? You're the best thing that's happened to me in a very long time; in fact, I think I'm in love. Actually, I know I am." She was hoping that he felt the same but knew only too well that men's minds worked differently than women's. "Well, say something" she urged.

"Is he still around, this husband?" he asked, sitting upright against the pillows.

"He's in Scotland somewhere. He went back to a former girlfriend. He decided that he couldn't live without her and should never have left her in the first place. In my opinion, for what it's worth, he smelt her money. He's lazy. It didn't take him long to engineer a reconciliation and live out the rest of his life in luxury. I don't have any rich relatives, so I'm never likely to have that problem," she laughed.

"No neither have I."

"Meeting you has made me realise that I should have instigated divorce proceedings a long time ago, but there was no need before I met you. I've decided to see a solicitor a soon as we get back."

"He never wanted a divorce then?"

"That's the strange thing about it, he....well, knowing him as I do, he's too mean to fork out the fees. I can imagine him sitting there, sipping his scotch, saying 'if she wants a divorce then let her pay for it.' That's the sort of person he is."

"You're well rid of him then. Come on let's get cracking or we'll get no supper."

They were provided with good home-cooked food and they all enjoyed themselves. They departed to the lounge where coffee was served in front of a roaring log fire. Lee telephoned Mrs Savage to arrange an interview the following morning. Mabel the housekeeper advised them, "Evelyn is still a little indisposed but she will see you tomorrow after breakfast around ten thirty, if that's alright," she said, with a firmness which told them it was that or nothing, like it or lump it.

"There's chocolate truffles in the tin if you'd like one, help yourselves. I'm off upstairs to bed now, so if you need anything, just let me know, said the housekeeper. With that, she left them to themselves to enjoy their evening. Linda was at a loss as to understand why her mood had plummeted since arriving a few hours ago, but on reflection she realised that it was because Chris hadn't said he loved her too. She had laid all her cards on the table, thinking that it was the best thing to do but now she was wondering if she should have kept her mouth shut. Had she given their relationship the kiss of death before it had even got started properly? She hoped not but had to admit to being more than a little disappointed that he hadn't declared his love for her, as she had done so openly. Still, it was early days and she wasn't going to give up on the relationship just yet. In the meantime she was determined to enjoy her weekend and resolved to buck her ideas up and stop being such a wimp. "Do you want me to disappear for an hour or two tomorrow whilst you chat to Evelyn?" she asked Jasmine. "I can browse around the town and get myself a coffee or something if you think I'd be in the way. I know police work is confidential."

"No that won't be necessary" Lee interjected. "It's an informal meeting. What we're after is contact names. She might not know anything but due to the length of time her nephew resided with her, I'm sure she must have picked up on a few things. Keep your eyes and ears peeled." He was sweating profusely and seemed to be fighting for his breath.

"Are you alright boss?" asked Chris, who was on his third truffle. "You look a bit out of sorts."

"I do feel a bit feverish. I might turn in early tonight but don't let me stop you three from enjoying yourselves if you want to go out on the town. Don't eat too many of those, you'll make yourself sick, they're very rich." He mopped his brow with his handkerchief.

"Do you fancy a brandy to have with your coffee?" Linda offered. "The barman's just opened up that little bar in the corner."

"That might be a good idea" he fished in his pocket for his wallet just as Chris jumped up.

"I'll get these. Linda can give me a hand." Just as they disappeared, Lee lay back in his armchair, closing his eyes. Minutes later he slumped sideways. Jasmine jumped up and felt for his pulse.

"He'll bring the drinks through in a minute" said Linda, on returning to the lounge. "What's happened?"

"I think he's passed out. We'll have to get him upstairs to bed. Go and fetch Chris, quick!"

"She's gone" said Tom, sitting himself down on Sally's sofa with a thud.

"Shirley? Gone where?"

"She packed three suitcases and left them by the front door for me to fall over when I got back from the supermarket run. She wants to be with Lionel she said, and that was it. Off she went. Just like that, without a backward glance."

"Oh Tom how awful. I don't know what to say."

"Well its water under the bridge now. I'm not staying in that flat a minute longer. I've been on to the housing department and told them. I never liked it."

"In a way, it's come at the right time hasn't it? There's nothing to stop us now is there? Off we go!"

"Are you still serious about upping sticks then?"

"Of course I am, but not without you. Are you up for an adventure Tom?"

"At my age, it's now or never. I'll not get another chance like this will I? Yes, let's do it before we change our minds!"

"Good, I'll put the kettle on and we'll celebrate with a nice cup of tea. Then we can make plans."

Dennis hoped he'd got the right address. He'd spent two nights in a hotel wondering what to do for the best but in the end he decided to take Marcie's advice and see if Peggy would put him up for a while. He'd insist on paying rent of course, that went without saying. He parked his car on the road and sauntered up the driveway to the front door. He noted that the garden could do with a good watering and weeding. That could be my first job, he thought. A statuesque girl about Marcie's age answered the door. She was wearing an apron and rubber gloves, obviously in the middle of some domestic chore. "Hello" she said jauntily.

"Sorry to bother you. Is Peggy at home?" he ventured nervously.

"Of course, come in" she beamed at him, her eyes sparkling like diamonds.

"I'm Candice, Marcie's friend from school. You're Dennis aren't you, Deidre's husband?"

"That's right. Gracious me, I didn't recognise you. How nice to see you. What are you doing around these parts?"

"I'm helping Peggy to get organised. Come through to the kitchen. Peggy, Dennis is here to see you," she shouted.

When Dennis entered the kitchen it was to see Peggy knelt on the floor with her head inside the oven, scrubbing brush in hand. "Oh Dennis, this is a surprise. Goodness I haven't seen you since your wedding to Deidre. Marcie's still in the hospital I'm afraid. Is Deidre with you?"

"Er…, no she isn't. I've been to the hospital and spoken to Marcie. Her face was still very bruised and swollen. I was quite shocked actually, as if she hasn't been through enough."

"Yes, quite. I'll put the kettle on if you just give me a minute to finish this, I'm nearly done."

Candice carried the tea tray into the lounge where Peggy and Dennis were chatting. She thought that he looked tired and strung out. On entering, she heard Peggy ask about Deidre.

"We've separated, I'm afraid. She's with someone else, a neighbour actually. It had been going on for a good few years but things came to a head and we had a huge row. Marcie told me to come to you. She said you might be able to accommodate me for a while, just until I sort myself out. Looking back, I can't help thinking that Deidre instigated that row on purpose. I'd lost my job you see. I was made redundant and she'd just emptied our savings account. She's bought a larger house. It was what she always wanted, she said. It's in what you would call an 'upmarket area.' I didn't want to move. There's only the two of us so why would we need a larger house? It just didn't make sense to me."

"She always was a headstrong girl. She may live to regret what she's done," said Peggy, rubbing her knees. The hard tiled floor in the kitchen had taken its toll and she was aching.

"I knew about the affair years ago but I just hoped it would sort of play itself out, if you know what I mean. I should have tackled the matter there and then instead of procrastinating. It's my own fault."

"Don't talk like that. I don't like the sound of this neighbour of yours. She'll come unstuck, you mark my words."

Candice laid the tea tray down on the coffee table. "Do you want some gel for your knees? Are they hurting?"

"They are a little. The gel's in the drawer in the Welsh dresser. Thank you."

"Stay as long as you like Dennis. Candice is staying with me too. She had to leave her flat as the owner was selling up. You can have the box room. Mind you, we'll have to tidy it up a bit!" she laughed.

Dennis immediately felt his spirits lifting as Candice handed him a slice of cake and mug of tea. As he bit into his cake he hoped against hope that Deidre wouldn't come looking for him if things didn't work out. Now that he'd actually made the break, he felt as though a great weight had been lifted from his shoulders. He wanted to taste the freedom. As if reading his thoughts, Candice asked, "So what will you do Dennis? I wouldn't rush into anything if I were you. Give yourself time to think things over. Make the right decision. Have you enough funds to tide you over for a bit?"

Peggy was wondering the same thing but didn't dare to ask. She smiled to herself. Candice was very direct in her approach she noticed.

"Yes, I got some redundancy money and I cashed in an insurance policy. It was money I'd put aside. Deidre knows nothing about it, thank goodness, or she'd have the lot off me. She has no conscience about stripping a man of his last halfpenny."

Peggy sipped her tea, thinking how some people managed to make such a mess of their lives and realising how lucky she'd been in having Arthur. It would never have occurred to either of them to walk away like that. Who on earth was Deidre trying to impress anyway, with her swanky house and a wardrobe full of designer clothes? Who on earth did she think she was? Of course, she didn't say any of this to Dennis. She thought he deserved someone better. Some women just didn't know when they were well off. They want excitement and passion. Arthur and I were both plodders, she thought to herself, but it suited us. We were happy with our lot and there's a lot to be said for that. When she eventually snapped out of her reverie, Candice and Dennis were discussing films and laughing fit to burst at some actor or other. After this she must have dozed off because when she next opened her eyes it was gone seven o'clock and there was a wonderful aroma emanating from the kitchen. Dennis was at the stove stirring the gravy and Candice was carving a chicken.

"Why on earth didn't you wake me?" said Peggy, smiling at the sight of a large plate of roast potatoes and buttered parsnips.

"I'm a dab hand at this gravy lark. Deidre never could get the hang of it. It was either thick and lumpy or too thin and watery," laughed Dennis.

Peggy fished about for something to do but gave up, finding it was all done.

"Well, actually Peggy, Candice has got something to tell you" said Dennis.

"Not bad news I hope? Please tell me it's not bad news, I couldn't stand it at the moment."

"No, it's good news in a way. I'll let Candice tell you. Come on let's eat before it gets cold."

They were on the cheese and crackers before the subject of Candice's news was raised again.

"I've been offered a two year secondment to another branch. It's a senior position and I'll be over the whole department. My boss thinks it will be good experience for me and has recommended me for the post."

"That's wonderful news Candy. You must take it."

"Thank you, I intend to. The only thing is it's in New York."

"New York? All the way to America!" gasped Peggy.

"Yes. I'm very nervous about it but if I don't take it I may regret it for the rest of my life. These opportunities don't come along every day."

"When do you start?"

"I leave this Sunday. I've to start straight away."

"What, so soon? Oh Candy I will miss you, just when we were getting so organised."

"Dennis is here now Peg. He'll help you. No doubt he'll make a better job of it than I ever could."

"You won't forget about me will you? And you'll come back?"

"Of course I'll come back! It's only a two year secondment. It'll soon pass."

"You'll write to us won't you Candy?" whispered Dennis. "Peggy's become very fond of you."

"Of course I will. I'll need somewhere to come back to won't I? Two years will soon pass. I'll be back before you know it. I'm nervous though."

"Have you been to The States before?"

"Only once with a boyfriend. It was New York actually. Bit of a disaster to be honest. We ended up rowing for most of the time. We were very young and headstrong. I don't think I could be bothered arguing now, I haven't got the energy" she laughed.

"You never know who you might meet over there. Mr Right might be just around the corner."

"Oh no, I'm not thinking along those lines at all Dennis. I value my freedom and my independence. I'm not sure I could go through all that again. The love of my life has been and gone. He was married and went back to his wife. I miss him every single day but I'm glad for his children. They need their father. Now I must go upstairs and get packing."

Dennis noticed the tears in her eyes and felt desperately sorry for her. It made him wonder if Deidre had ever felt that way about him. When he announced that he was leaving, she seemed relieved. There was no begging him to reconsider, just resignation that their marriage had reached the end of the road.

"Another cup of tea Peggy?" he asked, shaking himself out of his melancholy.

"Yes please Dennis. You will stay won't you Dennis? I've just got used to Candy and now she's leaving." She dabbed at the corner of her eyes with her handkerchief.

"I've nowhere else to go Peg. We'll be alright. We'll make a go of it. Don't worry. She's promised to keep it touch." "I've got a feeling she'll be too busy for all that" she said, resignedly.

"Yes, you might be right, but I think she's right to accept the post."

"Do you think Deidre and yourself...?"

"Get back together? No chance! The marriage was dead in the water a long time ago to be honest, but now that I've got my freedom back..."

"Would things have been different if you'd had children, do you think?"

"I've often wondered about that. Deidre didn't want any and I respected her wishes, although I was bitterly disappointed, I never mentioned it. It wouldn't have been fair. I thought perhaps that she'd change her mind eventually, once she reached her thirties, but she didn't. We did discuss it before we married. She just said she hadn't made up her mind about wanting them or not."

Peggy sipped her tea, thinking of her own miscarriages, three in total, resulting in only one son over the course of her child-bearing years. Still, he was a good boy and she felt truly blessed to have him, even though she didn't see much of him or the grandchildren. She hoped that Dennis would find love again, he deserved it.

Beth set the table, placing two soup bowls in the centre, together with the soup tureen. She hoped her father would like it as it was a new recipe that she was trying out. Hacking the bread into thick chunks, she placed the bread basket and the butter dish alongside the cheese, ham and pickles at the end of the table. It was the best she could do with the small amount of funds available. After the discovery of her mother's treachery, her father had insisted that she remain in her bedroom whilst he spoke to her mother. As soon as she heard her mother's key in the lock, she stood frozen to the spot with her ear to the door. Strangely, there were no raised voices. No shouting or arguing. An hour later there was a light tap on her door. She flew off the bed and opened it to see her father stood before her. Refusing to discuss what had been said between them, he merely gave her the option to stay with her mother or come with him. He was leaving immediately. What few possessions she had were quickly thrown into carrier bags. An hour later they were in the car heading for the motorway. They spent the night in a hotel and the following day he dropped her off at college before promising to fix up a flat. 'It's only temporary' he said, 'until we get organised.' So here they were in this tiny studio apartment. It was barely large enough for one person, never mind two, but it was clean and warm and she was happy to be with her dad. She wanted to try out the new recipes that she'd devised for her final exams which were in six weeks time, but lack of funds were preventing her from experimenting, so she would just have to hope that they worked out on the day. Knowing that her father was still paying the mortgage on the house made it awkward for her to ask for extra housekeeping money. The rent on the flat was exorbitant for such a small space but it was in a decent area and she was content. Hearing her father's key in the lock, she ran into the hallway to take his coat and briefcase.

"Good day dad?"

"Busy, but yes, how about you?"

"Only six weeks to go now! Then I'll have to think about a job."

"Have a rest first, you deserve it after all the hard work you've put in. How is Dean progressing?"

"A little better but he's still struggling with withdrawal symptoms. It's hard for him." She only visited him at the weekends as she was too busy during the week with college. It was the highlight of the week for both of them. Dean said she was the only thing keeping him alive and she felt much the same way about him. He was very different from Ashley but she saw that as a good thing. "Will you and mum divorce eventually dad?" she asked casually. She couldn't imagine them ever getting back together for a second time after what had transpired.

"I'm not even thinking about that at the moment Beth. I need some space. I feel wrecked."

"We need a holiday. I don't suppose there's any chance of that?"

"I'm working on it. There are a few people at the office who own chalets and caravans. It would have to be a freebie of course, which would mean a few favours in exchange. I'm not sure I'm up to that at the moment. It's taking me all my time to cope with my own workload. This smells good, what is it?"

"It's my new recipe. Tell me what you think. If it's any good, I'll use it for my exam. I'm so nervous dad. What if I don't pass?"

"You'll pass. Have confidence in yourself. Show me all your recipes and we'll go through them. I've done a fair bit of fine dining in my time over the years, so we'll go through them all together."

"Thanks dad."

Chapter Twenty-One

' "Mrs Savage will be down shortly."

"Oh, we thought...." said Jasmine.

"I'm Mabel the housekeeper. I've only been here a month. I had to leave my last post as the master passed away like. Forty years I worked for him, bless his soul. Mind you, he could be a cantankerous old so and so when the mood took him but Evelyn's a nice lady. She's had a few health problems of late, got to take things easy like, doctors orders."

Evelyn made her way down to the lounge sporting her dressing gown and bedroom slippers. "Do excuse me inspector but I'm not quite myself at the moment. I'll go back to bed when you've finished here." She chatted to Lee about his fainting fit the night before as Jasmine poured the tea.

"We've got Paracetamol and Aspirin if you need it," she said. "You look a bit washed out if you don't mind me saying so." Lee did indeed feel like death warmed up but was determined to get this interview over with.

"Regarding your nephew Mrs Savage, have you heard from him since he disappeared?"

"No inspector. I don't particularly want to either. He's my sister's child. He's not my responsibility. He was all sweetness and light to begin with, pleading and begging me to take him in and give him shelter. As soon as he got his feet under the table, he changed. I saw his true colours alright. He wanted me to give him money to buy drugs. I refused. That's when he started threatening me. It made me ill."

"Have you spoken to your sister about him since he disappeared?"

"Oh yes, several times. She made excuses for him, saying he's not a bad lad really. I can't help thinking that if she'd kept a tighter rein on him when he was younger, he wouldn't have got involved in the first place. She's fond of a drink is my sister, spends far too much time in the pub."

"The incident with the caravan exploding, do you think...?" said Chris.

"Oh yes, I think it must have been him. I'm only grateful that he didn't blow himself up in the process. I wouldn't want that, much as I detest his way of life. The day before he disappeared he was boasting about a large sum of money that was just sat waiting for him to get his hands on. When I asked him what on earth he was talking about, he clammed up. He knew he'd said too much. I tried to give him a good talking to, pointing out that no good would come of it etc, but he wouldn't listen. My sister blamed me for not handling the situation right. She said he would never have left if she'd been here. I'm sorry to say that she didn't seem overly upset about him disappearing. I suspect she was glad to see the back of him. He was always in trouble, even as a schoolboy."

"Can we take a quick look at his bedroom?" asked Lee.

"Yes of course. I haven't touched it since he left. My housekeeper went in to clean the first week she came to me but nobody's been in since. She'll show you up."

Lee nodded to Jasmine. "Take Linda with you. Two heads are better than one."

Jasmine and Linda followed the housekeeper up the staircase. "Nobody's been in here since I cleaned it," she told them.

"Did you notice anything whilst you were cleaning? Anything lying around?" asked Jasmine.

"You mean drugs? No, nothing. He didn't have much in the way of possessions, but I did notice he'd left his mobile phone behind. Whether that was intentional or accidental I wouldn't like to say. It's here in this drawer. Mind you, the battery will be flat now of course." She opened the top drawer of the bedside cabinet and handed it to Jasmine. "I expect he left in such a hurry that he clean forgot about it." She hesitated for a few minutes before heading for the door. "I'll leave you to it then."

"Thank you."

As soon as the door closed Linda piped up, "It's the same make and model as mine. I can charge it up on my charger."

"Have you got it with you?"

"Yes it's in my bag. I never leave in lying around in hotel rooms as I always forget to pack it and end up going home without it."

"Right, let's get it charged up. When it's fully charged, bring it to me."

"He may have left it on purpose you know," Linda said, taking the phone. "Especially if he knew he was going to be doing this disappearing act. Drop all his associates in it as an act of revenge."

"You could be right, but let's not jump to conclusions. There might not be anything on it that'll help us."

"What's your betting that there is, especially if he was a runner for a drugs gang, which I suspect he was? Perhaps someone owed him money or double-crossed him in some way?" She skipped form the room with eager excitement.

"Did you ever hear Billy mention any names whilst he was here?" asked Chris.

"He always left the room when his mobile rang, so I never got to hear what his conversations were all about, he made sure of that, but something strange cropped up one day whilst we were arguing. I told him he would end up in prison if he continued the way he was conducting his affairs. He was full of himself, all bluff and bluster. He looked at me in a very peculiar manner. 'They won't touch me' he said. 'How can you be so sure of that lad?' I said. 'There are cleverer people than you that have slipped up.' 'I know too much' he sneered."

"What did he mean by that?" Chris asked, scribbling away in his notebook.

"I never got to find out but when he went upstairs for his shower, I grabbed his phone and ran across the road with it. Mr Cosgrove had his young grandson staying with him. He's fourteen and such a clever boy. I got him to have a look and see if he could access anything but the phone was 'locked' he said, so he couldn't get into it, if you see what I mean, but he said that you could get around that and there were people who could 'unlock it' for a fee. I asked him if he knew how to unlock it but he didn't."

"So, you didn't hear him mention any names? Or anything that you think might help us with our enquiries?"

"I'm afraid not. I'm so sorry not to be of much help to you."

"Did he indicate where he might be heading when he left?"

"No. I didn't even know he intended leaving, he just disappeared. I got up one morning and there was no sign of him. He never came back."

"Were you worried?"

"Not overly worried, no. I asked my sister once if she was becoming an alcoholic and she hit the roof. 'How dare you insinuate such a thing!' she snapped. But I'm right officer."

"Thank you for your time Mrs Savage, we'll let you get back to your bed now. I hope you feel better soon" said Lee, draining the last of his coffee.

"We're pleased with your progress Mrs Green. We'd like to see you again in six weeks time to check on your eye but in the meantime, you're free to go," said Dr Singh, smiling.

Marcie's throat was bone dry and she felt sick. "Thank you" she whispered, almost inaudibly. Sister took the clipboard from the end of the bed and followed the doctor out into the corridor. Marcie stared at the closed door, willing it to re-open and for someone to tell her it had been a mistake and that she was to stay a little longer.

The moment she'd been dreading had finally arrived. She took out the plastic carrier bag containing her crumpled clothes from the bedside locker and proceeded to dress herself. Looking into her handbag for a hairbrush, she looked up to see Mabusi smiling at her from the doorway.

"Well my honey, it's time to say goodbye. Look after yourself."

"What do I do now?" she asked, failing to prevent the catch in her voice.

"What do you mean? Go home my dear."

"But the court case, are they coming to fetch me?"

"Are who coming to fetch you dear?"

"The police, I'll be starting my prison sentence I presume."

"Prison sentence? What on earth are you talking about honey? You were exonerated! There was insufficient evidence to convict you. The judge threw the case out. You're free!"

"Free? But, I don't understand. Are you sure?"

"Of course I am, absolutely sure, everyone knows. I spoke to that nice young policeman when you were first brought in. He seemed such a pleasant young man. Take my advice dear, ditch that husband of yours. He's no good."

"I already did Mabusi and thank you, for everything."

Chapter Twenty-Two

Linda was in her studio putting the finishing touches to the two lion statues that she'd been working on for the past month. She received the commission through a recommendation and although doubtful at first, she accepted the challenge and it had proved to be the best work she'd ever produced. 'At least I'll be able to have the central heating on this winter' she told herself. It had been three days since she returned from Ireland and she hadn't heard from Chris, despite having left two messages on his mobile. She was tempted to ring the station but changed her mind, not wanting to look desperate and needy. After carefully loading the statues into the back of the van, she set off to deliver them, hoping that they would survive the journey and arrive in one piece. Normally, a project like this would raise her spirits but the situation with Chris was laying heavily on her mind and she felt sad and depressed, telling herself that she'd totally misread the whole situation regarding their relationship. Her eyes filled up with tears but she fought it and knew she'd have to throw herself into her work and keep busy to take her mind off it. Checking the address in her work diary, she turned into a leafy private road which led into a long driveway. At the entrance stood two stone pillars. She stopped the van and stared as she approached them. Her statues were to sit on top of them and she smiled to herself, knowing that they would look good. She couldn't wait to see the effect and sped up towards the house. The driveway was almost a mile long and the manor house stood in all its splendour amongst acres of land. 'Very nice' Linda thought to herself, ringing the doorbell. A teenage girl opened the door, a slice of pizza in her hand. "Hello, are you Linda?" she asked, licking her fingers. "Dad's not around at the moment but he said to put the lions in the garage. I'll just fetch the key then we can drive around the back."

"Sorry to interrupt your lunch," Linda said, warming to the young girl, who seemed openly friendly.

"It's my breakfast actually. I can't wait to see them. Dad's left this envelope for you" she said, handing over a fat package. "It's the balance of the money he owes you. Turn left down this side of the house, the garages are at the rear. We're to use the one nearest the hedge."

As she opened the back doors of the van, Hamish shot out and proceeded towards the garages. "Hamish don't you dare disappear!" she shouted. "I'll never find him in these grounds!" she chuckled. "He's not a bad dog really but he does like to be outdoors and hates being cooped up inside."

"I love dogs. We've got four, two Great Danes and two Labradors, one golden and one chocolate." She pressed the remote control button and the garage doors opened. Between the two of them, they managed to get the statues inside and safely stored in the corner. "Would you like a cup of tea before you go?" she offered.

"That would be lovely, thank you. I've not had my breakfast yet."

She led them into a huge modern kitchen. Linda had never seen anything like it. It was like something you see in these colour brochures or glossy magazines. She sat at the large table and watched as the young girl busied herself with the teapot and cups. She noticed a pile of mail on the worktop and saw the name B.Mackleroy on the top envelope. The name immediately rang a bell and she knew where she'd heard it before. It was one of the names they'd taken down off Billy's mobile phone after Jasmine had unlocked it. Bunny Mackleroy. She wondered what the B stood for. Of course it couldn't be the same person she told herself. She was letting her imagination run away with itself, but all the same she was curious. "What line of business is your dad in?" she asked, as casually as she could.

"He's retired now. He used to be a painter and decorator for the local council."

Linda wondered where he'd got the money to afford a luxurious pile such as this. It certainly couldn't be through working for the local council. They didn't pay those sorts of wages. She reckoned he must have inherited it, or his wife had.

"Would Hamish like a couple of dog biscuits?" she asked.

"I'm sure he would, thanks." On seeing her disappear for a couple of minutes into the walk-in larder, Linda took the opportunity to rifle through the other letters in the pile and sure enough there was one at the very bottom in curly handwriting addressed to 'Bunny.' She felt herself go hot. Surely this lovely young girl's father wasn't mixed up in this drugs ring, was he? Even if he was, she couldn't bring herself to shop the man who'd been the means of such a good commission. She suddenly thought of Chris and was torn in her loyalty to him as a police officer. No, she thought, he can do his own digging, especially as he'd obviously given her the brush-off. She walked Hamish around for an hour before going home. Just as she put her key in the door, the telephone in the hall rang.

"Linda? It's Jasmine. Is Chris with you by any chance?"

"No, I haven't seen him since we got back from Ireland. Why?"

"That's strange. He was on two days off but he should have turned in for his shift today. He's not answering his landline or his mobile, any ideas where he could have gone?"

"No I haven't, sorry. I've got a key to his flat. Perhaps he's in bed ill or something?" she offered, her spirits rising in the hope that it was the real reason for him not contacting her.

"Can you meet me there in five minutes, just to do a quick check? The boss is panicking a bit. We're on the trail of this drugs ring and he was right in the middle of it. He's convinced that something's happened to him, copper's nose and all that." She rang off before Linda could answer. Putting Hamish's collar back on, she dashed back out to the car. On arriving at Chris' flat she noticed his allocated parking space was empty.

"No sign of the car" said Linda, that's his space there, pointing to the only vacant spot. The flat was empty. "You've got me worried now." They stood in the kitchen staring at each other, both of them lost for words. She thought about the commission for Bunny Mackleroy that she'd just completed and wondered whether to mention it. It seemed disloyal, especially as the money was good and it would save her from a very bleak winter, but if Chris was involved...or lying hurt somewhere...or locked up in a room somewhere...or whatever.

"What are you thinking?" asked Jasmine.

"Well, I might be getting a bit carried away with my imagination but I've just completed a commission for someone who called himself Ben. When I dropped off the statues, his daughter invited me in for a cup of tea and I noticed a pile of mail on the worktop addressed to Bunny Mackleroy. It was one of the names I took off Billy's mobile. It might be worth checking there."

"Give me the address," she said, getting out her notebook.

"Thinking about it, Hamish was sniffing around and stood barking for England outside one of the garages, the fifth one along from the left. I asked her what was in there and she said it was all her dad's stuff but didn't elaborate. You will let me know won't you, if you do find him? I'm really worried now. I thought he'd gone off me when I didn't hear from him."

"No chance of that Linda! He's dead keen, believe me. He never stops talking about you."

"Really?" said Linda, her mood suddenly brightening.

"We're on to this drugs ring. It's all stations go! We'll never get a better chance than this. We've got to nail it. Preferably before Huxley returns from his break," she smiled and then hot-footed it back out to her car, disappearing in a cloud of smoke.

"How did it go?" asked Gerald, giving his daughter a hug.

"Not bad, I think. Everything turned out the way I intended it to, so it just depends whether they liked it or not, but I worked really hard on my presentation as well, just like you said dad."

"Good. I'm sure everything will be fine. Now, as a little celebration, I've reserved us a table at the Italian."

"Is it bad luck to celebrate before I've got the results?"

"No, we deserve it. We've both worked hard. I need a drink."

"Dad?" she said tentatively.

"Yes?"

"How about if I go the hospital and speak to Marcie? Now that you and mum...."

"Oh I don't think she'll have me back now after the way I let her down so badly."

"You don't know until you try. What have you got to lose? She can only say yeah or nay can't she? At least you'll know where you stand. I really miss her."

"Yes Beth, so do I. So do I," said Gerald, resignedly. In truth he was finding it more and more difficult to find a reason to get out of bed in the mornings. He'd lost his enthusiasm for living. His wife's betrayal had sent him spiralling into a fit of depression like nothing he'd ever experienced before. He wasn't sure who he could trust these days. No that wasn't strictly true, for he knew he could rely on Marcie. He missed her desperately. Why had he been so stupid as to believe his wife's lies? The pleading and begging, the tears and words of remorse, telling him she was full of regret and taking the blame for everything, wanting to start afresh and make things right between them. It was all an act to drag him away from Marcie. She'd seen them together and didn't like it. Even though she didn't want him herself, she couldn't bear the thought of somebody else getting their clutches into him. He was blind to it all. He smiled at his daughter and was glad that he had her in his life. He knew he had to keep going, for her sake at least.

Lee showed his ID to the lady who opened the door. "We'd like to speak to Bunny Mackleroy if he's around" he said, not mincing words.

"Oh, I'm terribly sorry sir, there's nobody home at present. I'm the cleaner. The master called last night, asking his daughter to meet him in London, so she took the train early this morning." She opened the door and motioned for them to step inside.

"Any idea whereabouts they're staying in London?"

"He didn't say. They're not likely to discuss these things with me. He's a very busy man. There's always a lot of people coming and going, at all hours of the day and night sometimes."

"Are you able to give us any names and addresses, or contact telephone numbers?"

She scratched her head and seemed lost in thought for several minutes before opening a drawer in the hall table. She pulled out a telephone book, held together with an elastic band. "Don't know if this will be of any use to you. It's all I can think of. I have my duties to attend to you see. I did see the same faces now and again, like you do, but I couldn't tell you who they are. There was one name that stuck in my mind because it was unusual, 'Eugene' he called him, medium build with thinning sandy coloured hair. He was always smartly dressed and drove a black Mercedes. Very polite he was and well mannered, not like some of the others. A rough looking lot they were, some of them."

"Do you have the keys to the garages around the back? We need to take a look inside them."

"Ah, now wait a moment, I might just be able to help you there" she said, making her way into the kitchen. She rummaged through a couple of the drawers in the Welsh Dresser. As she was doing so, she had a feeling that she wasn't likely to see her employer or his family ever again. Her husband had nagged her for quite some weeks now to give the job up, telling her that Bunny had a bad reputation and he was up to no good. She'd hit back with the fact that he was her employer and paying her a decent wage, for that she was grateful and his young daughter was delightful.

"It's in a little red pouch" she said, tossing aside scissors and bits of string, rolls of masking tape and packs of batteries.

"I'll help you to look" said Jasmine, diving into the next drawer along. "Is this it?" she said holding up a small leather pouch.

"Yes, I think so. Are there keys inside?"

"There's a bunch here. We'll try them," she said following Lee outside. The housekeeper followed them out.

"It's this way officer" she motioned, pointing in the opposite direction to the way he was walking. "That's just the bin store, that side." Lee went straight to garage number five and tried all the keys in the lock, none of which fitted.

"That's strange" said the housekeeper. "I'm sure all the garage keys are on this key ring. I don't know of any other. Lucy used it all the time when stuff was being delivered."

"Lucy? Would that be the daughter?" asked Jasmine.

"Yes. She's a lovely natured girl. Nice disposition for a young person. We get on well. It was one of the reasons I decided to stay here."

"Did she ever talk about her father's business transactions? Mention any names?"

"No never. She loved horse riding. She rode nearly every day. There was one horse at the stables that she was very fond of called Merrylegs."

"Where are these stables?"

"Just up the lane. The road at the back of the house runs on to it. Husband and wife team run it. His name is Andy and his wife is Dortha. She's Danish I think."

There was a loud crack. Lee had succeeded in breaking the lock and heaved up the door. Curled up in the corner like a bundle of rags, was Chris

"Oh my goodness!" screamed the housekeeper.

Lee and Jasmine immediately ran inside and Lee felt for a pulse. "He's alive, call an ambulance. He's been drugged by the looks of things. There's a strange smell."

Chapter Twenty-Three

Dennis and Peggy arrived at the hospital only to be told that Marcie had been discharged two days ago, which sent Peggy into a flap.

"Where can she have gone?"

"Don't worry Peggy, we'll find her," he said, not at all sure that he knew where to start looking.

"Oh look, here's that nice young lady I was telling you about. Hello Beth, how nice to see you. Marcie's not here. She was discharged two days ago," she said. "This is Dennis, Marcie's brother-in-law. Dennis, this is Beth," she said. "How is that young man coming along? I notice he's not here either." She suddenly realised that she'd probably come to see him rather than Marcie and felt a bit foolish.

"Hello." She shook hands with Dennis before replying, "He's in a drug rehabilitation centre. I go at the weekends mainly, but now that I've finished my college course I'll be able to go in the week as well." She had secretly hoped to have a quick work with Marcie and tell her about her parents separating in the hope of them getting back together.

"You must tell me all about it. How did your exams go?"

"A lot has happened since then. I've left home."

"Really?" Peggy was a little shocked at this, Beth being so young. "You must tell me all about it. Would you like to come back to the house for some tea and cake?"

"Thank you." Beth knew that her father was in meetings all day today and would be late home for his evening meal, so she was glad of the company. It would be infinitely better than sitting in the flat all alone. Much as she liked the flat, it could be claustrophobic at times. She wasn't sure if it was advisable to mention Marcie's brief relationship with her father, after all he hadn't given his permission to make it public knowledge. The afternoon passed amicably enough with Beth telling them all about her catering course and the menus she produced for her final exam. Peggy was very interested to know what she intended to do now that she was qualified.

"It all depends on dad. My mother and he...they've recently separated. I want to stay with him."

Peggy mentioned her dream of running a B & B and they speculated on where would be the best location to attract the tourists. Dennis ran her back to the flat where she tried out a new recipe, hoping that her father would like it.

"Adrian? It's your dad here. Where are you? I rang the office but they said they hadn't seen you for about a month."

"I'm abroad dad. I'm very busy. What do you want?"

"Are you really abroad? Gosh, I wouldn't have guessed, the reception's so clear. It's just to let you know that your mother has left me. She wanted to be with Lionel."

"Well that doesn't surprise me one bit! You've only got yourself to blame. I haven't got time for all this, I'm busy."

"It was just to let you know that I gave the keys to the flat back to the housing association. I didn't want to stay there without your mother. I never liked it anyway. So, I thought I'd let you know in case you needed to contact us."

"Why on earth would I need to contact you?" he snapped.

Tom was tempted to say, 'the next time you run out of money would be just about right'. There was a loud 'click' and the line went dead. 'I don't know why on earth I bothered' he said under his breath.

"There's a gentleman to see you Lee. He won't speak to anyone else. He's been waiting over an hour," said the desk sergeant.

"Thanks, any chance of some coffee?"

"I'll get them" said Jasmine, heading towards the kitchen. They'd inspected the nine garages at Bunny Mackleroy's and found them all empty. He'd obviously been astute at moving all his stash, but where to? They'd searched all the waste land at the back of the house, together with every depot and warehouse in the immediate vicinity, with no results. Chris was rushed to hospital with the assurance that he was very dehydrated but otherwise should make a full recovery, much to everyone's relief. A dead police officer on top of everything else would be the death of them all, or at least their careers. Huxley was due back in twenty four hours, so time was running out. During the two days they'd spent in Ireland, the rest of the force had circulated the golf club and the Mayfair gentleman's club, after making a note of all the names Jasmine had dictated from Billy's mobile. The truth of the matter was that they'd nothing new to report and were no nearer catching the drugs gang. Word had obviously spread like wildfire and they'd all done a disappearing act or were lying low until the furore died down. The bar staff at both clubs remained non-committal, some professing to be new to the job and others saying they were far too busy to chat to customers or be on first name terms with them. Most of them were either lying or frightened of losing their jobs. Jasmine was pinning her hopes of finding Eugine, the gentleman mentioned by Bunny Mackleroy's housekeeper, but the bar staff had shaken their heads. Jasmine thought that perhaps he used another name when out and about and that Eugine was his real name. It was like looking for a needle in a haystack. Lee was suffering from a chest infection and refused to stay in bed but Jasmine had insisted that he take his antibiotics. She hoped the gentleman in the interview room had come to impart information. They could do with a bit of luck to set them on their way. Instinctively she wasn't sure they were even on the right track. Huxley wouldn't allow them more time, of that, she was certain.

"Sorry to keep you waiting. How can I help?" said Lee, sitting himself down at the desk opposite a well-dressed gentleman of slight build and wispy, sandy-coloured hair. He stood immediately on hearing the door click and proffered his hand.

"Eugine De Vere, you must be Detective Inspector Purslow?" he said nervously.

"Yes, take a seat. I've ordered some coffee."

"It's about Bunny Mackleroy..."

"I take it that you're acquainted with him? He seems to have disappeared. Have you any idea where we can contact him?" Lee studied his face for clues and got the distinct impression that all was not well between the two of them, irrespective of what had gone on previously.

"That's why I've come. I've known him for a good number of years. We used to work together for the local council. I was an accountant there, he was a painter and decorator, but we became good friends over the years. He's always been driven by money, if you get my meaning. What he earned with the council was never enough, he always had some scheme or other going on the side, to make a bit extra, but just lately he'd gone haywire and I told him so. We had heated words about it but he refused to take my advice. I told him he'd come unstuck with all of this, but he went ahead anyway. Two years it's been going on! Once you get involved with those thugs, they never leave you alone! He said I was fretting over nothing and that he could handle them, especially as Superintendent Huxley was a close friend of his. 'They can't touch me', he bragged. He really thought that he was above the law officer, but when I see what's happening to these youngsters on the streets, it makes me sick. I recently lost my granddaughter you see. She was only sixteen. She took an E tablet at some club or other. She collapsed and ended up on a life-support machine at the hospital. Four weeks later they switched it off. She was clinically dead anyway. We're all heartbroken and it's all down to scum like him!"

"You're referring to drugs I take it, just to be clear?"

"Yes officer! Yes! I told him not to get involved with these drug barons, but it was such good money you see, easy money, for doing relatively little. You've only got to look at the house and grounds he's got to see just how much money he's made. When I think of all those years I slaved away at my desk, forty in total, and what have I got to show for it? He used to throw that in my face every time I spoke to him. He found it amusing, said I was a mug and that life was out there for the taking. You just had to grab your opportunities with both hands he said and he'd no intention of passing up on anything that was coming his way. He really thinks he's invincible! Well no longer! Not after what happened to our lovely Amy. She was the light of our lives. I'll tell you where he's likely to be hiding and I know where's he's stashed all his booty!"

Jasmine entered with a tray of coffee and placed it on the table. She pulled up a chair and got out her notebook.

"This is Sergeant Simmonds, she's helping me with this case." Turning towards Jasmine he said "This is Eugene De Vere, he has some important information for us."

Chapter Twenty-Four

"Hello? Is that Adrian?"

"No, it's Roger."

"Oh, is Adrian there? I need to speak to him at once!"

"Who's calling please?"

"It's Shirley. I'm his mother."

There was a long wait before Adrian answered. "Mum where on earth are you?"

"I'm in your flat."

"What! How on earth did you get in?" he shouted, irritably.

"Your neighbour let me in with his key."

"Well, he'd no right to!"

"Listen darling, it seems that your father has vacated our little flat. There's another couple living there! He's deserted me!"

"Don't give me that nonsense mother. You left him to take up with Lionel, remember?"

"Oh that! No darling, it's all nonsense. Anyway, Lionel...well, he's changed. He's not the man I thought he was, that's all. He certainly didn't want me moving in with him. I've nowhere else to go."

"Well you can't stay there! Go back to the housing agency and tell them you want a one bedroom flat."

"I can't do that darling, I couldn't afford it and anyway, who'd look after me?"

"I'm too busy for all this!" he barked and ended the call.

"There's a couple of letters here for Marcie" said Dennis, placing them on the kitchen table. He'd organised her mail to be redirected to Peggy's address. "One of them has an Irish postmark, I notice."

"Oh, I wonder if it's from Mrs Savage" said Peggy, studying the handwriting on the envelope.

"Who's Mrs Savage?" asked Dennis. Peggy proceeded to tell him about the sale of the painting that Marcie had picked up form an antiques stall. She didn't see the need to hide anything from Dennis, he was family after all.

"Isn't that just typical of Marcie?" he said, sitting down with a thud into the nearest chair. "She never was interested in money, not like her sister Deidre. It's all she ever thought about. It's amazing how different two sisters could be in personality and temperament. One's so mean she wouldn't give you the dirt from under her finger-nails and the other generous to a fault."

"Yes" smiled Peggy. "Let's have a nice cup of tea then we must think about finding Marcie. Have you thought any more about where she could have gone?"

"I thought about writing to Candy. She might have a better idea. What do you think?"

"That's a thought. Yes, she might know. Judging from her last letter, she doesn't sound too happy in New York. There are too many memories for her. The break-up of a relationship is never easy at the best of times. She seems happy with the work situation though, thank goodness. I'll be so glad when she comes home."

"That's if she comes home Peggy. A lot can happen between now and then."

"Yes you're right. It's selfish of me to expect her to come back, but I'd got used to her. She was so organised and very much a 'hands on' sort of person, she gets things done." Ten minutes later she was fast asleep in the chair, so Dennis washed the dishes then proceeded to plough through the mountain of paperwork in the kitchen drawer. He'd settled all the unpaid bills and they were now up to date on that score but there appeared to be at least two years correspondence piled up. She obviously hadn't been coping for quite some time, probably since her husband died. He scribbled a quick letter to Candice and walked to the post box to post it, hoping that she would find the time in her busy schedule to answer it. He hadn't known her for very long but found that he was missing her too. Her energy and zest for life was infectious and she had a sharp wit like no other person he knew. He found himself laughing unselfconsciously when in her company. He hadn't done that for a very long time. Yes, he too hoped that she would come back to them.

"Are you sure this is the right place Lee?" asked Jasmine, eyeing the huge container depot spread out in front of them. There were rows and rows of container vehicles lined up against the walls on both sides. "If we've got to search this lot, we'll be here until next Christmas."

"It's the address Eugene gave us. Look for a container with 'Matusa' on the side."

"Matusa?"

"That's what he said, in green lettering. Let's see if we can talk to the night watchman."

"There's a porters cabin over there. There's someone inside. Pull over and I'll sound him out." She jumped out of the car and made her way across the yard, flashing her ID at the window, after tapping on the glass to wake him up. An elderly gentleman jumped to his feet and opened the window. Jasmine thought that he looked too old to be working at this time of night. She asked about the container and waited whilst he checked in a log book.

"Yes, it left this morning at eleven thirty. It's due to be shipped out this evening from Felixstowe."

"Ah" said Jasmine, her mood suddenly darkening. Bunny Mackleroy had moved too quickly for them once again.

"Have you any idea where the goods were headed, by any chance?"

"Yes I believe they were destined for the Greek island of Rhodes. I didn't like the chap who I had to deal with. He was very condescending, bordering on being downright rude actually. I was glad to see the back of him. We don't need his sort around here."

"Can you describe this gentleman?"

"Gentleman? He was no gentleman! He was a well-built chap, not the sort you'd pick a fight with. Dark hair, dark eyes, sun tan, leather jacket, signet ring on his little finger. He was smoking those awful Russian cigarettes and kept flicking ash all over my desk. Walked about as though he owned the place and he seemed in a terrible hurry. Wanted the goods shifted within twenty four hours, which is a tight turnaround for us, we normally like at least forty eight hours."

"Thanks. Sorry to have disturbed you."

"My pleasure. I'll pop the kettle on for my brew. That usually keeps me awake."

When Beth entered the ward at the rehabilitation centre, Dean's bed was empty. Her heart gave a lurch. Surely they hadn't discharged him already?

"He's in the day room dear," shouted the nurse. "His mother's with him. Go on through. The tea trolley will be around shortly." Beth smiled and thanked her as she made her way down to the far end of the corridor. She could hear Dean's mother's voice as she entered the door.

"Well you've only got yourself to blame for that lad!" she admonished. "After the way you behaved towards her, you can't expect her to come running around here."

"Hello" shouted Beth, giving both Dean and his mother a hug.

"Beth, thank goodness you've come. Try and talk some sense into this errant son of mine. I'm off now as I've an appointment in town. We'll catch up later in the week, when I've more time." In an instant, she was gone.

"Was it something I said?" asked Beth, laughing.

"Appointment in town my arse! She's off to the pub! It's opening time!"

"You can't really blame her can you? She must get lonely," Beth soothed, stroking his forehead and moving his fringe out of his eyes.

"She has the cheek to have a go at me, when really she's just as bad!"

"Don't let's talk about her, let's talk about us. You and me."

"Beth, I'm really scared" he said suddenly.

"Why? Why should you be scared? What is there to be scared of?"

"They're talking about discharging me from here."

"That's great Dean!"

"No it isn't! Don't you see? As soon as I hit the streets again, they'll come after me?"

"Who will?"

"The gang. The drugs barons. They're a violent lot. They'll do for me Beth. I'm a goner!"

"I'm sure you're exaggerating Dean. They wouldn't dare. Your sister's a police sergeant!"

"They won't offer me protection." He was lost in thought for a few moments before speaking again. "If you see Jasmine, will you tell her that I'm sorry? Sorry for everything. I treated her badly Beth and I'm ashamed of myself, but it wasn't the real me. It was the drugs you see. They made me violent."

"What happened exactly?" asked Beth, suddenly getting nervous. Perhaps she didn't really know Dean at all.

"It's a long story, but basically I was a runner. Money laundering, they call it. One of the dealers short changed me on one of the 'drops' to the tune of £500. I knew I'd be in dead trouble but I couldn't think of a way to make up the money. I asked Jasmine to loan me the money and she refused. I got angry and lashed out, with my fists. I'm not proud of what I did Beth, please believe me. It was only after she upped sticks and packed her bags that I realised that I was out of control and had to do something to break the cycle. When I met them to hand over the money I told them I wanted out and I wasn't doing it anymore. That's when all the trouble started. They didn't believe me when I told them about the £500. The next thing I knew I'd collapsed on my bedroom floor and my mother called the ambulance. The rest, you know. Please don't judge me Beth, I ..."

"It's alright. I understand, really I do. Look at the stupid thing I did. I haven't the excuse of being on drugs. I was just in an anguished state and couldn't see a way out."

"You're the only thing I've got to live for now Beth. Please say you'll stay with me" he pleaded, taking hold of her hand and gripping it tightly.

"That all depends" she teased him, smiling.

"Will you marry me? I've got nothing much to offer you at the moment, but that will change when I get myself back into the real world. We can build a new life together. It'll be a fresh start for both of us. Please say you will." He looked into her eyes with such longing that she hadn't the heart to refuse him. "When I get out of here, I'll have to disappear, go somewhere they can't find me. Somewhere they won't think of looking."

"Leave it to me. I'll think of something. Here's the tea trolley." It was only later, when boarding the bus to go home that Beth realised she hadn't given Dean an answer to his marriage proposal.

Chapter Twenty-Five

"We've missed the shipment at Felixstowe?" said Lee, banging his fist on the table.

"So what happens now?" asked Jasmine, at a loss as to how to proceed with the case, with no leads left to pursue.

"They've put a tail on the boat. It's all down to what happens at the other end."

"You don't sound too hopeful."

"I'm not. I'm losing ground with this case. Huxley's due back tomorrow. He'll close the case."

"Can he do that?"

"It all comes down to resources. Where best to spend the money. With nothing new to present and no new leads, we haven't a hope in hell of continuing with this investigation. It's not justified."

"We tried our best."

"Yes but not nearly hard enough obviously."

"Fancy a brandy with your coffee?" Jasmine offered. She had to find a way of lifting him out of this doom and gloom attitude. It really wasn't like him. All his fighting spirit seemed to have deserted him.

"Aye, go on then. We'll go to the hospital tomorrow and see Chris. He should be back in the land of the living by then."

"Are you alright? It's not like you to be so negative."

"Oh, take no notice of me Jaz, I'm just overwhelmingly tired."

"Too tired for an early night?"

"Is that an offer?" he smiled, chancing his arm, hoping that he hadn't misunderstood her meaning.

"It might be" she winked and went to the cupboard to fetch the Cognac.

Dennis loved his new life at Peggy's and couldn't remember when he'd last felt so relaxed and happy. For the first time in his life he hadn't got to turn out of his bed and make his way to the office and the freedom was infectious. 'I could get used to this new life' he mused to himself as he washed the dishes. He made a pot of coffee and took it into the lounge where Peggy was sat staring into the flames of the fire.

"I'm so worried about Marcie. Where can she have gone Dennis?"

"Did she have any other close friends, apart from Candice? Or relatives?"

"Not that I know of, that's what worries me. She really didn't have anywhere to go." She sipped her coffee before continuing, "Have you heard from Deidre by any chance? She wouldn't have gone there would she? I know they weren't close or anything but still..."

Dennis couldn't help but laugh. "No Peggy! That's the last place she'd go believe me! I'm not even sure where Deidre is. Having put the house on the market and put a deposit on this new place."

"Where exactly was this new house? Was it in the same area?"

"We didn't get that far. She organised it all on her own without consulting me. I wasn't involved. She will have moved in with you know who by now."

"What foolish, impulsive behaviour. She always was headstrong, even as a child. I only hope she doesn't live to regret it."

"It's not my concern anymore Peggy. It's the life she's chosen for herself, so she'll be happy." Dennis knew that his redundancy package wouldn't last indefinitely and that sooner or later he'd need to find a way of procuring an income. Having made a break for freedom, he was reluctant to give it up, but tried to remain hopeful of finding something he enjoyed doing. His soul was crying out for change and he was determined to get it right this time. He knew that he had to make it work.

"You will stay won't you Dennis?" Peggy asked, earnestly. "I couldn't bear it if you left. Not now."

"I'm not going anywhere. These last few weeks here with you have been the happiest of my entire life so far. I will need to find employment of some sort though. I can't live on fresh air."

"Oh no not yet Dennis. Let's wait until Marcie's home then we can discuss it together."

Dennis was wondering what difference it would make when Marcie returned, but didn't say so out loud. A loud knock at the back door interrupted his thoughts.

"Who can that be at this time of night?" asked Peggy, looking concerned and hopeful in equal measures. Her mind was still focused on Marcie, although she knew in her heart that the girl wouldn't just turn up unannounced like this.

Dennis opened the door to find a young lady holding a small dog, a dachshund to be precise. She asked if Peggy was in and had she got the right house.

"Hello, Suzy isn't it?" said Peggy, suddenly brightening on finding a new visitor.

"I'm so sorry to disturb you like this but we didn't know what else to do. Is Marcie here with you by any chance?"

"I'm afraid she isn't at the moment," said Dennis, tickling the dog's ears. "And who's this little chap?"

"This is Milo. Marcie used to look after him. He belonged to the couple next door but they disappeared, leaving him behind. Marcie took him in and fed him but when she....well, the day she had to attend court for the hearing she asked me if I'd mind him until she got back, only...well, the landlord's sold the property since then and I'm afraid I'm not in a position to keep him you see. My father-in-law's critically ill so Mike and I are moving to the bungalow to look after him. He's already got two dogs so there just isn't room for Milo as well."

"We'll take him!" said Peggy. "He knows me. We used to walk him around the little park in the town centre when I called for tea on Sunday afternoons. I'm a member of St Mary's church on the corner and I used to call after the service."

"I'll get his things from the car." She deposited Milo on the kitchen floor and flew out to the waiting car, emerging two minutes later with a dog basket containing a lead and a few soft toys. Mike appeared with a cardboard box full of tins of dog food, a blanket and a chewed ball.

"Won't you join us for coffee?" Dennis offered.

"No, we'd best be off, we're all packed and ready to leave. Thank you so much for taking Milo. He's a dear little thing and I couldn't bear to take him to the dog's home. The estate agent told me where to find you. A bit naughty of him I know but I bribed him."

They watched the car disappear up the road in a puff of smoke before turning to see Milo sat staring at them from under the kitchen table.

"His car needs a new exhaust or something," observed Peggy.

Dennis swept Milo up in his arms. "Well young man, this is your new home now. Come on let's find you something to eat."

Chris climbed into the back of the taxi, having been discharged from the hospital. He was desperate for a hot bath and some decent food.

"You on that case?" asked the driver, swinging the taxi out of the hospital car park.

"Which case would that be?" asked Chris.

"You're a copper aren't you? That court case? That pair of twisters Adrian Green and Roger Moorcroft?"

"What about it?" said Chris evasively.

"I used to ferry your oppo around quite a lot. Ken Huxley."

"Oh really?" Chris was suddenly all ears.

"Yeah, he and that Bunny Mack...what's his name?"

"Yes I know who you mean. Were they friends then, do you reckon?"

"Friends, I should say so! Drinking buddies they were. Always down at that Mayfair Gentleman's club, drunk as skunks most of the time, thick as thieves if you ask me. They got chucked out of the golf club you know, for drunk and disorderly behaviour."

"Did they?"

"Yeah, and him a copper too" he chuckled. "He might be a superintendent but he couldn't talk his way out of that one! They're a bit particular up at the golf club you know. They won't stand for any raucous revelry. They like to attract a better class of personnel, if you understand me."

"I do" said Chris, now in his element.

"To be fair, it's that Mackleroy fella' I can't stand. He's arrogant."

"Have you known him for a long time then?"

"Years, we go back a long way. He's changed recently, though. He never used to be like that. In the old days, he was just one of the lads but in the past couple of years he's suddenly acquired status and it's made him bumptious. Huxley, by contrast is just a first class idiot. No disrespect, I know he's your boss and all that." He rattled on in a similar fashion for a good twenty minutes before pulling into Chris's driveway. Chris gave him a huge tip and thanked him.

"Well that went better than expected" laughed Bunny. The Romanian driver of the truck seemed more than usually nervous and was hopping about from foot to foot.

"Relax man, we're in the clear. I told you, they can't touch us. I've got connections in high places. He'll see us right. Now, all we've got to do is shift this lot."

"Shouldn't we...how you say...lie low for little bit. Let dust settle," said the Romanian. "I have family in Romania. I not do time in prison."

"You won't my friend. Trust me."

"How can you be so sure?"

Bunny tapped the side of his nose and keyed in the code on the security lock. The iron gates started to slowly slide open. The Romanian's eyes nearly left his head when he saw the amount of stuff stored inside, all of it illicit drugs with a street value of millions. He started to sweat and feel extremely uncomfortable, suddenly getting an attack of conscience. He had a wife and three small children of his own and wondered how they would react if they discovered he'd been dabbling in drug-running, for surely this lot would be destined for sale on the streets and in the local nightclubs. What on earth had possessed him to get involved with this man who had offered him easy money? He saw it as the answer to all his problems, being able to return home to his family, telling them that he'd worked hard in England. But this? This was all too much, even for him. It was grotesque, immoral and totally wrong. He also knew that he was in it up to his neck for Bunny Mackleroy wasn't the sort of man to take no for an answer. He wouldn't be allowed to just walk away from it all now. Not being able to see a way out of his problems, he was resigned to his fate of eventually ending up locked away for years to come and felt the nausea rising up in his throat, for when push came to shove, it would be his head on the chopping block and not Bunny's. It was no wonder the man was in high spirits, for his 'friend' in the police force would make sure that the blame lay elsewhere. He was in a win-win situation, whereas he himself was in a no-win situation.

Chapter Twenty-Six

Marcie walked through the reception area of The Grand Hotel and turned right out onto the promenade which led into Lytham. It was a walk she used to do with Gerald. The memories came flooding back without prompting. It suddenly occurred to her that they had never discussed the future. Perhaps she'd got the whole relationship wrong and she was just a distraction, rather than a partner for life, which was what she was hoping for. Had she expected too much? It certainly seemed like it. Telling herself that she'd got the memories to look back on, which was something to savour at the very least, she didn't regret any of it. It was the one part of her life that she'd do exactly the same again, given the circumstances. Smiling to herself, she thought of Candice's words of approval when she heard about Gerald. Her words of warning regarding Adrian, however, went un-heeded. The fact that she was free and not facing a prison sentence had done nothing to lighten her mood, which puzzled her. She should be dancing on air, full of the joys of spring at her new found freedom, so why did she feel suicidal? Her appetite had disappeared, she wasn't sleeping well and her energy levels were low. An over-whelming desire to get away from everything had dominated her thoughts and before she knew it she'd checked in, using her credit card. A poster on a hoarding, advertising a play at the little the-atre broke her reverie and suddenly she was transported back to all the plays they'd attended together, the conversation flowing easily between them. They would discuss all their favourite playwrights, poets and composers, artists and authors, often talking well into the night, time forgotten. He was certainly well read and was quite simply the most interesting man she'd ever met on that score. Adrian, by contrast was a closed book. When asked what novels or films he liked he would tell her he'd hadn't time for all that, work being his priority above everything else. If you wanted to succeed in life he said, you had to put all thoughts of entertainment out of your mind. She had no idea what music he liked, what books he read – if he indeed he read at all, which she doubted, which type of music he liked or even what hobbies he had. His work seemed all-consuming and he certainly had a preoccupation with Roger. Practically every other sentence made reference to him or his methods. She marvelled at the books and plays that Gerald recommended. They were always enjoyable and to her taste, whether this was by design or accident she had no idea but she was eternally grateful. Her repertoire had expanded enormously because of it and her life was all the richer. He also had an extensive knowledge of art, having studied all the great masters at university. On a visit to The Louvre in Paris, he'd talked her through the history of art, rattling off details as though he was an expert, which to her mind, he was. How on earth did one acquire and retain such knowledge, she often asked herself? The memories continued to flood back, tumbling into her thoughts without warning, her face wet with tears. Before she knew it she'd reached the windmill at Lytham, having no recollection of how long she'd been walking. She spotted a gentleman sitting on the bench facing the coast. It was his shoes she noticed first, brown Oxfords. Gerald used to wear them. As she approached she took note of his dark grey overcoat. It was just like the one Gerald used to wear. Hastily brushing away her tears with the back of her gloved hand, she was determined to be civil and say hello. She had to snap out of this melancholy and get back into the here and now. He seemed not to notice her at first, until she paused just long enough to smile, then he suddenly shot off the bench and lunged towards her, his face a mask of anxiety. He was certainly thinner than she remembered him. He had a rather sad, haunted look about him.

"Oh, Marcie! Thank goodness I've found you!" he said, wrapping his arms around her shoulders in a tight bear hug. She was so startled that she almost toppled backwards.

"Gerald! My goodness, I never expected to see you here. Have you come in search of me?" she felt both puzzled and alarmed, hoping that there hadn't been some catastrophe which required her urgent attention.

"Beth has taken to calling at Peggy's when I'm working late. They said you'd disappeared and they had no idea where you were. They're really worried about you, as I am. Are you alright?"

"Yes, I suppose so," she said nonchalantly. "How did you know where to find me?"

"I took a chance. It's the one place we used to love. It's our place. I called at The Grand and booked a suite. Would you like a pot of tea?" In all the time she'd known him, she'd never heard him offer her a pot of tea. He only drank coffee.

"Tea, Gerald?"

"Oh yes, I'm quite the connoisseur you know." He was smiling now and taking her arm, guided her towards the town centre. Five minutes later they were seated in a small tea shop. The waitress brought china cups and saucers together with a plate of scones and an enormous teapot.

"I'm feeling a little light-headed," he said, "that and the fact that I've not slept well for weeks. Everything's gone wrong Marcie. I've been such a fool. Will you ever forgive me?"

Marcie made no reply, not trusting herself to give the right answer, for she had no idea what he was going to say next. Was he asking her to forgive him for leaving her the way he did and going back to his wife? He poured out the tea and plated up one of the scones and handed the plate to her. She'd never known him to eat during the day, so this was strange behaviour indeed.

"My wife stitched me up. Stripped me of everything I possessed and took the lot. All I possess are the clothes I'm now wearing. I was a complete fool for trusting her and believing her lies. Of course, she was still seeing him behind my back. Beth and I caught her red handed one night when we went out for a meal. When I confronted her she didn't bother to deny it, just made out that she couldn't give him up as her feelings for him were too strong. Beth and I are in a rented studio flat on our own. I gave her the option of staying with her mother or coming with me and she packed her things immediately. She's finished her catering course now, so she's qualified. When Beth said you'd disappeared, I went into a blind panic. I was afraid that I'd never see you again. It was then that I knew my future belonged with you. I should never have gone back to her and I'm so sorry for leaving you the way I did. Believe me Marcie when I say that I tormented myself day and night before making the decision, but her pleas of begging me to give her another chance finally got to me. I thought of Beth and how breaking up the family home would affect her. I just wanted to do the right thing. I've made a terrible mess of things and....well, heaven knows Marcie, I've precious little to offer you now but I must ask before it's too late. Would you consider marrying me? Once our divorces are through? I have a little nest egg put buy. It's secreted away somewhere. She doesn't know anything about it, or she'd have it off me. I can't touch it until the divorce papers are signed, but it should be enough to buy us a little cottage somewhere. It's not much I know, but I do believe we could be happy. Would you like that? Please say you'll marry me Marcie. We'll start again. We'll build ourselves a new life."

Marcie was stunned into silence. Had she really heard the words she'd been longing to hear for such a long time? Was it sensible to rush headlong into another marriage so quickly after the first disastrous one? Realistically, the alternative was to spend the rest of her days alone. "I've made a mess of things too" she said, placing her hand on top of his. "I've nothing much to offer either. All I possess are the clothes that I'm wearing, so we're both in the same boat." They laughed at this. The earnest look in his eyes, the look of longing, hope and expectation etched in every nuance of his face made her realise that she hadn't been wrong about him after all. "I will marry you Gerald, as long as you don't expect too much! I can't cook and I'm terrible at housework, according to my mother."

"Oh, who cares about all that?" he said, lacing his fingers in hers and raising his cup to a toast. "Here's to us!" They clinked cups and tucked into their scones.

Bunny was losing his temper with the Romanian, who was suddenly becoming demanding and uncooperative. He was refusing to accept their usual terms of 50% now and 50% on completion of the drop. Instead he was demanding the whole lot up front or he wouldn't do it. It was to be his last assignment he said because he was returning home to Romania.

"Alright suit yourself mate" snapped Bunny, "I can soon find someone else to do it."

The Romanian turned on his heels and headed back out towards the gates. He'd reached the road and was just about to head off into the night when he heard the words, "Alright, you win." Ten minutes later he was in the cab and on his way. He now had enough funds for a flight back home and a decent nest egg to impress his wife with. He drove the truck into a side road at the back of the railway, then checking the cab to make sure he hadn't left anything personal behind, boarded a train to London.

"Mr Mackleroy? We'd like a word please" said Lee, showing his ID.

"What's all this about?" said Bunny, looking about him shiftily to see if any of the neighbours had seen the police car.

"Can we come in?"

"No you can't, I'm a bit busy at the moment."

"Fair enough, we can conduct our conversation here on the doorstep or down at the station if you prefer."

Bunny opened the door, stepping to one side to allow them to enter. Jasmine stifled a gasp as she clocked the decor and furnishings. It was like walking into Buckingham Palace. They weren't invited into the lounge to sit down so Lee launched straight into the attack standing in the hallway.

"We've had a complaint from a gentleman, grumbling that a large lorry has been parked outside his house, blocking his driveway."

"What on earth's that got to do with me?" barked Bunny, starting to sweat.

"We've traced the lorry back to you. Don't bother denying it, we've finger printed it. It contained a huge assignment of illegal substances."

"I don't know what you're talking about!" he snapped. "I'll be speaking to Superintendent Huxley about this, its harassment!"

Jasmine produced a photograph and handed it to him. "Ever seen this man?"

He studied it for several seconds before handing it back, "No."

"Right, that will be all for now" said Lee. "Thank you for your time. We'll be in touch."

Jasmine placed the photograph into a plastic wallet. They now had his fingerprints.

Bunny was furious. The Romanian had obviously done a runner, leaving the whole consignment behind, which was now in the hands of the police. He cursed himself for being taken in so easily. He should have realised he was being stitched up. Not only that, he was now out of pocket and the drugs barons would be after him, of that he was certain. He'd have to disappear, and quick! But where could he go where they wouldn't find him? He'd placed his daughter at her mother's in London. He was convinced that she'd have made her way home by now, having missed riding her favourite horse Merrylegs but there was no sign of her ever returning. Knowing full well that he'd neglected her over the last few years, leaving her to her own devices far too often he knew that she was probably having a good time at her mother's. His ex-wife was a social butterfly with a huge amount of friends. What young person wouldn't want to be part of all that? Looking about him, he suddenly wondered if it had all been worth it, but it was too late now. His fate was sealed and he couldn't see a way out this predicament. He hoped, rather than believed that a quick telephone call to his old friend Huxley at the station would at least solve the problem of him being arrested. He'd always come up trumps for him in the past, so he'd no reason to think otherwise now.

Chapter Twenty-Seven

"Do you reckon that's the last of his stash?" asked Jasmine, as she dished out the soup.

"We can't be sure of anything where Mackleroy's concerned" said Lee.

"I can't see how he's going to wriggle free on this one. We've enough evidence to convict him. He's involved. I can't see how Huxley can carry on protecting him the way he has either. He might be his best buddy but there's a limit...surely he wouldn't put his own job on the line....?"

"Huxley will save his own skin, come what may."

"But it's all wrong Lee! He's supposed to be an upholder of the law and yet, here he is protecting a criminal who's supplying the streets with drugs. I mean, look what's happened to Dean. It's ruining young people's lives. Has the man no conscience at tall?"

"Probably not, that's why he's risen to the top the way he has. You have to be thick-skinned."

"Yes, but even so..." There was silence whilst they tucked into their soup. It was home-made, one of her mother's recipes and an old family favourite. She'd also made some bread using her new bread maker. "It's a pity we weren't able to track down this gang. That would have been icing on the cake, for sure."

"If Mackleroy goes down he'll name and shame the lot of them."

"You think?"

"I know it. He'll not go quietly and he'll make sure everyone else involved goes down with him."

"Trouble is how do we track them all down? They could be anywhere."

"It's amazing how everyone up at that Mayfair club closed ranks. It makes you wonder if they're all in on it."

"Either that or they're just protecting their best customers. It's bread and butter to them, after all. They probably couldn't afford to be losing their best payers who have been members for years. It's funny because when Chris and I went to the Golf Club, all the men were reluctant to talk but the women were friendly. Not knowing what their men folk got up to was a plus in their book. It meant they could live their own lives exactly the way they wanted to without too many questions being asked, and boy do they live the life! Going away for spa weekends with all their chums, getting their hair and nails done, going for facials, racking up the account at Harrods for their winter and summer wardrobes. I tell you Lee, it's a different world!"

Lee scratched his head. "I can't help thinking that we've overlooked some important detail that's staring us in the face."

"You feel that too? I've tried to go over every detail of every report on this case and re-read all my notes form all the people we've interviewed...and...nothing."

"They're all lying, probably through fear. They've got to carry on living around here and if word got out that they'd grassed, their lives wouldn't be worth living."

Jasmine got out the cheeseboard and a jar of pickles, placing them in the centre of the table. Lee poured them both a glass of cider just as his phone rang. He took the call and said, "That was Linda. Chris has been discharged from the hospital, he's at home."

"Great. Will we go and see him today?"

"No, we'll let him rest. Tomorrow will be soon enough. The lad's had it rough. We've nothing new to report anyway. Let's hope he's done some thinking whilst he's been languishing in that hospital bed because my brain's mashed."

"That information Eugene DeVere gave us....did they check it all out? Thoroughly I mean?"

"Supposedly."

"And?"

"Nothing. They reckon they didn't find anything."

"That doesn't sound right to me Lee. You don't think they could have been paid a back-hander to keep their mouths shut?"

"It's a possibility. There's more corruption about than you think. Money talks, especially when you've a big mortgage and a wife and kids to support. It's easy money."

"How the hell are we supposed to do our jobs properly with all this going on around us? It's like trying to plait sawdust. I'm slowly beginning to think that Chris's idea of setting up a private detective agency is a good idea. He found some premises you know, a little office in the town centre. I went to view it with him. It's got everything. He's looking into applying for a licence to set it all up."

Is he? Well, after what's happened to him, I wouldn't blame him if he decided to move on. He's met Linda now. Police work is notorious for wrecking relationships."

"Well it's not going to wreck this one" she said, kissing him on the nose.

"What time did your dad say he'd be here?" asked Peggy, who was getting impatient. She wanted to make sure that Marcie was alright. She knew she'd get no rest until she had seen for herself that her friend was indeed in good health and unharmed. She didn't trust Adrian to leave her alone, even though the court case was over.

"About six o'clock, depending on the traffic," said Beth, checking the vegetables which were roasting in the oven. It had been five days now since her father departed for the coast, saying that he'd find Marcie. "They've had a lot of catching up to do."

"Well couldn't they have done all that here?"

"They might have wanted to spend a little time together, on their own," soothed Beth, smiling. She now looked upon Peggy's as her second home, coming straight there after visiting Dean.

"Yes I suppose you're right? Where's Dennis?"

"In the garden, I asked him to pick me some fresh mint for the sauce."

"They're here" said Dennis, suddenly appearing in the doorway and handing Beth the herbs. "I'll go and let them in." Peggy jumped up from her chair and went over to the window but she couldn't see much as it was already going dark. Making her way into the hallway behind Beth, she almost tripped over Milo who sped full pelt into Marcie's arms the minute she stepped over the threshold.

Dennis couldn't help laughing, "He's not forgotten you! I think he's pleased to see you!" There were hugs all round before they finally settled themselves in the lounge for a well needed cup of tea. Dennis handed Marcie the mail from her flat, giving her a full account of the story behind Milo being handed back into their care. He'd placed the one in the brown envelope postmarked Ireland on the top of the pile. "This one looks important" he said. "In my estimation brown envelopes usually mean trouble."

"Oh dear, don't say that Dennis, I couldn't take any more bad news."

"Take no notice of him Marcie dear. He's only joking" Peggy admonished, flicking the tea towel in his face.

"Oh lord! You were right Dennis. It's a solicitor's letter!" said Marcie, the colour suddenly draining out of her face.

"Give it to me" said Gerald, "I'll deal with it." He took the letter from her and there was silence until he spoke the words, "It's about your friend Mrs Evelyn Savage. She passed away three weeks ago. They're asking you to contact them at your earliest convenience."

"Do they say what it's about?" she whispered, tentatively.

"Who's Mrs Savage?" asked Beth looking from her father to Marcie, then from Dennis to Peggie.

"It's a lady I bought a painting off in the market stall a while ago. We kept in touch," said Marcie, not wanting to go into too much detail about what had actually occurred between them, for it was meant to be kept secret and the less people knew about it the better as far she was concerned.

"Does she live....I mean did she live in Ireland then?"

"Yes, she moved there shortly after I bought the painting. It's where she was born and I would imagine it always felt like home, whereas England didn't."

"Would you like me to ring them for you, tomorrow?" asked Gerald.

"No, thanks all the same but I think I'd better do it myself." She began to feel uncomfortable again and hoped that she wasn't in more trouble. She didn't trust Adrian and never knew what he was going to do next.

"It can't be anything to do with Adrian or Roger," said Gerald. "They've done a runner if the staff are to be believed. They've not been around for weeks now and the workers haven't been paid. Rumour has it that they've absconded abroad somewhere."

"That doesn't surprise me one bit" snapped Marcie. "I never met a more selfish pair. All they ever think about is themselves!"

Gerald placed his arm around her shoulders. "It's not your concern anymore, thank goodness."

"You forget Gerald, I'm not divorced yet. Perhaps I need to take a leaf out of their book and start thinking of myself a bit more instead of worrying about everyone else the way I have been doing for the past fifty years!"

"Wise words," said Peggy. "Now let's eat whilst everything's fresh."

"What sort of mood's he in Sid?" asked Lee.

"Bad tempered. I'd watch your back if I were you?" said the desk sergeant.

"Good holiday?" Lee breezed into Huxley's office and sat himself down, mentally bracing himself for a fight.

"Not particularly" he barked, throwing files to the corner of his desk.

"Don't you get on with your in-laws then?" said Lee, attempting to humour him.

"My wife wants to move down there permanently."

"Well, what are you waiting for? Just go. You're nearing retirement anyway. Be kind to yourself, you've worked hard all these years, you deserve a break."

Huxley ignored his comments and launched straight into his attack about a complaint from Mackleroy, citing gross misconduct and harassment.

Lee played him at his own game and ignored him, producing a copy of a report from his folder and shoving it towards him across the desk.

"What's this?"

"It's a copy of one of your reports. We interviewed this girl and she assures us that this conversation never took place."

"Well she lying," he said, without even looking at Lee or the report.

Lee sat in silence, waiting until Huxley made eye contact with him before saying, "This is just the tip of the iceberg. We've unearthed enough evidence to request a full investigation and conduct an enquiry into this whole case." Lee held his nerve, knowing full well that he was bluffing. Bunny Mackleroy had obviously wasted no time in contacting his best buddy to get him off the hook. The fingerprints on the photograph matched the fingerprints which were all over the van. It was hard evidence. "How long have we worked together? Forty years? Take my advice, cut your losses and tell your wife you're up for it. Disappear. She'll love you for it. Mackleroy's in a no win situation here and it's about time you severed all ties with him."

"When I want your opinion on my private life I'll ask for it!"

"You can't go on protecting him the way you do. Sooner or later questions will be asked, particularly regarding the information that your wife provided you with regarding Marcie's bank account. Marcie told nobody about that money, nobody at all. There's only one way you could have got that information, from her. Run for the hills now whilst you still can, with your dignity and reputation intact. I say this as a long standing colleague and ...friend."

"Get out of my office!"

"I meant it kindly. You and I have a lot of history. We understand each other well. Don't put all that on the line. At least give some serious thought to what I've said. I may not be around myself for much longer. I might be moving on." He left the office without a backward glance, not really caring what Huxley would do next."

"What's this?" asked Beth, taking a folded piece of paper from Dean and sitting in the nearest chair in the day room, which was where he spent most of his time now.

"It's all the car registration numbers of the gang. They're circling the grounds at night, I've seen them. They're waiting for me Beth. They know that sooner rather than later, I'm going to be discharged from here, then they'll pounce. I won't stand a chance!"

This all sounded a bit far-fetched to Beth who wondered if he was imagining things. "Are you sure it's them?" she asked, searching his face for clues.

"Oh it's them all right! Believe me."

"How many are there in total? The gang, I mean?"

"There are eight of them that I dealt with on a regular basis."

"Are they all local lads?"

"They're not lads Beth. They're grown men, hardened criminals and not the sort of people you'd want to meet down a dark alleyway."

"Then we'll have to form a plan for your escape. I've got a few ideas. It might be our only chance."

Dean liked the way she referred to his problems as 'our only chance,' indicating that they were now a team and they'd work through this rough patch together. He knew that he'd never survive without her now and was eternally grateful for having met her. She really was a girl in a million. "I want you to give these details to my sister. It's the all the car registration numbers."

"Jasmine?"

"Yes. These men are still active, all of them. They've been at it for years. She might be able put a tail on them or something."

Chapter Twenty-Eight

Marcie waited until the house was empty before telephoning the Irish solicitor's office. Her fingers shook as she held the receiver, not knowing what on earth she was about to hear. She'd awoken with a headache and felt nauseous. Taking one of her little blue tablets to ward off one of her attacks, she decided to get it over with and face up to whatever it was that life was throwing at her. There was nothing else for it. There seemed to be an interminable wait after she gave her name to the receptionist and she almost put the receiver down in a sudden attack of nerves, her bottle momentarily deserting her. The solicitor thanked her for contacting them and introduced himself as Declan Monaghue, referring to 'her good friend Mrs Savage.'

"She wanted you to have the house. It's quite a large property with three acres of land. In her will she stated that she always felt that the property was rightfully yours and she wants it restored to the real owner, namely yourself. She never forgot your kindness."

Marcie was too stunned to speak and sat staring into space as if she'd misheard. When she didn't speak, he continued, "I should point out at this stage that a family member is contesting the will. This of course will delay things. He's promised to come in and speak to us sometime this week. We won't know the exact position until then, but we will keep you informed." Marcie thanked him and then she rang Gerald at his office, as promised. He was about to go into a meeting so their conversation was short. "We'll talk about it tonight over supper" he said. She held the receiver in her hand long after he'd hung up. His soft velvety voice always had a calming effect on her. Her mood hadn't lifted, as expected. She still felt very low in spirits and couldn't see a way forward, thinking that she'd be better off dead. Making her way into the kitchen, she made herself a cup of tea and filled a hot water bottle, carrying them up to the spare bedroom where she'd spent the previous night. Curling up under the duvet, she suddenly wondered how her sister Deidre was faring. Where on earth was she? Had she hooked up with the neighbour, as Dennis had intimated? There had been no word from her, but she supposed that was normal, she hadn't really expected her to keep in touch but ever since the court case she secretly hoped that her sister would find a kind word or deed. It would be nice to have a loving sister, someone she could rely on for moral rearmament and support. That was the thing she envied the most when observing other people. Scribbling a short note for Peggy, she left it on the bedside table and willed herself to fall asleep.

Chris was getting irritated. Linda was fussing unnecessarily in his opinion. She hadn't left him alone for two minutes. When he snapped at her to 'stop fussing' she said she was terrified of losing him and hadn't slept a wink when he was in hospital. They ended up laughing about it and she jumped under the bed covers fully clothed, wrapping her arms around him. Hamish, thinking it was all a game, jumped up onto the bed too and finding a comfortable spot at the bottom of the bed, fell asleep. The telephone on the bedside table rang.

"I'd better take that," he said, sitting upright. "It might be Lee or Jasmine."

"Don't you dare go back to work yet!" she hissed, just as he picked up the receiver.

He winked at her and after saying hello, discovered that it was his friend Mantos from Greece. There followed much bon'homie and laughter, followed by a lengthy silence. He signalled for Linda to pass him a pad and pen. He was scribbling away on the pad for quite some time and eventually Linda went downstairs to make some coffee. When she went back upstairs he was still on the telephone making notes so she placed his coffee cup on the bedside table and went into the bathroom to have a shower. She spent twenty minutes blow-drying her hair and re-entered the bedroom just as he hung up. He leant back against the pillows and seemed lost for words. After several seconds she said, "Everything alright? Your coffee's gone cold. Shall I make you another one?"

"Yes please, I just need to go through this lot," he said, ruffling his hair and rifling through the pad, which he'd half filled with his notes.

Dean hung about in the hallway until he spotted the young nurse he'd befriended during his stay at the treatment centre. "I need your help," he whispered, taking hold of her elbow and steering her into a side corridor.

"Of course Dean, what can I do for you? It's your last day here isn't it?"

"Yes, I've officially been discharged." He looked about him to make sure that no one was listening in to their conversation before continuing, "Look, I know this might seem a strange request, but for reasons that I'd rather not go into, I don't want to exit via the front door. Is there a back way, where nobody will see me?"

She stared at him for a few seconds, her big brown eyes searching his face. After a few seconds she smiled and said, "Come with me." Dean followed her down to the end of the corridor. She led him into a small galley kitchen, first checking that it was empty before closing the door behind them. She opened a glass panelled door which led out into a small courtyard. Walking over to the wooden fence which ran down to a wooded area at the back, she beckoned for him to follow her. She quietly removed two of the wooden panels in the fence and told him to squeeze through. "It leads out into the woods. If you follow that path, you'll eventually come to the main road. It takes about thirty minutes to reach the town centre. We nurses use it all the time when we can't get day-passes. We look out for each other." Dean thanked her and headed off into the night.

"Hello darling, it's me. What? Fed up already? No, no, look I've been giving some thought to your idea about moving to the Lake District. Your parents are getting older and it's our responsibility to look after them. We'll talk more tonight when I get home but I just wanted to let you know. You look for a suitable property and I'll talk to the estate agent and get our house on the market. What? Oh, quite a number of things actually. What? On no, I'll pack it in. It's about time anyway. Retirement's not far off for me and the time's right. We'll do it. Yes, yes that's fine. Bye darling."

Mrs Huxley couldn't believe her ears at the sea change in her husband but was secretly jumping for joy. She immediately telephoned her parents to give them the good news and drafted a letter to hand in at the bank, tendering her resignation due to relocation. Running upstairs, she delved into the bottom of the wardrobe to retrieve the brochures from the estate agent that she'd secreted away. She'd almost decide to go without him. By four thirty she'd arranged viewings on four properties in the area nearest her parents.

Beth knew that she was being watched and was careful to continue her usual routine of visiting Dean every day, even though he was no longer there. Arriving just as all the nurses were in their daily meeting with matron when they handed over to the afternoon staff, she sneaked into the day room and sat talking to whoever was around. If the dayroom was empty she read a magazine and pretended she was waiting for someone. If she timed it right, she was on her way home just as the nurses came out of their meeting, slipping out unseen. Jasmine had warned her not to hang around on the streets on her own as she was in danger of being kidnapped and held to ransom. 'These thugs won't think twice about forcing information out of you' she told her. Beth wondered how on earth they'd got to know that she was visiting Dean and thought that Jasmine must be exaggerating, but even so, she knew she couldn't take any chances. 'They'll get to know soon enough that Dean's been discharged and they'll hunt him down, but hopefully by then he'll have had a few days to make his escape," she said, unconvincingly, for these drugs barons seemed to have eyes everywhere. Nothing seemed to get past them. They made it their business to know everything that was going on in and around their patch. Fortunately, the bus stop was practically right outside the front entrance and with the help of the timetable she managed to hop on without waiting around. She made her way straight to Peggy's and let herself in with her key. There seemed to be a small light blue car following her up the road as she got off the bus. Telling herself she was imagining things, she peeped through the curtains in the lounge, making sure that she remained unseen. Sure enough, the car turned around at the end of the cul-de-sac and disappeared. She made a note of the car registration number and telephoned Jasmine.

Dean had walked all the way to the caravan site, which took him about five hours. Making his way into the woods at the back of the camp, he found the tree that he'd marked with his penknife. It took him a while to prize off the section of bark. He looked furtively around him to make sure that he wasn't being observed before removing the rucksack he'd planted there all those years ago. Surprisingly, it was still intact and with trembling fingers he unzipped the top section and felt inside. The moneybag was still there. He forced his hand inside it and felt the banknotes. Bingo! Zipping the bag back up, he swung it onto his back and went on his way. An hour later he'd reached the bus terminal where he boarded a bus to the coast.

Billy sat in his bedroom nursing the worst hangover that he'd ever had. Having run out of his own supply of Cannabis, he'd cadged some off a friend. He couldn't seem to hold down a job these days and was always short of money. He collected his unemployment giro once a fortnight but it didn't last two minutes. His only hope was to get his hands on that huge estate that his Aunt Evelyn owned. The appointment with the solicitor was at ten o'clock the following morning, which gave him twelve hours to sober up and make himself decent. Everyone in the pub last night was talking about the death of Mrs Evelyn Savage. He now regretted boasting that he was in line to inherit the entire estate. He smoked the tab his friend Peter had given him but it tasted different form his normal supply. "What the hell's this rubbish you've given me mate?" he'd joked.

"What on earth would you do with an estate that size Billy? I mean honestly, it's all got to be maintained you know. It'll be hard work. It wouldn't do for me mate" said Peter.

"I'd employ staff to do all that wouldn't I," said Billy.

"Oh eye? And where would you get the money to pay all the staff? Mrs Savage had no money in the bank. Everyone knows that."

Billy knew that he was right. There were only just enough funds in her account to cover the cost of the funeral. How on earth she'd been living all these years was a mystery. "She has a housekeeper, so she found money for that."

"Yes, out of her pension according to Lillian at the post office."

"Good grief is there no privacy in this village?" he snapped, ordering himself another pint at the bar.

"Seriously Billy, I'd think twice before taking on a property that size. Even if you sell it, the drugs barons will be after you. You're in too deep mate. I can guarantee that within six months you'd have nothing left. They'd hound you until there was nothing left then toss you on the scrap heap."

Billy cursed the day he'd ever got involved in the first place. It was all that Bunny Mackleroy's fault, boasting about his new house and all the fancy holidays in the Caribbean. 'Don't be a mug lad. Live the life. It's all out there for the taking. If you don't take it, somebody else will.' Those were his very words and before he knew it he'd been sucked in. Now there was no escape. He turned over in his bed and pulled the covers over his head. He was shivering and couldn't seem to get warm. Suddenly he started sweating and he felt very peculiar. He tossed and turned in his bed for the next five or six hours, not knowing what was happening to him. He was drenched in sweat and he couldn't seem to keep still. What the hell was in that tab he'd smoked last night? He'd have something to say to Peter the next time he saw him. Eventually the sweating stopped and he started to feel sick. The next three hours were spent with his head down the lavatory. He'd never been so ill in all his life.

Chapter Twenty-Nine

Gerald decided to dodge a meeting at the office and get on his way earlier than usual. He arrived at Peggy's to find Beth at the stove making dinner.

"You're early dad" she said, kissing him on the cheek.

"I'm slowly losing interest in the job to be honest. Everything's getting on my nerves, particularly the Managing Director who seems to think he's ruling the universe."

"Peggy's in a bit of a panic. Poor Marcie's had one of her attacks and has spent all day in bed. She's in the lounge with Dennis, you go through and I'll make some coffee. Dinner will be another forty minutes yet, at least."

Peggy jumped up the minute Gerald walked through the door. "We were just discussing this," she said handing him a brown envelope with an Irish postmark. "I think it might be another letter from that solicitor."

"We don't think Marcie's in any fit state to be dealing with this at the moment" said Dennis.

"Then I'll deal with it." Gerald ripped it open and sat reading it for a good five minutes before placing it on the coffee table, just as Beth came in with the tray. Dennis and Peggy sat patiently, waiting for the news.

"Is it good news or bad news dad?" Beth handed her father his coffee and sat down on the sofa.

"Well, good I think, although it does contain some sad news regarding her sister's boy."

"That would be Billy, I presume?" Peggy knew about the difficult time Evelyn had experienced at the hands of this hedonistic young man.

"Yes, you're right. He was the one contesting the will, as you know. "

"What's happened to Billy?" Dennis asked.

"It appears that he choked on his own vomit after a heavy drinking bout. The post mortem showed a mixture of illegal substances in his blood stream. As he was a known drug user, the judge ruled 'accidental death.' I don't suppose we'll ever know what really happened."

"This seems to be happening more and more these days," said Peggy, shaking her head. "What a waste of a young life. They ought to bring back conscription. Make them do two years in the forces. That would get them off the streets."

Dennis was eager to know if Marcie was now the owner of the estate. "Does that mean Marcie's home and dry then?"

"Yes, it would appear so. It's all going through probate. They're drawing up the papers for her to sign, so as soon as she's fit enough to travel she can pick up the keys from the estate agent."

"Could I go with her please dad?" asked Beth, eyes as big as saucers,

"I vote that we should all go," said Gerald. "I'd like to see this house. I believe there are several acres of land too. What do you say Peggy? Dennis?"

Chris arrived at the station early and was busy typing up his report when Lee and Jasmine turned up.

"Couldn't you sleep?" Lee joked, placing a coffee and a bacon sandwich on his desk.

"Didn't I always tell you that things would turn up trumps?" chirped Chris, grinning from ear to ear.

"Why, what's happened?"

Before he had a chance to speak, Jasmine came rushing in with the news that Huxley had decided to retire. All the staff were clucking like hens as to who was going to fill his shoes and their fingers were all pointing in Lee's direction. Lee shook his head in disbelief. So he had taken his advice after all. That proved one thing only - that he was guilty of the charges Lee had laid at his door. Either that or he'd decided to protect his wife, who could have been in serious trouble. All the same, Lee was pleased that he had decided to do the sensible thing, given the circumstances, for he knew that things could have got very messy with no guarantee of what the outcome would be.

"What on earth's brought this on all of a sudden?" asked Chris.

"His wife's parents are elderly and need looking after" said Jasmine, sipping her coffee, "I must admit it's rather surprising though. Maybe that break away was just what he needed to make him see things differently. I suppose there's bound to be a time when you've just had enough, even if you love your job. His wife's a few years older than him. She was due to retire at the end of this year anyway. Maybe she gave him an ultimatum. Perhaps she'd decided to go on her own anyway, with or without her husband?"

"You could be right" said Lee. He knew that if they did offer him the post, he would have to give it some serious thought. Word hadn't got around yet about his relationship with Jasmine and he knew that if they were going to remain together as a couple, as he very much hoped they would, then one of them would have to leave the force. Maybe it would be a good idea for Jasmine to hook up with Chris in his private investigation business after all. They were interrupted by a commotion in the reception area. Jasmine opened the door to see three officers marching arrestees to the interview rooms. She dashed back to reception to speak to the desk sergeant. "Who were they?" she whispered.

"Drugs, that's the second lot they've brought in. Those car registration numbers you gave us have turned up trumps. We've been following them for ages, stands to reason that sooner or later they'd lead us to their hoard. Today's the day it seems. Watch this space." She dashed back to give the good news to Lee and Chris. The station was abuzz with activity. Twenty minutes later another six were brought in. Lee, Chris and Jasmine were called into the interview rooms, where they spent the whole day taking statements and typing up reports. By nine o'clock in the evening they'd made twelve arrests. Huxley was nearly doing handsprings in the corridor.

"Come on" ordered Lee, grabbing his jacket. "Let's get home to our beds. Chris, join us for supper. I want to hear what this good news is that you were about to tell us before all this kicked off." As they made their way out into the car park the desk sergeant called Lee back.

"Huxley is asking to speak to you before you go" he shouted through the window.

Tossing the car keys in Jasmine's direction, he said "Wait in the car."

"What can he want at this time of night?" she muttered.

"So what's the plan?" Lee said, pulling up a chair and looking about him to see if anyone else would be joining them in the meeting.

Huxley went over to the door, peered out into the corridor to make sure they were alone before closing it and sitting down at his desk. Lee thought he looked distraught, with no sign of the previous euphoria at their good fortune in making so many arrests in one afternoon. He ran his fingers through his hair and dropped his head in his hands. Lee waited a few moments before breaking the silence.

"It's Bunny isn't it?"

"He knows too much."

"So what? What can he do, and who'd believe him anyway?"

"We go back a long way. If I don't get him exonerated, he'll make trouble. He's got contacts, and I don't mean the friendly sort."

"We can't exonerate him without releasing all the rest of gang. If we let him go, the gang will go after him."

"What the hell am I going to do? I can't see a way out of this! What a mess!"

Lee was tempted to say that he'd no right to have got involved in the first place and couldn't help feeling that whatever direction they decided to go in, it wouldn't end well.

"Did he honestly think he could get away with all this indefinitely? That's a bit naive if you ask me. It's the sort of behaviour you'd expect from a teenager, not a grown man with a family to support. His friendship with you has given him a false sense of security. He thinks he can do exactly as he pleases and just walk away."

"That's why I feel so guilty. Don't get me wrong, I never encouraged him or anything like that, but I didn't discourage him either. Strangely, I never thought it would come to this."

"The way I see it, there's only one thing you can do."

Huxley looked up for the first time, his eyes searching Lee's face for clues.

"You're going to have to do one."

"You mean disappear?"

"Tell them at HQ that you've got domestic problems and need to vacate your position immediately. Then clear out your desk and be away on your toes before anyone can put a trace on you. You don't need to tell anyone where you're going. It's none of their business."

"It'll never work. They'll not release me just like that. There would have to be a good excuse."

"Then invent one," said Lee, nonchalantly. "I can't see an alternative way." He was finding it difficult to feel any sympathy for the man sat in front of him. If there was one thing he hated, it was a bent copper. He'd had a good run for his money and his past was now catching up with him, but for all that, he wouldn't like to be the one to grass on him. He didn't want that on his conscience. They were interrupted by the desk sergeant who wanted to put a call through. It was Huxley's wife. He waved Lee away, stating that they would speak further tomorrow. When he returned to the car

Jasmine was eager to know what Huxley wanted.

"I think I can guess" she said. "He's got to find a way of getting his buddy off the hook."

"You've got it in one." He turned the ignition key but didn't move off immediately.

"What'll happen to him?"

"Who? Bunny or Huxley?"

"Both."

"Oh, who knows Jaz? What does the future hold for any of us? It's all a lottery, this wheel of life."

"That's very philosophical. What's brought all this on?"

"I can't help feeling that I'm being selfish, hanging on to you the way I have been doing lately. After all, you're so much younger than me. You've got your whole life ahead of you, whereas I am middle-aged. My life's half over."

"I'm not complaining" she smiled at him and ruffled his hair playfully.

"All I'm saying is that if you wanted to move on, then I won't stand in your way. It just wouldn't be fair."

"Move on where? Are you asking me to move out of the flat?" she said, not quite believing what she had just heard.

"Hell, no, that's not what I meant at all. I just don't want you to feel obligated."

"I'm here because I want to be. End of conversation."

Turning to face her, he said softly, "Would you consider becoming my wife?"

"Wow, is that a proposal? The answer is most definitely yes!"

"Are you sure?"

"I'm sure!"

"Are you sure you wouldn't rather be inside, where it's a bit warmer?" said Gerald, rubbing his hands together to keep warm.

"No thanks. I need some fresh air." Marcie leant her head against his shoulder and watched the swell of the Irish sea. She'd always loved the sea. It had a calming effect on her, even when it was choppy, which it wasn't today. There was even a hint of sun trying to break through the clouds, casting light onto the deck. Dennis appeared with a tray of tea, followed by Beth with a tray of sandwiches.

"Where's Peggy?" asked Gerald, taking the tray from her.

"She's looking for the ladies. She's so excited about the house. She's talked of nothing else ever since that letter arrived from the solicitors. It's really perked her up," Beth laughed.

"I hope she's not going to be disappointed" said Marcie. "We don't know what state it's in. It might need a lot doing to it."

"Well, it's amazing what a good lick of fresh paint can do" said Dennis, handing out the tea. He was secretly looking forward to getting stuck into a project. He needed something to take his mind off his broken marriage. There had been no word from Candice either and he was surprised at how disappointed he was. He desperately hoped that she hadn't forgotten him so soon.

Peggy appeared, smiling from ear to ear. "Gosh, this takes me back to when I was first married" she gushed. "I've not been on a ferry for over forty years!"

"Where did you go?" Beth was eager to know. "Was it your honeymoon?"

"No it was our first anniversary. We went to the Isle of Wight. It rained every day for a fortnight, but we still enjoyed ourselves. Our honeymoon was one night in a B & B in Blackpool. It was all we could afford at the time!" she chuckled. "Despite our lack of funds, they were happy days. Well, they were for me anyway." Beth laughed. She couldn't imagine life without Peggy now. She couldn't imagine her life without Dean either and wondered where he was right at this minute. Having never been on a ferry before, she was enjoying every minute, knowing in her heart that Dean wouldn't let her down like Ashley. He would be waiting for her. Dennis produced a map of Ireland and proceeded to study it with Gerald, the two of them discussing popular tourist spots and places of interest.

Marcie was still feeling low in spirits and she couldn't work out why. Gerald was back in her life so she should be on cloud nine, but she wasn't. Her life hadn't worked out how she'd planned. All she'd ever wanted was to carve out her own little niche somewhere. To have a place that she could call her own, something to work and live for. Was that too much to ask for? Peggie broke her reverie.

"Are you alright Marcie? You're still not well, I can tell. I said it was too soon, but would they listen? Men are all the same. Have a sandwich, you'll feel better."

"No thanks Peggy, I'm not hungry, just thirsty."

"You must build your strength up, you're not strong and I don't want you going downhill again. When we get settled we'll do some proper cooking. Good old fashioned stews and casseroles. I was brought up on them. You can't go wrong with that sort of fare. Well, it certainly didn't do me any harm."

"You're quite right Peggy" said Beth. "I'll look out some recipes. I was thinking....if there's a reasonable amount of land surrounding this property, we could build an allotment and grow all our own fruit and vegetables. We can plant herbs and lettuces, tomatoes and cucumbers and such." She was thinking that Dean could look after this side of things, but didn't say so out loud.

"That's a wonderful idea" said Peggy, draining the last of her tea. "That's if the soil's good enough. We'd be self sufficient and all organic. They spray everything with insecticides these days; you don't know what you're eating half the time."

Marcie rested her head against the wall and closed her eyes, willing herself to fall asleep. A strange feeling washed over her and made her shiver, as though someone had just walked over her grave. She immediately thought of Adrian and wondered where he was. Having instigated divorce proceedings, the solicitor had informed her that she had good grounds for divorce, citing irreconcilable differences, but as she didn't know his whereabouts, serving him with the paperwork was proving impossible. Part of her hoped that he'd found happiness with Roger, but somehow she doubted it. Roger wasn't the easiest of people to get along with and she feared that Adrian would always be at his beck and call. It was an unequal partnership. She drifted off to sleep dreaming about her brother Peter and wished that he was still here to comfort her.

181

Chapter Thirty

Lee turned the steaks over on the grill then chopped the mushrooms and tomatoes.

"Steaks on a Monday?" laughed Chris, rubbing his hands together after spying the chips coming out of the oven.

Lee smiled and contemplated whether to break the news about himself and Jasmine. "We've got some news actually Chris, but it can wait until later."

"Oh heavens, don't tell me Huxley's worked one of his specials..."

"No, nothing like that, but first we want to know what your good news is."

"Thinking about it, it's a double edged sword really. There's good news and bad news."

"Oh?"

"You can read the report for yourself when you get to the office tomorrow. I've put a copy on your desk."

Lee plated up the steaks and took them to the table where Jasmine was pouring out the beer. They'd forgotten to buy the wine, there being only bottles of stout in the fridge. They were just finishing their meal when the subject of Mantos arose again, having got sidetracked by all the arrests they'd made that afternoon. They were all in agreement about the fact that Huxley wouldn't be able to help Bunny this time.

"Of course it's only the tip of the iceberg really" Lee continued. "How many more of the gang are still out there? We've no way of knowing."

"Yes but we've made inroads. We can pat ourselves on the back for that at least," said Chris, who was ever the optimist. "And of course there's the other good news. Now that really is worth celebrating...sort of."

Jasmine poured the coffee. They'd run out of milk so she'd opened a tin of evaporated milk from the cupboard. There was obviously a bad side to this story and she wondered what had occurred.

"So what's this other news Lee?"

Lee glanced across at Jasmine and took hold of her hand. "Jasmine's agreed to be my wife. We wanted you to be the first to know."

"Gosh, I wasn't expecting that boss. Congratulations." He stood up and kissed Jasmine on the cheek before shaking Lee's hand. "Linda and I...well, we'll have to wait a bit. She was married quite young and they separated but never divorced. Things are underway to rectify that. Of course, he might decide to be awkward and refuse to sign the papers, which Linda thinks is more than likely, but we're happy as we are. I'm moving into her cottage next week." He picked up his coffee mug and said "Here's to us."

Dean ordered his mum her usual pint of Guinness from the bar. "Here you are mum. Make it the last one because we need to get Smart settled for the night, then tomorrow we'll get the map out."

"How much longer before we head towards the big house?" she asked, enjoying every minute of her mini holiday with her son, especially all the stops and the local pubs along the way. Dean had met her off the ferry then hired a horse and gypsy caravan. They'd been on the road for about five days now and she never wanted it to end. Their horse Smart seemed to know all the roads and trotted along quite happily. She thought back to the day Dean told her that he was planning to disappear. Her heart plummeted to her boots. "You can't leave me on my own Dean!" she pleaded. "Where will you go? What will you do? How will I get in touch with you?" she demanded. After much confrontation, Dean agreed that she could come with him, providing she was prepared to rough it a bit and travel at night with very little luggage, just one small holdall. She readily agreed and left the house at midnight, leaving via the back door and crossing the fields which led to the back of the bus station, where she spent the night in the waiting room, drinking coffee from her flask. At six o'clock in the morning the bus station cafe opened and she ordered herself a bacon sandwich and mug of hot tea before boarding the bus to the train station. From there she boarded the train to the coast and took the ferry to Ireland, as planned.

"Two more days should do it" said Dean, "Then we can make our way to Donegal and find the house. Beth will be there, so it'll all be fine, don't worry." He patted her hand and smiled at the woman facing him, hardly recognisable as the mother he knew in England. Happiness radiated out of her every pore. He'd never seen her so animated. He supposed that was largely due to the amount of alcohol they'd been consuming, also the fact that this little adventure was probably the most exciting thing that had happened to her in years. He also knew that he would have a job keeping his mother out of the pubs once they got settled, but for all that he was glad to have her with him. She was good company and they rubbed along well enough together. He had to make it all work somehow. He knew in his heart that Beth would understand why he couldn't leave his mum behind. One day he would explain to Beth what had happened at the caravan site and how lucky he was to have survived the explosion. His friend Billy had told him of a caravan site near Morecambe bay. Adrian had inveigled a large amount of money out of the company's coffers and stashed it in the green and blue caravan nearest the toilets on the far side of the campsite. Dean asked him how he knew all this but Billy just tapped the side of his nose. They hatched a plan between them to break in and steal the loot before anyone else got to it. Looking back now, he couldn't believe how naive and foolish he'd been but he was high on the drugs by then and acting irrationally. They waited until closing time at the nearest pub before sneaking into the back of the camp site and waiting until the night watchman went to fill his kettle from the tap in the offices at the side of the camp. Breaking in was easy and with torches they conducted a thorough search of the caravan. After a couple of hours they gave up. "It's not here, are you sure you've got it right Billy?" said Dean.

"I'm sure. He's obviously moved it or changed his mind at the last minute. I'm not hanging around here, I'm off! I've got better things to do with my time than waste it around here on a wild goose chase. Are you coming?"

"What, at this time of night? It's two o'clock in the morning. Can't we kip down here for the night and move off in the early hours before it gets light?"

"And be seen by all and sundry? Use your loaf."

"I'm dog tired" said Dean. "I'll just grab a couple of hours on the sofa."

"Suit yourself. I'm off."

Dean woke up at five o'clock in the morning. It was just getting light. He made his way into the kitchen to see if he could find anything to make himself a brew with and as he passed the kitchen table his foot caught on a piece of linoleum that was curling up at one end. 'That needs taping down' he thought, 'someone's going to come a cropper otherwise.' As he took hold of the corner, it came away easily in his hand to reveal a piece of wood underneath. He lifted the wood out and saw a rucksack buried beneath it. On grabbing the bag, he headed out of the door to take a closer look inside. He'd just got his feet on the grass verge when there was an enormous bang and the whole caravan burst into flames. He was thrown into the bushes face down, the bag still in his hand. Apart from a few scratches he was unharmed and couldn't believe his luck when he saw the caravan wreathed in flames. He'd never know to this day how he'd managed to escape being blown to pieces, but he was alive and luck was on his side, as he opened the bag to reveal a huge wad of banknotes.

"Is that your horse outside mate?" Dean turned to see an angry lady facing him.

"Yes, why?"

"It's eaten half my hedge. Would you mind moving him, before the whole lot disappears!" she spat, turning on her heels without waiting for an answer.

"Come on mum, drink up, we'd best be off."

She was just about to protest that it was only ten o'clock but thought better of it. She wouldn't put it past Dean to send her packing back home on that ferry if she didn't do as she was told. Draining the last of her Guinness, she wrapped her coat around her and grabbed her bag. "The poor lad's probably half starved. Did you feed him earlier?"

"Course I did. Come on." When they got Smart back on the road Dean decided to have a quiet word with his mother about her drinking. "Look mum, I know this is going to be hard for both of us, but if we're to make a go of this – and I sincerely hope that we can, then I've got to stay off the drugs and you've got to stay off the booze. It's not going to be easy for either of us but it's for the best. You do see that don't you? I nearly died in that hospital."

"You don't need to remind me son. Those weeks were the worst of my life. The thought of losing you nearly crucified me. No, we'll make a go of this lad. I'll not let you down and if you slip back onto your old ways you'll have me to answer to. Let me at least enjoy these last couple of days eh? What are they like, Beth's family?"

"I've only seen her father once. He came to visit her whilst I was in the hospital but I didn't get chance to speak to him, unfortunately. He appeared well dressed and he spoke very well. He's educated I'd say. Not exactly our class Mum but Beth is the one I'm marrying and I don't want to make a bad impression, if you see what I mean."

"She's a lovely natured girl. You're a lucky lad Dean. It's a fresh start for both of us. What will we do if..."

"Don't mother! You were going to say 'if she's gone off me' weren't you? It'll be the end of me, that's what!"

Chapter Thirty-One

Dennis was more than impressed by the amount of land surrounding the house. Plans to turn some of it into an allotment were forming nicely in his mind. Mentally making a note of all the fruit, vegetables and herbs that would grow in this rich soil, in his mind he'd already moved in. There were three outbuildings which were in good condition. These could be turned into accommodation for the ramblers. A lick of paint was all that was needed to freshen them up. Meanwhile, Beth and Peggy made straight for the kitchen, which was huge. A Range cooker and an Aga graced one wall together with a large grill and hotplate, two microwave ovens and an expensive looking food mixer and blender. Together they rifled through all the cupboards and drawers, inspecting the cutlery and equipment. They made a note of all the jars and packets in the pantry, then sitting down at the table, made a list of all the staples they would need. Gerald headed straight downstairs to inspect the wine cellar, which was well stocked. Marcie went on a tour of all the rooms, which were tastefully furnished and surprisingly spacious. There were eight bedrooms, the largest one being on-suite with a little sitting room overlooking the bay. The views were magnificent. She sat down on the bed and suddenly thought of Adrian. There was no way she'd be able to keep all of this, she thought. Once Adrian got wind of it he'd have the lot off her. She knew this for a fact. He was ruthless in his pursuit of money, which was a great pity for she loved the house. There was a touch of real class about the whole set up.

"Oh there you are" said Beth, breathless from running up the stairs. She sat down on the bed next to Marcie and asked her if she was feeling alright.

"Oh don't mind about me Beth. I've got a lot to think about that's all."

"Dad's booked a table at the pub in the village. Peggy's very tired so we'll have an early night. We've so much to talk about in the morning." Marcie smiled as she watched Beth skip back down the stairs. Seeing her so happy was heart-warming. She couldn't help but wonder if this blissful bubble would burst if Dean failed to materialise. 'I hope he doesn't let her down' she said to herself as she descended the stairs. It could prove to be one disappointment too many.

It was gone eight o'clock the following morning when Marcie finally made her way downstairs to the kitchen for breakfast. She hadn't slept well and felt groggy and low in spirits. Having laid all her cards on the table last night in the pub, she'd voiced her opinions regarding Adrian getting his hands on the house and selling it. The others all agreed that it was a distinct possibility, as they were legally still married. It put a damper on the whole evening. Hours ago they were full of hopes and dreams and possibilities, now it seemed unlikely they would ever get the chance to put their plans into action to run the B & B.

"Beth and Dennis have gone to the corner shop for milk and bread" said Gerald, who was tipping coffee beans into the grinder. "We've got cereals, fruit and yoghurt."

"That sounds lovely." She made her way over to him and laid her head on his shoulder, winding her arms around his waist. "I'm sorry I ruined our evening last night. It did rather put a damper on things didn't it?"

"What we need is professional advice. I suggest we go back to the solicitor's office and have a word. We need to know where we stand legally. I'll come with you."

"Peggy what on earth are you doing?" said Marcie on seeing her friend scrutinising rows of jars and bottles with a magnifying glass.

"Checking the 'best before' dates on this lot. We don't want botulism," she said firmly.

The kitchen door burst open and Beth ran through it, eyes wide with excitement.

"Marcie, you'll never guess what's happened!" she gushed, so breathless she could hardly get the words out.

"What on earth has happened Beth?" asked Gerald.

Dennis, following close behind her, produced a newspaper from the bag he was carrying. He laid it flat out on the table for them all to see. "Read this, if you will. Front page news!"

Gerald picked up the paper and immediately saw a photograph of Adrian with the headline "Local businessman dies in police raid." They all crowded around as he proceeded to read the whole article. It was a full five minutes before he put the paper down and enlightened them as to what had occurred.

"A shipment of goods that left Felixstowe was picked up by Adrian and Roger's boat, The Marigold. They lay in wait until it was dark before entering the port at Rhodes. By that time the area was surrounded. The police were waiting for them. They were both on board, caught red handed, but before they could make any arrests Roger jumped over the side and made a swim for it. Adrian dived in after him, but not being a strong swimmer, soon ran out of steam. By the time they fished his body out of the water, he was dead."

"He's dead?" exclaimed Marcie.

"I'm afraid so. Roger was picked up about a mile further along the coast. It took six officers to restrain him and get the handcuffs on him. He put up one hell of a fight. They compounded the boat. There was cocaine and barbiturates with a street value worth millions. Roger's now awaiting trial. It made the local news. An officer named Mantos has been hailed as quite the local hero and possibly in line for promotion. It's the biggest haul they've ever had. Adrian's mother is on the way over there to bring his body back."

"What a waste" said Peggie, shaking her head, "Now his poor mother's got to clear up the mess, and all for what?"

"Roger's got a lot to answer for if you ask me" said Dennis. "It's all his doing. He dragged Adrian in."

"No doubt" said Gerald. "I hope they throw the book at him. He'll be looking at a lengthy prison sentence."

Marcie picked up the newspaper and began to read the article for herself, not quite believing what she'd just heard. "Adrian's mother will no doubt blame me for everything. She'll come after me with a pick-axe."

"Not if I've got anything to do with it she won't!" barked Gerald.

"Let's get the breakfast going" said Dennis, unloading the groceries onto the table. Beth placed some bread under the grill and filled the milk jug.

"It does sort of throw fresh light on things now doesn't it?" said Beth sheepishly, for she didn't want to upset Marcie in any way. Adrian was her husband, after all.

Marcie threw the paper down and said, "How stupid of him! He can't swim! He never could. His mother told me. He was scared of water as a child and never learnt but I suppose the alternative was unthinkable. The police must have been following them or had a tip off or something. I mean, how did they know where to start looking?"

"There are forces at work that you and I will never know about. He was a bad egg. I'll never forget the way he treated you, but for all that I wouldn't have wished him dead. I'm so sorry. This must be awful for you."

"That goes for all of us" said Dennis. Marcie was numb with shock. Adrian was dead. So she was free at last.

"I wish it didn't have to end like this" she said wearily. "I kept hoping that he would come to his senses and I don't know, sort himself out and get on the straight and narrow somehow."

"Well I'm sorry Marcie but I'm finding it hard to feel sympathy for the man. He cheated a lot of people out of a lot of money" said Peggy. "There are youngsters on the streets, dying from drug abuse. He had no conscience whatsoever."

Marcie wandered outside into the garden and looked up at the sky. The sun was just starting to appear through the clouds, casting light onto the patio. Sitting on the stone wall, she noticed a blue tit in the cherry blossom tree. It seemed to be looking straight at her. Looking back over her life so far, all she had ever wanted was to feel loved and cherished. Most of her young life had been spent trying to gratify her parents, who only had eyes for her sister Deidre. Trying to please them was a wasteful and thankless task, she eventually realised. The blue tit had found himself a big fat juicy worm and was carrying it off. She watched him fly off into the trees beyond. Somehow or other she had survived her ordeal and here she was living to tell the tale with the chance of the love of a good man. She made a pact with herself never to be beholden to anyone ever again. This house would remain in her name. It was hers and hers alone. Who knows what the future may hold? Could they all make a go of running the B & B for the ramblers? She certainly hoped they could, after all, they'd nothing else to put their efforts into. Wandering back into the kitchen, she saw Gerald looking at her anxiously.

"Are you alright?" he said, coming towards her and wrapping his arms around her.

Dennis, Beth and Peggie were all looking at her, concern etched on all their faces.

"Yes. Yes I am." she smiled at them and sat down at the table to tuck into her breakfast. Five minutes later the kitchen door opened and a lady in an apron appeared.

"Oh, I'm so sorry," she said. "The estate agent did tell me you were coming but I didn't know which day you'd be arriving. I had hoped to get the place cleaned up a bit before you came. I'm Mabel, Evelyn's housekeeper."

Marcie shot off her chair and introduced herself. "You will stay on won't you Mabel? We'll be running the B & B once we get organised, so we'll need all the extra help we can get. This is my family, Gerald, my fiancé, his daughter Beth, Dennis my brother-in-law and my very good friend Peggy."

Mabel's face broke into a wreath of smiles. "That's very kind of you. Are you sure?" The relief was etched into every nuance of her features. The very thought of having to find herself another position had weighed heavily upon her mind, for she wasn't as young as she was and good positions were hard to find these days.

"There's a lady and gentleman heading up the driveway. They'll be arriving shortly." She said, turning towards the window.

"It looks like Dean, Beth. Not sure who the lady is. Is it his mother?" said Marcie.

Beth ran outside and raced across the grass towards the man she knew would never let her down.

Chapter Thirty-Two

Jasmine was just filling the kettle for their morning coffee when a loud hammering at the door interrupted her. Chris swept past her in the doorway without waiting to be greeted. His face was flushed and there was a thunderous look about him.

"Chris, whatever's the matter? What's happened?"

"Where's Lee?"

"He's in the shower. He'll be just a few minutes. Sit down and have some coffee."

She poured three cups and sat him down forcibly at the table whilst trying to read his face. Had something happened to Linda? Had she walked out on him? She immediately dismissed this as he wouldn't come barging around here to speak to Lee about it. No, it had to be something to do with work, which only meant one thing, Huxley. She waited patiently for Lee to appear. Two minutes later, he appeared.

"Hello Chris. Everything alright?" he breezed. He sat himself down at the table and sensing the frosty atmosphere, looked straight at Chris and said, "Shoot."

"Huxley's released Bunny. He reckons he reported the van stolen twenty four hours before it was found."

"Which is a complete lie," said Jasmine flatly. Lee continued to wait for more information before speaking. He couldn't believe the stupidity of it. The man had just signed his own death warrant. How long did he think Bunny would last once the gang got to know about his release?

"What's more, he's talking about releasing all the others too."

"You've got to be joking?" said Jasmine, incredulously. "The reports are all on file."

"No they're not" said Chris, flatly.

"What do you mean? What's he done with them?" demanded Lee, beginning to get annoyed.

"Deleted the whole lot and erased all the files. It's as if they never existed."

"We'll be the laughing stock of the whole neighbourhood if they get away with this" said Jasmine.

"Right" said Lee, standing up and grabbing his coat from the hallway. "Come on. This calls for a confrontation. He's not getting away with this. Has the man lost his wits?"

"He's running scared" said Chris. "I always knew he was as weak as water. How are we ever to hold our heads up after this? The gang will have us over a barrel."

Twenty minutes later they were seated in Huxley's office after bull-dozing in on- masse before waiting to be invited.

Lee's face was like thunder. He leant across the desk so that his face was inches away from Huxley's. "What the hell are you playing at?" he spat.

"I will not be intimidated by you or anyone else for that matter. Let's just get one thing straight shall we? I'm the Superintendent of this branch, not you. So don't you forget it."

"Six weeks we've been working on this case" said Chris. "All our hard work wiped out, just like that! It reads as though we've just been sat on our backsides doing nothing."

"You can't let Bunny dictate to you like this. Where's your sense man?" demanded Lee.

"He's right sir......" any sympathy Jasmine had for the man was slowly draining away.

"I'd keep quiet if I were you. If you know what's good for you." Huxley gave her a hard stare.

"Ok, if that's the way you want it," said Lee nonchalantly, getting up from his chair.

Huxley looked at him with fear in his eyes. "Where are you going?"

"You're on your own from now on. I'm finished here." He swept out of the room without a backward glance.

"That goes for me too," said Jasmine, following Lee out of the room.

"And me," said Chris. All three of them marched along the corridor towards the reception desk where they threw their ID's down before marching out towards the car park.

"You can't do this!" bellowed Huxley, from the doorway of his office, but nobody was listening.

Dennis loved his new life in Ireland. With Dean's help, they'd converted a good portion of the surrounding land into an allotment. Gerald had made a written record of the entire contents of the cellar, sorting it all into categories, beers and ales, wines and champagnes, liqueurs and spirits, mixers and soft drinks. Mabel and Dean's mother Eileen had cleaned the entire house and sorted out the linen store, whilst Beth and Peggie tackled the kitchen and pantry. After much discussion, Gerald had decided to return to England to work out his notice. The licence to run the B & B had been renewed and they had been granted a licence to serve alcohol in the evenings. Opening one of the rooms as a dining hall at the weekends would bring in extra income. Marcie was apprehensive about the whole thing, having many reservations as to whether they could make it work. The others however, did not seem in any doubt. The house was in a good location and mid-way on a well established rambling route. A constant stream of ramblers could be seen daily from their bedroom windows, which all looked out over the bay. Marcie wished that she could feel even a frisson of excitement for the project, but she couldn't. All she could see in front of her were days of hard work and toil, which was something she was hoping to escape from. Gerald had assured her that once the breakfast was over, the rest of the day would be theirs to do as they wished. The other members of the household would keep everything running smoothly, with only the weekend evening meals to worry about. As she waved him off at the station, she wondered if she would ever see him again.

Sergeant Jayne Hardman was just finishing her shift, having completed all her reports for the day. Her back was aching and she was looking forward to a hot bath, followed by a nice glass of wine by the fireside. On passing the desk constable in reception, she noted the three ID's on the counter top. "What's all this?" she asked. Peter gave her one of his 'looks' before declaring, "You missed all the fun. Lee, Jasmine and Chris have all walked out."

"What? When was this?"

"Earlier today. Huxley's nearly combusting."

"Give those to me" she ordered, stuffing them into her handbag. "I'll get to the bottom of this."

"It's over the arrests we made. Huxley's deleted all the files off the system…"

"Has he indeed!" She marched out to the car park with a smile on her face.

"Coffee at yours?" suggested Chris. "We need to talk."

"Aye, come on." Lee jumped in his car and sped out of the car park practically on two wheels. Ten minutes later they were seated in the lounge licking their wounds. Nobody spoke for a full ten minutes. Chris was thinking that his only option now was to take on the lease for the office in town and chase up his application for a licence to run his private investigation business. His conscience was telling him that he didn't possess the knowhow or experience required to get it off the ground and make it work. He'd only been with the police force for a short length of time and he knew that a certain level of expertise was required in order to appear professional. He wondered if Jasmine would join him. Could the two of them make it work? All of a sudden, his get up and go seemed to have deserted him. Jasmine's only concern was for Lee. She wasn't bothered for herself but she knew that Lee loved his job and had over thirty year's pension to think about. It was a lot to throw away. Lee was puzzled at the mindless stupidity of Superintendent Huxley. He'd obviously falsified the report that Bunny has supposedly made the day before the van was discovered. Releasing twelve detainees for drug trafficking was a grave and serious offence and one that he just couldn't condone. He didn't want his name anywhere near this scenario. The more he thought about it the more he was convinced that he'd done the right thing in walking away. Suddenly the doorbell rang.

"I'll go." Jasmine jumped up, glad to be doing something. Sergeant Jayne Hardman was standing on the step.

"Can I have a word?" she said, switching her radio onto mute.

"Sure, come in Jayne. I suppose you've heard what happened?"

"I want Lee's version."

"Lee, its Jayne. I'll make some fresh coffee."

Chris jumped up and offered her his seat. "I suppose you heard what Huxley's latest stunt...?"

"Yes," she interrupted. "That's why I'm here. He's not getting away with this. I had an idea he would try something like this, that's why I backed-up all the files. Those reports are going back on the system. I'll let the courts decide if Bunny Mackleroy is telling the truth or not about the van being stolen. There's a whole Pandora's Box I can open against Huxley. What he's got away with over the years due to his seniority in the force is scandalous."

Lee knew that Jayne had an axe to grind against Huxley as she was the only other candidate in line at the time of the promotion to Superintendent. Huxley won the prize, but even so, everything that she'd just said was true and he'd back her all the way in court if he had to. He'd always had a good relationship with her over the years and found her to be thorough and dedicated. The force had seen off her marriage, which he knew was probably down to the demands of the job, much the same as his own marriage in point of fact.

"It's good to know I've still got some friends left" said Lee, scratching his head. "Where on earth do we go from here?"

"You can get these back on for a start," she commanded, fishing the three ID's out of her bag. Lee could feel the relief flooding through his veins.

Chapter Thirty-Three

"It's a letter for you Marcie. Beth says it's her dad's handwriting" said Dennis, handing her the envelope. "There's one here from The States for me. I wonder if it's from Candy."

"Oh, open it quickly!" shouted Peggy, seating herself down next to him at the kitchen table, washing-up momentarily forgotten. He ripped it open and started to read. Peggy waited patiently, the suspense nearly killing her. Judging by the frown on his face, she thought it probably contained news that they didn't wish to hear. Had she decided to stay in New York? She hoped not, as she would be so disappointed. Somehow, life just seemed easier and more fun with her around to take care of things. Dennis turned the page over and read the back of the letter, then turned it back again and re-read it from the beginning. Eventually he put the letter down on the table top. Peggy was tempted to snatch it up and read it for herself but just managed to stop herself in time. The letter wasn't addressed to her, so she'd no right.

"Hmm..." he said.

"Bad news?" said Beth, placing a pot of tea on the table.

"She took ill in the office and was taken to the hospital for tests. They've removed some gallstones. She said she still feels like death warmed up due to a post-op infection, but at least the pain has gone."

"Mrs Percival at the Post Office had gallstones. She said the pain was worse than childbirth!" said Peggy. Dennis handed her the letter then turned to Marcie.

"What's news with Gerald?"

"They're making him work two months notice, due to the seniority of his position."

"That doesn't surprise me." Dennis knew all about office politics as he'd experienced it himself over the years.

"Oh, and he sends his love Beth. He's going to write to you at the weekend when he's got some spare time. I expect he'll be eager to learn all about Dean."

Beth's face broke into a contented smile. "He loves it actually, especially working outside on the allotment. He's even drawn up some plans for the rest of the garden. What's Candice going to do when she comes out of hospital? Is she going back to work?"

"She doesn't say. I'd better get back outside to give Dean a hand. He'll be wondering where I've got to." Picking up the watering can from the shed, he made his way over to the tap on the outside wall and proceeded to fill it. His thoughts were full of Candy and hoped with all his heart that she'd join them in Ireland once her two year secondment was over.

Dean was studying his plan of the whole garden. The allotment was now completed. They'd planted just about every vegetable they could think of, together with a few fruit trees and herbs. All that remained was to get the rest of the space looking good so that their guests could sit out in the summer. In the short space of time that he'd been in Ireland, he couldn't believe how different his life was. He loved working alongside Dennis and between the two of them they whipped the grounds into shape. It was a lot of hard labour but he wouldn't have it any other way. For the first time in his life, he was able to put his head on his pillow at night and sleep soundly. His mother seemed happy too, having made a good friend of the housekeeper. They tackled the laundry and the cleaning between them and offered their services in the kitchen as and when required. Things were slow to begin with but due to the inclement weather the previous week things had finally got off the ground, with all the guest rooms occupied. Dennis made a sign out of a spare piece of wood, offering rooms and breakfast, which he left on the grass next to the footpath. The passing ramblers were wet, cold and hungry. "Ah, you're open again! Thank goodness! The nearest pub is miles away," they wailed. After the initial intake, word must have spread like wildfire amongst the clubs as they were now operating an 'all day breakfast' service in the dining room, which was proving very popular. Marcie decided to hire out one of the spare rooms, after receiving enquiries from various groups. They now had regular bookings for the local craft society, an art club, a reading group, knit and natter, country dancing, amateur photography and music appreciation. This proved to be a complete game-changer for Marcie, as she was meeting so many interesting people. Slowly, she could feel her mood brightening and the melancholy of old was gradually dissipating. She knew without a doubt that Gerald would also enjoy this side of the business and she couldn't wait to tell him all about it. Her previous reservations about whether it would all work had proved unfounded. For the first time since she arrived on Irish soil, she began to believe that they could make a go of it. The situation surrounding Adrian's death was still weighing heavily on her mind and she was eager to know all the details surrounding events leading up to Roger's arrest.

"Oh, there you are Marcie. Are you alright?" Peggy placed a mug of tea down in front of her.

"I was just wondering...would you think it in order for me to invite Dean's sister over for a few days?"

"You mean Jasmine, the police woman?"

"Yes" she laughed. "I just need some sort of closure and I can't do that at the moment. I'm not sleeping well. Adrian's mother will be blaming me for everything, no doubt. You know Peggy, all I ever wanted was ...well, I just wanted to be loved and to give my love in return. I loved both my parents unconditionally, but it wasn't reciprocated. Then I dived headlong into a most unsuitable marriage to a man that was only interested in my money. If only he'd shown me a modicum of kindness or respect, I could have born it all much better. Why am I such a poor judge of character, I wonder?"

"You're not the first woman to choose the wrong man Marcie and you won't be the last. It's life. My advice is to draw a line under it and chalk it all down to experience. Live in the present and look to the future. That's what I'm doing. Look at what we've achieved in the short time we've been here. Things are shaping up nicely. Would you like me to ask Dean to drop Jasmine a line?"

"Yes please Peggy. Thank you. Thank you for everything. I've never said this before, but if it hadn't been for you standing by me... well, I wouldn't be where I am today. Why don't you invite Andrew and Ivy over for a break? The children would love it."

Peggy's face lit up at the mention of her son and grandchildren. "It would be nice to see them all. Yes, I'll write this evening after supper." Marcie watched her as she skipped along the corridor back to the kitchen. She hoped that Andrew would find the time to visit his mother.

Lee arrived at the office to find Chris already at this desk with his head in a file.

"What's that you're studying?" he asked, looking over his shoulder.

"The copies I made of Marcie's diary. There are some strange initials at the back. Look." He turned over the page for Lee to see, then continued, "I've ticked them all off against the names of all the six employees who asked for their money back from Adrian and Roger. There are two sets of initials left over. BM and KH. Can you guess who they belong to?"

"Bunny Mackleroy and Kenneth Huxley. It could be coincidence of course but it seems unlikely. I just knew those two were more involved somehow. No wonder Huxley wanted the case wrapped up. He didn't want us digging too deep."

"What we need to find out now is whether they got their investments back. I was tempted to suggest that we pay another visit to the solicitor who handled the court case, but it wouldn't really do any good would it? He was adamant that he only represented five employees. No outsiders. We're not likely to get anything out of Huxley and his chum are we? They'll never admit to being involved, unless we can provide proof, which we can't. Where on earth do we go from here? There's no sign of Huxley this morning. According to Jayne, he's been summoned to the Commissioner's office for a debriefing. How on earth is he going to talk his way out of this one?"

"It's out of our hands now. We've done everything we can. I spent all night reading the reports from the National Crime Agency and Border Force. Adrian's boat contained four million pounds worth of cocaine. After our tip off, they'd been monitoring Roger's movements for some time before catching them in the act red-handed."

"Mantos has been highly commended for his involvement in their capture. He's invited me and Sally over to stay for a few days. When's your next meeting with Huxley?"

"It was meant to be at ten o'clock this morning. I'll go and speak to Jayne instead and find out what's happening."

Chapter Thirty-Four

Gerald had just completed his last day at the office, having handed over to his replacement a month ago. Ironically, they'd replaced him with a very glamorous young lady. Gerald wasn't sure about her but she certainly had lots of confidence and a certain arrogance about her that demanded respect. He smiled to himself, thinking that he'd like to be a fly on the wall during the next few weeks to see how his boss fared with this fiery young piece. He packed up all his and Beth's belongings in a large trunk and sent it on ahead by sea in the hope that it would arrive in Ireland before he did. Having vacated the flat, he was spending his last night in a hotel and was looking forward to a nice glass of wine with his evening meal. The ferry was booked for six o'clock the following morning. He'd read Marcie's last letter over and over, gleaning more and more out of it every time he read it. Things were moving very quickly and he wanted to be part of the growth and development. He was disappointed that Beth hadn't written to him but she never was very good at letter writing and he supposed that Dean was taking up most of her time. As he made his way into the dining room he noticed a familiar face sat over in the far corner next to the radiators and she appeared to be alone.

"It's Candice, isn't it?" he ventured, hoping he'd hadn't made a mistake. She looked thinner than he remembered her and there was a distinct paleness to her skin with dark circles under her eyes.

"Gerald?" was all she ventured.

"You don't look at all well my dear. Can I get you a drink from the bar?"

"No thank you. I've just returned from The States and only been out of hospital about a week. Is Marcie with you?"

"No, there're all in Ireland. The B & B's doing really well. I'm driving to the ferry tomorrow. May I join you?"

"Please do."

He seated himself opposite her at the table and ordered himself a glass of wine and a jug of water with ice and lemon for Candy. "So you've been ill then?"

"It was a two year secondment but I asked to be released early when I fell ill with gallstones. The operation went well but I picked up an infection which has left me very weak. I was on an antibiotic drip for ten days. I've hardly eaten a thing this last month. I still haven't got my appetite back. I must say the company were marvellous about the whole thing. I got six months pay in lieu and they even paid me my bonus. I couldn't have asked for more. The day after my operation a huge bouquet of flowers arrived on the ward together with an enormous basket of fresh fruit and a card signed by the whole department. It was lovely. I gave all the fruit to the nurses, but enough about me, tell me what's happening with you."

"My wife and I have separated, for good this time. I should never have gone back to be honest. I'm going out to join Marcie in Ireland. My daughter Beth is already over there. She passed her catering exams."

"Good for her! She'll be happy then."

"I do hope so. There's a new boyfriend on the scene. He's had a few problems with drugs, but to be fair he does seems to be a reformed character these days. I'll be keeping a close eye on him. What will you do now? Are you going back to the States?"

"They want me back. They've given me a month off to get myself fully fit. I could go back to finish my secondment but I'm undecided. New York has unsettled me. My soul is crying out for change. Do you ever get that feeling?" They ordered their food and spent the rest of the evening reminiscing about old times.

"Where's the boss this morning?" Chris asked, handing Jasmine her coffee.

"He's been summoned by the Commissioner. He took the train early this morning."

"I don't like the sound of that."

"What good is there to be had in all this? He's booked himself an overnight stay."

"If you want to eat with Linda and me tonight, you're welcome."

"I'm on three days off after today. I've had a letter from Dean. He's invited me over to Ireland."

"Go. It'll be good to build bridges."

"Yes, I know. I'd like to see mum too. Would you and Linda come with me? I'm nervous about that ferry. I've got a feeling someone is watching my movements."

"What makes you think that?"

"I don't know..."

"I wouldn't get the leave at such short notice. Why not wait until Lee comes back, then you could both go together?"

"Have you thought any more about the lease on that office in town?"

Chris closed the door and sat down opposite her desk, pulling his chair up close. "As a matter of fact, I have. I've signed the lease and the licence is going through. I should hear within the next few weeks. Look, I'll be honest with you Jaz I need you and Lee to come in with me, old hands and all that. Do you think he'd consider it? I haven't got his talent or experience."

"You'll never know until you try."

"What about you?"

"I'd do it like a shot. It all depends on what the Commissioner has to say to Lee."

Chris stared at his shoes, suddenly feeling self-conscious, before saying, "Forgive me for asking Jaz, but will you and Lee be starting a family after you're married?"

"That's very unlikely Chris, to be honest with you. Lee's too old and I'm not sure I want to go down that route. It's not that I'm against motherhood or anything.....just that.....well, his job doesn't exactly lend itself to domestic bliss. I'm thinking of the long, unsociable hours, being on call 24 hours a day. It's the reason his first marriage broke up. His wife got fed up. He does love his job though. He always said he wouldn't want to do anything else."

"If the Commissioner offers him the Superintendent's job, would he take it?"

"Oh, I should think so. Although, having said that, Jayne must in the running for it too."

"That's what I was thinking. Is he staying in London tonight?"

"Yes."

"Right, that's settled then. Come to Linda's for seven thirty. We can discuss things further after dinner."

"Thanks Chris, I'd like that. I won't sleep tonight."

"Will he ring you after the meeting, do you think?"

"No, I told him not to. We'll chat tomorrow."

Chapter Thirty-Five

Deidre noted the 'for sale' board in the front garden before making her way up the path to the front door and ringing the bell. She waited a few minutes before ringing it again, keeping her finger on the buzzer this time. Peering through the lounge window, there was no sign of life inside. She assumed that Peggy must be out. Wandering around the side of the house, she tried the back door, which was locked. She gave a loud knock before shouting loudly, "Peggy! Peggy are you there?" Standing on tiptoe, she peered through the kitchen window.

"Can I help you madam?"

She turned to see an elderly gentleman stood at the gate, watching her.

"Oh, yes. I was looking for Peggy. I presume she's out."

"She's been gone for quite a while now. The house has been empty for some time."

"Oh. Where did she go?"

"I've no idea I'm afraid. I did speak to the estate agent the last time he was here. He said Peggy's son owned the house and he was selling up."

"It's my sister Marcie and my husband that I'm looking for, to be exact."

"Sorry, I can't help you there. Perhaps if you ring the estate agents, they might be able to help you." He watched her as she trudged back up the lane towards the bus stop, knowing full well where the family had gone but decided not to get involved. After all, it was none of his business. It was the second lady who'd come looking for Peggy. Two days previous, there had been a much older lady who'd arrived in a taxi, looking for Marcie, who she referred to as her daughter-in-law. He gave her the same treatment and hoped they would eventually get a nice family settled there. It didn't surprise him in the least that Peggie had decided to move on. She must have been very lonely since her husband died. He wished now that he'd paid more attention to the situation and visited her now and again, but somehow he never got round to it. He stood for a long time looking at the beautiful rose bushes in her front garden. He was going to miss Peggie and he hoped that she was happy, wherever she was. He made his way up the lane to the bus stop, having decided to speak to the estate agent about these two ladies snooping around looking for Marcie. 'I'll warn him that they might be paying him a visit and to be on his guard and to not give too much information away as to their whereabouts,' he told himself. The elder lady, particularly, looked as though she might cause trouble.

Lee arrived home to find the flat empty and presumed Jasmine had gone off to work. Dumping his overnight case in the hallway, he went into the kitchen and made himself a coffee. He knew that he had some serious thinking to do about his and Jasmine's future. Suddenly the buzz of the job didn't seem so important to him anymore. It was a contributing factor to the collapse of his marriage and he didn't want the same thing to happen again. Grabbing his coat, he headed for the outdoors, hoping to clear his head. Passing through the town centre, he carried on walking until he reached the wooded wasteland which led onto the motorway. His soul was restless and his instincts were telling him that it was now or never. The very thought of losing Jasmine was more than he could bear. From the very day she'd moved into his flat, he'd felt a sea-change within himself. This was how life was meant to be. When he thought back to the days after his wife walked out on him, the lonely days and nights, the miserable existence where life lost all its meaning and purpose. He supposed that there were people all over the world feeling the same at some point or other in their lives but now that he'd got a chance at real happiness, he'd be a fool to let it go. By the time he got back to the flat it was going dark and approaching four o'clock. He'd been gone for nearly five hours! He rushed upstairs to take a shower, which is where Jasmine found him.

"Ah, you're back then," she said, running towards him and planting a kiss on his lips. "I've missed you. Did you miss me?"

"What do you think?" he smiled and wrapped his arms around her, giving her one of his bear hugs.

"How did the meeting go?"

"Actually, I let Jayne do most of the talking. She had a few things to get off her chest."

"Was Huxley there too?" she asked, sitting on the bed next to him, whilst he dried his hair.

"No, it was just the three of us. He didn't commit himself, but I got the distinct impression that they'd had their suspicions about Huxley for quite some time, but like he said, there was no concrete evidence, so they had nothing to confront him with. The decision lies with him as to where he takes it from here. They could just let him go with a clean slate, pension intact and let the courts decide whether Bunny and his other cronies are to be locked up or not."

"What's he like, the Commissioner?"

"I've met him on a number of occasions, over the years, but I can't say that I know him really well. That's what makes him so difficult to read. Of course, we've no idea what sort of relationship he had with Huxley either, but I can't see them being best mates. They're as different as chalk and cheese. They socialise in very different circles, if you know what I mean."

Jasmine waited a few moments before collecting her thoughts. "I spent the night at Linda's cottage. Chris wanted to talk to me about the private investigating business. He's signed the lease for the office and got the licence under way but he's worried that he doesn't possess the experience or expertise to make a go of it on his own. That's where you and I come in. He wants us to join him. I'd like to give it a go but I said I'd ask you first. What do you think?"

"I'll give it some serious thought over the next few days. Right now, I'm dog tired and need some rest."

"Do you feel up to a few days in Ireland? Dean's asked me over. Marcie wants to talk to us about Adrian. She's only been given the very briefest outline of what went on. I think she'd appreciate a chat with us so she can finally put the whole thing to bed for good. It would also be a chance to build some bridges with Dean. Mum reckons he's turned over a new leaf since meeting Beth. He's finally found his happy ever after."

"I'm happy for the lad. We just need to make sure he doesn't slip back into old habits. I've seen it happen before. As to the investigating business, it's looking more and more attractive. Jane would get the Super's job if I turned it down. I think she's ready for it."

"Do you think Bunny will cause trouble if he's dragged to court? He seems the type and I had a very funny dream about Jane the other night, someone broke into her house and tried to strangle her. It was as clear as day and I woke up in a hot sweat. Do you think we ought to warn her?"

"I've already done that. She knows the score, but all the same, I'll ring her again in the morning for a chat. I'm not sure I can get time off to go over to Ireland, but I'll see how the land lies. We might be able to wangle an extra day around our days off. Do you fancy the pub tonight? It's steak night."

"Lead me to it!" she laughed.

Linda made her way into the police station and addressed the desk sergeant, "Could I please speak to Sergeant Simmonds?"

"Have you got an appointment?"

"No."

"Could I ask what it's in connection with madam?"

"It rather personal and it is urgent."

"I'll just find out where she is, if you'd like to take a seat. I've only just come on duty."

Five minutes later she was sat in interview room one with a cup of tea and a biscuit.

"Linda, what on earth's happened? You look as white as a sheet," said Jasmine.

"Is Chris around this morning?" she asked nervously, looking furtively at the door.

"No, he's out on a call. What is it?"

"I tried to tell you last night in the pub but I couldn't get you on your own without Chris overhearing."

Jasmine eyed her friend, trying to read her face for signs of what was to come and failing miserably.

"I've been a bit careless you see, with my pills. I did the test and.....well, I'm pregnant. Oh Jasmine! Whatever am I going to do? It wasn't planned."

"Are you sure? Have you had it confirmed?"

"Yes. There's no mistake. You know Chris better than I do Jaz. How do you think he'll take it?"

Jasmine smiled and then started to laugh.

"What's so funny?" said Linda indignantly, fearing that her friend had failed to see the seriousness of her plight.

"That makes two of us! I can't believe this. What a coincidence!"

"What, you mean...."

"Yes, although I've not had mine confirmed yet, but I'm pretty sure. I did the test and it was positive. I'm as regular as clockwork normally. I haven't broken the news to Lee yet. I'll have to pick my moment. Right now he's got a lot on his mind. I say Linda, why don't you persuade Chris to ask for a few days off and the four of us can go over to Ireland for a few days. Dean's invited me. We can tell them then. What do you say?"

Linda started to laugh too. Now that she had a partner in crime, things didn't seem nearly so black. "Leave it to me!"

Chapter Thirty-Six

Gerald looked down at the small suitcase containing the sum total of all that he possessed. Momentarily dwelling on all the beautiful suits and shoes that he used to possess before his greedy wife got her hands on them all, the crisp shirts, gold cufflinks, silk cravats, leather belts and gloves, not to mention his overcoat which had been tailor made for him in Saville Row during a trip to London. He felt truly ashamed that he'd only got the one suit now and a mackintosh to keep the rain out. Being smartly dressed had been drummed into him by his parents from a young age. 'What on earth would they say if they could see me now?' he wondered. Candice had reminded him that he wouldn't need anything but a good pair of denim jeans and a few sweaters for his new life in Ireland. The very thought of not having to dress smartly didn't sit comfortably with him but he supposed that he would get used to it in time. He had no notion of what his new life would involve or what he'd be doing on a daily basis but he was looking forward to finally being with Marcie. His heart was doing somersaults and he hoped that hers was too. He'd missed her terribly and his life just didn't seem complete without her in it. Last night he'd driven to a nearby riverbank and tossed his old mobile phone into it. He didn't want anyone from his old life contacting him, least of all his greedy wife. He'd also switched his bank account, knowing how she liked using her credit cards freely. Her new man could fund her lifestyle now, and good luck to him, he'll need it. Once the honeymoon period wears off, he was convinced that she'd revert back to her old bad-tempered self for she had a very controlling nature. No man would put up with that for long, it was too stifling. She suffocated the life out of people. When he first met her he assumed it was because she cared but once he married her, he realised that she didn't have a caring bone in her body. All she ever cared about was herself. For the first time in his life he felt free. He was starting a new life with the woman he loved and the future would be what he chose to make it, and make it he would. He'd risen to prosperity before and he was absolutely convinced that with Marcie at his side, he could rebuild his life and rise up again. He poured himself a tot of whisky from the mini-bar and climbed into bed, eventually falling into a deep sleep.

Chapter Thirty-Seven

Linda and Jasmine sat on the deck sipping their cups of tea and eating their sandwiches. Lee and Chris couldn't get leave until later in the week, but were hoping to join the girls for an overnight stay at the weekend. Jasmine was looking forward to seeing Dean and her mother again and to breaking the news to them about her pregnancy. The thought caused her some trepidation and she hoped that her mother would overlook the fact that she wasn't married yet. Fortunately it was a warm day and the sea was relatively calm, so there were no howling winds and driving rain to force them inside like the last time they'd sat on the deck. She had no such qualms about breaking the news to Lee, for he was quite simply the best man that she'd ever met. Yes, Lee was fifty years old and the pregnancy wasn't planned but she knew without a doubt that he would look after her.

"Have you had any morning sickness?" asked Linda, taking a bite of her cheese salad sandwich.

"Shh...not yet! Don't mention the word 'sick' whilst we're on this boat please!" she laughed.

"No, I haven't either. Is that a good sign or a bad one?"

"Good I hope."

"I'm nervous about breaking the news to Chris. How do you think he'll take it?"

"Put it this way, you needn't worry, Chris is potty about you. The only fly in the ointment is the fact that he can't marry you until your divorce comes through."

"I'll be glad when all that's behind me. Divorce is such a messy business, but still we can enjoy ourselves for the next few days can't we? Whatever happens, we've got each other. Here's to us," she said, lifting her cup.

Jasmine lifted her cup, "To us."

"Anything I can do boss?" Chris asked as he watched Lee turn the steaks over on the grill.

"There's beer in the fridge, open a couple of bottles." He took the roasted vegetables out of the oven and tipped them into a serving dish. "Take these plates through and I'll join you in a second."

Chris sat down at the table, admiring the impressive cheese board, complete with grapes, celery and crusty bread. It seemed strange to be eating without the girls, but he knew it was his chance to tackle Lee about the investigation business. He wasn't prepared to do it without Lee's help and he might need some persuading. Tonight would give him that chance to talk freely and openly without any outside interference. The decision had to be Lee's. Before he had a chance to speak, Lee interrupted his thoughts.

"I can't help feeling dissatisfied about this whole Adrian Green case. It was a most unsatisfactory ending."

"We got him in the end though. Well, I mean at least we got Roger Moorcroft. The rest of the gang are due to be sentenced. If it wasn't for me looking in Marcie's diary, we'd never have known about that boat. Surely the Commissioner was pleased about that?"

"You can never tell with him. He plays his cards close to his chest, gives nothing away, but I can't help feeling that we've missed something. There's a whole gang of them out there still at large. If this was to be my last case....well, I wanted to go out on a high."

"Why bother? You've an incredible track record. This case had been going on for years, without a result. That's why they brought you in. Yes, it's unfortunate that Adrian drowned in the way he did but that was down to his own stupidity. In that moment of blind panic, it must have crossed his mind that life was never going to be the same again, whatever happened. Seeing Roger swim away from him without any regard for him whatsoever must have stung a bit. What else could he have done under the circumstances? He only had two choices. Stay and be arrested or make a run for it. It'll be interesting to see what happens to Roger now. Adrian's mother's already been over there causing trouble, from what Jayne tells me. I'd love to have been a fly on the wall during those exchanges." He fell silent for a few minutes whilst he tackled his steak, then he continued,

"Did I hear you right? You said something about it being your last case."

"I said 'if' Chris. That's what I wanted to discuss with you. I'm more than ready for a change. Not only that, if I'm to make a go of it with Jasmine, then I need to think about the future. My first marriage broke up because of my dedication to the force. I was never at home. I don't want the same thing to happen again with Jaz."

Chris couldn't contain his joy. "So, it's on then? Are we in business? What you've just said rings true for me too. I don't want to stay in the police force if you go. We've built up a special bond. I'm sure we can make a go of the investigation business if we really put our minds to it."

The doorbell rang, breaking up their tete-a-tete. Chris sprang to his feet, "I'll get that."

It was Jayne. "Sorry to disturb you. I'm glad you're both here. I want to discuss something with you. I didn't sleep last night."

"It's alright Jayne, come in. We're just having our supper, would you like to join us?"

"No thanks, I ate earlier, just a coffee please." Chris noted that she looked troubled, which wasn't at all like her. He knew instinctively that something serious must have occurred. She sat down at the table opposite Lee and apologised once again for disturbing their evening.

"You're always welcome to drop in anytime Jayne, you know that. Has something happened?"

"You could say that." She hesitated for a few minutes before continuing, hanging her jacket on the back of the chair and throwing her bag onto the floor.

"The Commissioner's offered me a job as Deputy Assistant Commissioner."

"Wow Jayne that's fantastic! Congratulations!" Chris couldn't believe what he was hearing. "You deserve it after the way you've worked all these years."

Lee remained silent, knowing full well that there would be strings attached. He was right. Her next sentence confirmed it.

"But there's a snag. A big one and I'm not sure I can...."

"I think I can guess what you're going to say," interrupted Lee. "You've to drop the case against Bunny Mackleroy. Huxley's in too deep. Bunny will spill all the beans if he doesn't get what he wants."

"That's not right, surely?" said Chris, incredulously.

"In a nutshell, yes it is."

"Well, I don't often give advice Jayne but on this occasion I'm going to. Walk away from it. You've not worked all these years just to throw your integrity down the drain like this. The Commissioner's not the man I thought he was if he goes along with this charade of Huxley's. It makes me think he's not lily-white himself, but I suppose he hasn't got where he has without cutting a few corners, but this is strictly not on."

"Phew!" Jayne let out a sigh and started to laugh. "I thought I was going mad for a minute or two. I'd already made up my mind but I just wanted your opinion."

"But what will you do now?" Chris was concerned for her. "If you turn it down he might make life difficult for you."

"Yes, you're right Chris, he would and he will. I've had another offer. I wasn't sure at first but this has made my mind up for me and I'm going to accept it."

"You don't think he's just testing the water, to see how you'd react?" asked Chris.

"That crossed my mind too" Lee poured her some coffee before continuing, "but I don't think so. There's more to this than we know about. I don't want to get involved. I don't trust either of them. You can't get away from the fact that they both carry a lot of clout. They wouldn't think twice about saving their own skins. Even if there was to be a full investigation, who do you think the courts would believe? No I reckon we need to leave them to it. It's the only sensible thing to do. So Jayne, what's this offer you've had?" He was curious, as the police force had been her life and he couldn't imagine her doing anything else.

"You know I've always loved dogs.....well, Dan and I bonded over coffee one morning. I agreed to look after his two dogs when he went away at the weekends on his fishing trips."

"Yes, we heard about that," Chris laughed, wondering what was coming next. "Yours died recently didn't it?"

"Yes I miss her more than words can say. Eighteen years I had her. I still talk to her every day. I keep her photo on my bedside table." She went quiet for a few moments, lost in her reverie when Chris spoke.

"And?"

"Oh, sorry, yes. A few weeks ago Dan told me about this animal rescue centre in Dorset. The couple that run it are elderly and want to pass it on to someone who will carry on the good work. He wants me to help him run it. There's a nice little cottage and around five acres of land, stables, the lot. But that's not all...," she smiled, not at all sure how they'd react to her other news. "We started having our evening meals together and we've become close. He's asked me to marry him. So...I'm engaged, as of yesterday."

"Well, I think that's terrific Jane, congratulations!" Chris kissed her on the cheek and then added, "Hopefully, it won't be too long before Linda and I are doing the same."

"You're very quiet Lee. What do you think? Am I mad to even think about it at my age?"

"It doesn't really matter what either of us think does it? It's your life, but seeing as you asked, I can't think of a better career change for you. Knowing you as I do and your love of dogs, I think it would suit you very well and I've known Dan a long time. He's not only a good copper but he's also steady and reliable and altogether a thoroughly nice person. Mind you, you'll have to keep him well fed...he likes his grub!"

"Don't I know it? I'll keep him in check. We'll be too busy to be eating all the time. Since Dan came into my life, I've realise what was missing. I'm not getting any younger and the thought of spending the rest of my days alone terrifies me."

Lee knew the feeling well. Since Jasmine came into his life the world had become a more colourful place and he treasured it more than anything.

"So that's all four of us moving to pastures new," laughed Chris. He took a swig of his beer before continuing, "But I don't suppose it'll bother them in the slightest. There's always someone waiting in the wings to take our place isn't there?"

"I'm not going to lose any sleep over that" Jayne laughed, "I've given the best years of my life to the force, my marriage included. It's time for me to consider what I want for the future and ever since Dan mentioned the sanctuary, well... I just want to get out there and get stuck in!"

Lee's mobile rang, just as Jayne was about to leave.

"Purslow. Oh, hello Mike, what's occurred? Right, whereabouts are you? We're on our way!" He threw his phone into his top pocket before jumping to his feet. "Get your coats you two, we're needed."

Chapter Thirty-Eight

Jasmine sat in the small library, which was situated on the first floor at the back of the house, the views from the window giving a good pastoral scene of wild flowers, cherry and oak trees. There was something wild and untamed about it that Jasmine found strangely calming. She'd experienced her first bout of morning sickness and had forgone her breakfast in favour of a pot of tea, which sat in front of her. Marcie was just settling in the first batch of visitors to the hall. Today was the local art society and Linda, being an artist, had elected to join in the class. She poured herself a cup of tea and nibbled on a ginger biscuit as she watched the squirrels scrambling about rummaging for food. A huge variety of birds graced the trees, their dawn chorus soothing her senses. Marcie burst in, full of apologies.

"Sorry to keep you waiting Jasmine. Are you feeling any better?" she asked, seating herself down in the leather armchair opposite her.

"Yes, thanks. Can I pour you a cup?" she proffered the teapot.

"Yes please, I've been up since six. I'm parched." She waited a few moments before adding, "I'd like to know what Adrian had to say for himself when you interviewed him. What did he say about me? As you can imagine, I'm having difficulty drawing a line under all this. His betrayal has left me mistrusting of all humanity. If only he'd consulted me. If he was in difficulties I would have moved heaven on earth to help him out of whatever predicament he was in. Why did he have to do what he did? I was arrested and frogmarched out of the office by two police officers, which left me horrified. I was locked up in a cell then fingerprinted and grilled for over five hours. I have to tell you Jasmine, I was terrified."

Jasmine hesitated before replying, "Don't overreact to all that. It's all routine procedure. We have to follow up on all possible leads to get the information we need. Lee conducted Adrian's initial interview and the general consensus was that he said very little, knowing full well that lack of information and evidence would lead to him being exonerated. We consulted psychiatrists and behaviour experts, who went over every detail of the case. Adrian was a professional liar who knew how to manipulate people. He preyed on the weak and the vulnerable by turning on the charm, so they put their trust in him, believing he was doing them a favour and would look after everything. Once they parted with their money, his job was done and he no longer cared. He became infatuated with Roger, who was the love of his life. Roger is a control freak who has no conscience about anything. If you want my advice Marcie, I would forget about the whole episode. Easier said than done I know, but those two cheated a lot of people out of a lot of money, breaking up marriages and ruining people's lives. There were suicides."

"Did Adrian know about Roger's drug dealing?"

"I can't believe that he didn't know. Not for one minute. Adrian's own parents failed to ask the right questions before parting with large sums of money to 'bail him out.' Perhaps if they had done so, their son might still be alive today. It was Roger that was the driving force behind it all. Adrian was employed to do all his bidding and was responsible for destroying all the computer files and paper records. They didn't show an ounce of remorse for anything they'd done or any of the people they'd thrown out of work. Adrian had ample time to rectify things, if he'd wanted to. He could have saved the company, but he chose not to."

"Why could he not see what was happening?"

"He probably did but his feelings for Roger were too strong. He couldn't help himself. He was totally infatuated."

"So, when it got to court....?"

"Quite simply, there wasn't enough evidence to make a conviction. It was all muddled and after several hours the jury were confused. None of it made any sense. The judge threw the case out."

"I've berated myself for not having read the situation correctly. Why could I not see that his relationship with Roger was more than mere infatuation? I'm sure the others in the office knew. Why didn't someone warn me?"

"Would you have listened it they had?"

"I might have, eventually, but it's of no consequence now is it? I've got an uneasy feeling about all this Jasmine. I don't trust Roger anymore than I trusted Adrian. When is he due to appear in court?"

Jasmine sipped her tea. She didn't want to go into all the finer details of the case because she knew it would cause more upset. Marcie had suffered enough torment to last a lifetime. "He's been deported back to England and is...well, he seems mentally unbalanced. It could be the trauma of everything that's happened or he could be bluffing. Either way, it looks likely that he will be sent to a secure unit where he can be carefully monitored." Helping herself to another biscuit, she tried to steer the conversation into a different direction. "When does Gerald arrive?"

Marcie smiled as she said, "His boat docks at four o'clock tomorrow afternoon. I just hope he can settle here. Beth's talked of nothing else for the past week. She's doing a special tea, Lobster Thermidore, it's his favourite."

"That sounds way out of my league! He's obviously got expensive tastes."

"He'll have to get used to more basic fare from now on! Why don't you get some fresh air? If you walk to the right of the oak tree, you get a lovely view of the bay. It's quite spectacular, even though I do say so myself."

"Yes, I might just do that. Thanks for making us so welcome, our room's lovely."

"It's the crime reading group this afternoon. You can join in if you like. I always sit in, it's good fun and they're a great crowd.

There's about ten of us, usually."

"I'll see what Linda wants to do first, but it sounds good."

"We usually do soup and sandwiches for lunch, it's easier when there are large numbers to cater for. Do join us, around one o'clock."

Jasmine threw her jacket on and headed for the hallway. Hamish was sat staring at the front door. "You're waiting for your walk are you?" She ruffled his ears and clipped on his lead. The cold wind nipped at her ears and nose, but it was welcome and refreshing. The view of the bay was wild and rugged with waves crashing against the rocks with vengeance. She spotted an ice cream van in the small car park and headed towards it. Hamish's tail went into overdrive as he attacked his cornet with glee. Jasmine bought herself an ice lolly and sat on the wall, suddenly wondering if she'd totally misread Lee. Up until this moment she'd been certain he would react favourably about the pregnancy, but now she was having her doubts. He was middle aged after all. Her confidence was slowly draining away from her and she started to feel very nervous. Lifting her face up towards the sun, she closed her eyes and let the wind swirl around her, telling herself not to be so dramatic. It was probably down to her hormones playing tricks on her again. Even so, she would have to break the news to her mother and brother too, realising that she'd need to pick the right moment. She just hoped there wasn't going to be an almighty row followed by a lecture. That was something her mother was good at, being a regular church goer, she might see it as an act of...well, she didn't know what. She could hear her mother's voice admonishing her, 'Pregnant, to a man twice your age, with no wedding ring on your finger? Oh Jasmine, you have let me down.' Making her way down to the bay, she sat on a flat bit of rock, watching the waves rolling in and out, crashing onto the shore, creating lace-like patterns on the sand. Hamish nestled in beside her. She tucked him under her arm and rested her head onto his soft fur, hoping that he wouldn't make a jump into the sea, as she knew she'd never be able to rescue him. They must have been there for quite some time before she heard someone calling her name.

"Oh, there you are! They sent me to fetch you, lunch is ready. Are you alright? We were getting worried."

Dennis sat down beside her, glad of a few minutes break from the back-breaking task of sorting out the allotment. "It's lovely here, isn't it? You lose all track of time."

"Hello Dennis. Yes, it's lovely. I'm fine. Are you enjoying yourself here?"

He hesitated a few minutes before replying, "I am actually. The girls have done a grand job in getting things organised. The hiring out of the hall is bringing in a steady income and with the catering as well, we're extremely busy. I practically fall unconscious at night when my head hits the pillow!"

"I was like that when I first joined the force. Being on my feet all day and running around all over the place takes some getting used to. How does my mother seem? Is she happy do you think? Settled?"

"Eileen's made a good friend in Mabel. Marcie kept her on as we need all the help we can get. The pair of them are inseparable, both being Irish you can imagine the banter that goes on between them all day long. It makes for a lively atmosphere. If it hadn't been for her, I think your mum might have felt a bit out of place. Beth and Peggy are so busy in the kitchen, they've rarely got time for anything else, but they're happy doing what they enjoy and love. They've always got their heads together planning new recipes and trying out new things to see if they work."

"There's a lot to be said for that. Come on, we'd best get back or they'll be sending out a search party for us."

He helped her up and tucked her arm under his, taking Hamish's lead, they strolled back up to the house.

Chapter Thirty-Nine

Lee swung the car off the main road onto a piece of waste ground tucked at the back of the factories on the industrial estate. He circled around the entire estate three times before spotting Mike nursing his radio and looking distinctly nervous. He waved them over and led them to a small dilapidated looking warehouse. Most of the windows were boarded up, except for one.

"Take a look boss. Huxley's in there with Mackleroy. I might be barking up the wrong tree, but if my source of information proves to be correct, I reckon those boxes contain the last of his hoard. He's trying to work out how to get rid of it and fast. I'm not sure how to tackle this sir. If I'm wrong then we're going to look pretty stupid."

"I'll risk that" said Lee, eyeing up the situation inside. Huxley and Bunny were sat on overturned wooden crates facing each other and appeared to be deep in conversation. "Mackleroy's awaiting trial for drug trafficking, so what's the Chief Superintendent doing in a disused warehouse like this – having a tea party?"

"Those are my thoughts exactly. I'm game if you are. I can't wait to hear his excuse."

Chapter Forty

Dean was just about to climb into bed when he heard a tapping at his door. He opened it to find Jasmine wrapping her house coat around her.

"Sorry, were you asleep? I just wanted a chat with you and mum before I leave. Mum's just clearing up in the kitchen. Can you come down?"

Dean scratched his head and hoped he wasn't in for a lecture as he'd only just settled into his new life and he didn't want reminding of his old one, which he felt was well and truly behind him now.

"Alright, give me a couple of minutes."

He shuffled sheepishly through the kitchen doorway to find his mother retrieving a bottle of Madeira wine out of the cupboard over the sink.

"Would you like a tot of this Jaz? It's for cooking really but they won't miss a little glass each?" said Eileen.

"Er....no thanks mum I'm off the booze at the moment. That's what I wanted to talk to you about. Sit down, both of you."

"Ooh, this sounds serious. You're not ill are you? We always used to enjoy a little tot now and again, do you remember, when your dad was alive? No, of course you don't, you were too young, silly me." She put the bottle back in the cupboard and sat down, kicking off her shoes. "My feet ache something rotten at this time of the day. I don't think I'll ever get used to being on my feet all day."

Jasmine waited a few minutes before deciding to just plunge straight in.

"I've got some news and I wanted to share it with the two people who mean the most to me in the whole world."

"Who would that be then?" Dean grinned.

"It's you two, of course! Lee's asked me to marry him. We've not set a date yet."

"Congratulations sis. Wow, at long last you've finally found someone to take you on!" he leant over and threw his arms around her, giving her a kiss on the cheek.

"Are you sure about this Jasmine? He's a good few years older...." said her mother.

"Yes mum I'm sure. Quite sure. That's not all actually. I've just discovered that I'm pregnant. Lee doesn't know yet, I've not told him and it's not the reason we're getting married. It's definitely not a shotgun wedding. I'd already agreed to marry him before I knew I was expecting." She held her breath, awaiting the lecture which was sure to follow. There was no turning back now.

Her mother's face lit up, creasing into smiles."Oh Jaz! My first grandchild! I'd quite given up hope. Oh love, I'm delighted. If Lee makes you happy then that's good enough for me. When were you going to break the news to him?"

"This weekend but he's busy on a case and can't come over just yet."

"Take some time off. Phone in sick and stay with us a bit longer. Marcie won't mind a bit."

"I'm tempted actually. I'm so tired mum."

"What will you do about your job? Will you stay in the force after the baby's born?" Dean asked, filling the kettle and setting it to boil.

"There are big developments afoot there actually. It all depends how things pan out but I've got another option which I'm considering."

Placing the teapot on the table, Dean set out the mugs. "We'll celebrate with a cup of cha." He was silent for a few minutes whilst he poured out the tea before deciding to come clean about the stash of money from the caravan. It was lying heavily on his mind and he wanted to be rid of it, wondering if it would be best to just hand the whole lot over to his sister to take to the police station. She could make up any story she liked as to where it had come from. Having the money in his bedroom was proving to be too much of a temptation, not that he'd ever go back on the drugs as he was determined to stay clean, more for Beth's sake than his own. The thought of losing her would be the end of him. He knew that for a fact.

"There's something I want to get off my chest too."

"Dean, you've not been up to anything have you?" His mother's face suddenly took on a haunted look.

He spent the next hour telling them both about his visit to the caravan site with Billy, leaving no stone unturned, right up until the explosion which wrecked the caravan and almost blew him to pieces in the process. His mother was horrified but held her tongue. She was just glad that her precious son had survived and was here to tell the tale.

"Dean, you need to get rid of that stash of money." Jasmine couldn't believe the stupidity of her brother but knew that he was in the throes of drugs and not in his right mind when all that was going on. "You do realise that if the police decide to do a raid on this place and that money was found on the premises, Marcie would go straight to prison. She stood trial remember. They'd assume she was guilty after all, even though she was exonerated due to lack of hard evidence. They wouldn't hesitate and if Bunny Mackleroy goes down he'll name everyone that was involved and that includes you."

"Good grief Jaz what are you saying? Do I need to disappear? I thought the case was now closed. What do I do? You've got to help me, I'm scared. Did anyone follow you over here on the ferry? If the gang come after me, I'm well and truly finished." He was starting to sweat and turned pale.

"Roger's awaiting trial, so the case is still ongoing I'm afraid. Some of the gang are under arrest. They'll stand trial in due course. Roger's case got deferred due to health issues. He's not the sort of person to take the blame for anything. As to anyone following me over here, it wouldn't surprise me one little bit. Who else knows about this money?"

"Nobody."

"Not even Beth?"

"Especially not Beth. I did toy with the idea of explaining it all to her but thought better of it. What do I do Jaz? Mum?" His eyes darting form his mother to his sister.

"Don't look at me son. What do you reckon Jaz?"

"Time isn't on our side, we need to act fast. We'll discuss it in the morning after breakfast."

"I'll never forgive myself for lashing out at you like that Jaz. It's haunted me ever since. It was only after you'd left that I realised I needed to sort myself out. I'm truly sorry, really I am. I was terrified of the gang you see. They threatened me. I truly believe they'd have killed me."

"Bury it. It's all in the past now. We must look to the future. I just wish Lee were here, he'd know what to do. I'll ring him tonight and ask him when he's coming over. If he can't make it then we'll have to think of something between us. In the meantime, make sure that money is well hidden where nobody will find it."

"How much money are we talking about here?" his mother asked. "I could do with a few new clothes and of course I've only got my little pension to survive on…"

"Mum! We'll discuss it in the morning after I've had a good think, in the meantime, not a word to anyone about this. Promise me…?"

"Of course dear, sorry, I don't know what came over me. I got carried away with myself for a moment or two. Pay no heed to me I'm just a silly old lady."

"You are nothing of the kind. Now come on, let's get to our beds." Jasmine collected the cups and the teapot and took them over to the sink. Dean's news had shaken her and she wasn't sure how to handle it. She wished that Lee had been able to make it. He had a way of looking at things and solving problems better than anyone else she knew. That's what years of experience in the force did for you she supposed.

Linda was already asleep by the time Jasmine slipped under the covers. She noted the bucket standing on a newspaper by the side of the bed and wondered if her friend was feeling as rough as she had been these past few days. The sheets felt soothingly cool against her skin as she lay back staring up at the ceiling. Despite her troubled thoughts, she was asleep within minutes.

Chapter Forty-One

Lee showered and dressed in record time. He'd overslept again for the third day in a row. Jasmine was the early riser and he'd got out of the habit of setting his alarm clock. He wasn't looking forward to this morning's meeting with the Commissioner, which was scheduled for ten o'clock. Making his way down to the kitchen, his body felt as heavy as lead. He'd stayed up late last night typing his final report together with his letter of resignation. What a fiasco last night had turned into, but at least this way he could leave with his record intact and a full pension, which was all he wanted. He and Mike were just about to break into the warehouse and find out what Huxley was about, when the Commissioner arrived and ordered them to let him deal with it. He would certainly have something to say about that in the meeting this morning and after all his years in the force, he was going to make sure he left with a clean slate. Mike was livid and felt as though the wind had been knocked out of his sails and wanted to know how the Commissioner had found out so quickly. Had someone at the station tipped him off? There were dark forces operating under his very nose and he didn't like it. Lee was going to make sure his efforts were recognised. It was the least he could do for the lad as a parting shot. Mike was right, there was no way the Commissioner could have know about this if he hadn't been tipped off by someone at the station. Someone was feeding him information about everything that was going on. It was like working for the Mafia and he was glad to be going,

Chapter Forty-Two

Superintendent Kenneth Huxley was seething at the amount of staff handing in their resignation, leaving him without any experience in the force. He blamed DI Lee Purslow for this. Within the week, after accepting Purslow's resignation, he'd lost Sergeant Jane Hardman, Constable Christopher Potter, Constable Daniel Denny and Sergeant Jasmine Simmonds. They were the backbone of his team. He relied on their dependability, integrity and experience. What a mess. Agreeing to the meeting with Bunny at his warehouse had been a huge mistake and one he regretted. Bunny was threatening to reveal everything if he didn't get him exonerated. His only hope was that the Commissioner would treat his threats as incoherent ramblings of a man thwarted in his hour of need. If proof were needed, it could be found and Huxley was well aware of this. The Commissioner himself wasn't squeaky clean but who would the courts believe when it all came out, as it inevitably would? Why on earth hadn't he taken Lee Purslow's advice and cut and run when he had the chance? He'd made things ten times worse for himself by agreeing to help Bunny as a last and final act of mercy. He was in it up to his neck and could see no way out now. He jumped in his car and drove home with a pounding headache. As he pulled up in the driveway a wave of nausea washed over him and he was sweating profusely. He really didn't feel good. His wife met him in the hallway.

"I expected you an hour ago Ken, where have you been? I'll get your supper organised."

"No, don't bother, I don't want anything. I don't feel good. I'm going up to bed."

Before he had chance to mount the stairs he double over with chest pains and hit the floor. The ambulance arrived twenty minutes later but he was already dead.

Chapter Forty-Three

Gerald arrived early the following morning with Candice in tow, just as Jasmine called the whole family into a meeting before breakfast. Dean's confession about the money was still on her mind. Several issues came to light during their discussion. Firstly, Gerald asked Marcie if she was happy with the way things had turned out and if she wanted to continue with things as they were. After much contemplation she admitted that it wasn't what she had in mind for her future but had enjoyed meeting all the ramblers and club members. She couldn't exactly class them as friends but they were good company. Dean admitted to feeling restless and unsettled. Beth and Peggy were feeling under pressure as the breakfasts and lunches were hectic. Dennis suddenly felt the sand shifting from under his feet. He looked across the kitchen table to where Candice was sat and tried to read her thoughts.

"Don't worry, I'm not going anywhere without you Dennis." She beamed at him, her green eyes sparkling like diamonds.

"Dean and I are a team. I'm not going anywhere without him," Beth declared, taking hold of his hand.

"I hope I'm going to be included in your future plans," wailed Mabel, suddenly feeling panic stricken at being left stranded. She looked across at Dean and Eileen, hoping for reassurance from her new found friend. She wasn't disappointed.

"Yes, we're a team too. We're staying together, also I want to be nearer to you Jaz, especially now. I want to be part of my grandchildren's lives."

"I think we're all getting a bit carried away with ourselves here," said Marcie, placing her arm around Peggy's shoulders. "Whatever we decide, I vote that we all stay together. I can't lose any of you now."

There followed a loud chorus of "Here, here!"

"We'd better start the breakfasts," announced Marcie. "We'll talk again later once it's quietened down a bit. Meanwhile, I'll get my thinking cap on and see what I can come up with."

After seventy two hours in police custody, Bunny was released, on Huxley's orders. He'd undergone intense interrogation but revealed nothing of any consequence. He sauntered out of his cell with a swagger and a spring in his step, knowing very well that if Huxley didn't want to ruin his illustrious career spanning fifty years, he'd have to get him off all charges. As he entered the high street, he resisted the urge to celebrate his freedom in the pub and made his way home. He hadn't felt this good about life in a long while. Putting his key in the lock, he stepped over the mountain of mail on the hall carpet and made his way over to the mini bar and poured himself a large whisky. He sipped it slowly whilst contemplating his next move. He'd had it with this drugs scene. It was time for a rethink about what to do next. Having got used to the high life, he wasn't about to give it all up now. No, he'd find some other way to make himself lots of money, just like other business entrepreneurs before him. It was all out there for the taking, you just had to grab it. He'd no intention of grafting either. Sweated labour wasn't for him. He would get other people to do all the hard work whilst he creamed off the profits. There were winners and losers in this life and he was the leader of the pack. Yes sir, he'd find a way to make himself lots of money. If people were impressed by his estate now, just let them wait and see what the future had in store. They hadn't witnessed anything yet. The best was yet to come. He downed the rest of his whisky with a smile on his face.

"Good morning Mr DeVere, the usual is it?"

"Yes please Janice." He took his newspaper and folded it under his arm, tossing the coins onto the counter. As he walked past the pub back to his car, he seethed with resentment at the events of last night. He hadn't slept well. He kept seeing Bunny Mackleroy's smug face. His elbow was propping up the bar as he chatted to all and sundry, as though he was everybody's best friend. Why had they released him without charge? He intended to confront Huxley and ask him what on earth he was playing at. His young niece would still be alive if it wasn't for the likes of Bunny and his cronies, peddling drugs to fund their luxurious lifestyles. It was obscene. He'd left the pub without finishing his pint. He parked his car in his driveway and entered the kitchen. His wife had left him a note to say she'd taken the cat to the vet's for his injection and would be back in about an hour. Setting the kettle to boil, he spooned coffee into his favourite mug, surveying the shabbiness of the kitchen and indeed the whole house in general. The entire place needed updating and the thought filled him with shame. Fortunately his wife wasn't the materialistic sort and was happy as long as everything worked. He blessed the day he met her, for she was undoubtedly the best thing that had ever happened to him. Settling himself by the fireside in the lounge, he sipped his coffee and opened his newspaper. He nearly choked when he saw the headlines on the front page. He read the article three times just to make sure his mind wasn't playing tricks on him. The hair on the back of his neck stood on end and his scalp began to tingle. Huxley was dead, natural causes, a heart attack at his home last night. He placed the paper down on his lap, a slow realisation permeating his soul. Bunny's world was about to unravel. His lifelong friend in the force couldn't save him now.

Lee was ten minutes late by the time he arrived at the station for his meeting with The Commissioner. Jayne intercepted him in the corridor just as he was about to enter the main interview room. "You don't need to rush, he's not here."

"Oh, is the meeting cancelled then? Has there been an emergency?"

"You could say that," said Jayne. "Come in here a minute whilst I update you." She motioned for him to follow her into a smaller side room. She sat down in one of the chairs and motioned for him to sit in the chair on the opposite side of the desk.

"What's occurred?" asked Lee.

"Huxley's dead."

Lee was too shocked to speak. Had one of the drugs gang finally caught up with him? Had Bunny finally snapped and lost his temper?

"It's not what you're thinking. It was natural causes. He keeled over at home. He had a massive coronary and died instantly."

Lee ran his hands through his hair, suddenly thinking of Huxley's poor wife who had been so excited at moving into the new house near to her parents.

"I'm very sorry to hear that, truly I am."

"That's not all. Bunny Mackleroy's in the cells. He was arrested and brought in last night. The Commissioner has been served with a formal notice, allegations of gross misconduct and dishonesty. He's facing investigative proceedings and is suspended."

Lee stared at her in disbelief. After all these years, his past had finally caught up with him but knowing full well that he could still wriggle off the hook. Of course, he'll deny everything. Suspension didn't necessarily mean conviction, but undoubtedly his career as Commissioner was over, at least for the time being.

"Well that puts a different slant on things."

"Doesn't it just? Bunny's determined to take everyone else down with him, naming everyone he was in contact with. That includes Jasmine's brother Dean, so you'd better warn him. Superintendent Paisley is here to speak to you. She's been seconded from one of the other branches to stand in for The Commissioner."

"Give me a minute whilst I ring Jasmine," he said, dashing out into the corridor.

Chapter Forty-Four

"The police are here again," announced Brian, to no-one in particular. They'd called twice already that week, wanting to talk to Dean Simmonds. "They've got a warrant to search the premises and grounds,"

"Well good luck with that," barked Norma. "No mean task with a place this size. How many of them are there?"

"There's just the two of them."

"Good grief, it gets worse. Is that all they could spare?"

"I must admit, I'm not at all happy about any of this but what can we do?"

"Nothing let them get on with it."

"What if they find something?" asked Janice, suddenly feeling nervous. "Will we all be arrested?"

"I've no idea what it is they're looking for, they won't say, but they can't arrest all of us. The Ramblers have over a thousand members now and as we've formed a co-operative, we're all joint owners of this place. Show them in Brian, the sooner we get this over with the better," said Norma, sounding more confident than she actually felt.

"How on earth are we to search a place this size boss? It'll take us a week," said the young constable, not relishing the enormous task awaiting them.

"We do one room at a time lad," said the inspector. He marched through the door without waiting to be invited in. Brian met them in the hallway.

"Where do you wish to start gentlemen?"

"The bedrooms," barked the inspector, brushing past Brian and marching upstairs without a backward glance. Brian watched the young constable trailing in his wake and actually felt sorry for the lad. He knew the bedrooms were all empty as the previous occupants had only just vacated the premises.

"Where are they?" asked Janice, looking over Brian's shoulder.

"They've gone upstairs."

"They won't find anything there, the bedrooms are all empty," assured Norma. "They'll be back down within the half hour. I'll get the coffee ready."

"I say, they won't start digging up the garden will they?" asked Brian, getting more anxious by the minute. The inspector's brusque manner had unnerved him, but he supposed he was only doing his job and couldn't afford the niceties of politeness in these circumstances; after all, they were probably all suspects in the eyes of the law. He just wanted to be better informed about what was going on.

"They might just do that if they don't find what it is they're looking for," advised Janice, with no real conviction that she was right. "You don't think its drugs do you? I mean, what else could it be? Or large sums of money perhaps? Marcie was released without charge after the court case wasn't she? Knowing her as we do, she wouldn't do such a thing, she really wouldn't."

"I agree," said Norma. "She's a gentle soul. I'm good at character reading."

Brian laughed, "That's your twenty years as a prison warder speaking. I suppose when you're surrounded by criminals on a daily basis, you begin to understand how they think and behave."

"Spot on!"

"I'm really nervous," said Janice. "I won't settle until they're off the premises. I'm not unpacking my stuff until they've gone for good. They're not rifling through my things. I'm keeping my case in the car boot."

"They'll search that as well, if they're thorough. We're all under suspicion. Don't fret Janice, we're innocent remember. Whatever's gone on before we arrived is no concern of ours," assured Norma.

"It might be our concern if they find something on the premises," Brian said, beginning to feel distinctly uncomfortable.

"Where do we stand re the law, if they do find something?" asked Janice innocently. "OK so we convince them we know nothing about it, but it's still on our premises and as we are the owners..."

"Let's not jump the gun. I suggest we just wait it out. I'll put the kettle on. We'll drown our sorrows with a restorative cup of tea," laughed Norma, her jovial manner masking the truth of the matter in as much as Janice could be right.

"Surely they would have taken it with them wouldn't they?" added Janice. "I mean, you wouldn't leave it here for the police to find would you? In all honesty, if there was something, and I say 'if' then I can't see them leaving it here, but maybe they intended to come back for it once all the hoo-ha has died down."

Brian merely nodded and flopped into the nearest chair to wait it out. There was no point in starting any jobs if they were all going to be carted off to the nearest police cell. An hour passed before Norma said "Brian, go up and ask our guests if they'd like a cup of tea or coffee."

He found them in the main bedroom, looking forlorn and careworn.

"Norma has asked if you'd like some refreshment."

"Yes please." chipped the young constable, without looking up from the wardrobe he was rifling through.

"Get on with your work lad!" barked the sergeant.

"Well I'm having one. He'll have one too. Thank you. We'll be down shortly," He turned to Brian and smiled. "We'd like another word actually."

"Very good sir." He turned and made his way downstairs. "They're coming down. They want to talk to us again."

"I'll leave you and Norma to do all the talking," said Janice. "I'm bound to put my foot in it. Not that we've anything to hide."

Upstairs, the sergeant was getting more and more frustrated. How on earth were they expected to find anything in an estate this size? What were they meant to do? Rip up the floorboards? Dig up the gardens?

"We need to find out where the family suddenly disappeared to. It's highly suspicious if you ask me, suddenly absconding like that. Leave the talking to me lad, come on."

Brian and Janice were getting increasingly nervous at the sergeants probing questions, most of which they couldn't answer. Norma however, seemed to be enjoying herself and displayed no sign of nerves.

"All we know inspector," she said, flicking cigarette ash into the fire, "is that Marcie was unwell. She suffered these blinding headaches which knocked her off her feet for days on end, so it was decided, after a family meeting, that they'd move on and try their hand at something else. Also it was common knowledge that she was separated from her husband Adrian, who was demanding his half of the property. When he died, his mother took up the fight with his solicitor. The mother is worse than the son if you ask me. A nasty piece of work that one. As to where they went to, no one knows, they didn't say. They had no choice but to sell up really. She wasn't in a position to buy him out. We had to call a meeting with all our club members, advising them of the sale of the property and it caused quite an uproar I can tell you. It's the best thing that's happened around here in years as Marcie made such a good job of running the place. We didn't want to give it all up you see, so we put it to the vote about forming a cooperative and buying it between us."

"And where did you raise all the money, might I ask?"

"Well that's the thing you see. The Ramblers have over a thousand members. We all chipped in what we could to put the deposit down and the rest is on a mortgage. The estate agent in town handled it all. They were marvellously helpful actually."

"What's the name of this estate agent?" asked the young constable, getting out his notebook and pencil.

Norma gave him the details and refilled their coffee cups, handing round the biscuits as she did so. The sergeant was scowling like a spoilt child that had just been smacked for being naughty, knowing full well that his boss wouldn't be happy about any of this and would no doubt blame him for not handling the situation correctly. The young constable was secretly cursing that wretched Bunny Mackleroy, sending them on a wild goose chase like this. What exactly they were expected to find in a place this size was anybody's guess. He helped himself to another biscuit off the plate and stirred two sugars into his second cup of coffee, determined to enjoy the temporary sojourn before his sergeant put a stop to it all.

Chapter Forty-Five

Roger Moorcroft was sectioned under the mental health act and committed to an institution. Bunny Mackleroy was sentenced to twelve years in prison for drug smuggling and money laundering. After three months he was found hanged in his cell, having committed suicide. The police made sixteen arrests, all of which resulted in custodial sentences ranging from eighteen months to five years.

The police raided the estate in Ireland extensively for several months, after which they had to abandon the task due to lack of funding, having found nothing incriminating. The budget simply didn't warrant spending more money on something, which when boiled down to it, was mere hearsay. The take-over by the ramblers proved to be legitimate with all the relevant paperwork in order. No money or drugs were found, even after sniffer dogs were brought in. Case closed.

The morning after their meeting, Peggy took to her bed, distinctly unwell. It was then decided by all concerned, to up sticks and leave Ireland for good. As soon as Peggy was back in the land of the living, they headed back to England. Gerald booked them into a suite at the Grand Hotel at Lytham St Anne's on the Fylde coast. On the second day Gerald received the alarming news that Malcolm, his good friend of many years had drowned in a boating accident. The boat was left to Gerald in his will. It was the boat crew who imparted the news to him, having skippered the launch for the last decade; they were worried about losing their jobs. Dean, on hearing the news, decided to come clean to Gerald about his involvement with Bunny Mackleroy and offered to use his hoard of money to pay the crew their wages, impressing upon him the urgency for him to disappear before the authorities came looking for him. Within three days they were on their way to Cornwall to join the boat, leaving no forwarding address. Lee and Chris joined them for a long break before starting up the detective agency. As they lay sunning themselves on the sun deck, Lee squeezed Jasmine's hand. "I didn't realise how much I needed this break Jaz."

"Are you happy about the baby? I didn't do it on purpose. I must have forgotten one of my pills."

"I never thought I'd be a father. I'm overwhelmed but overjoyed too. We've been truly blessed."

They continued to cruise around for three months, enjoying glorious sunshine, swimming in the sea and eating delicious food prepared and served by the crew.

Malcolm's barn conversion in Devon had been left to his only daughter Charlotte, who intended to run it as a B & B. Her boyfriend wanted to take over the running of the place, which was something Charlotte wasn't going to allow. It was hers and she intended to run things her way. After a series of rows, he upped sticks and left. She begged him to reconsider and assured him that things would be different once they were married, after which, all decisions would be made jointly. He then became abusive and said he had no intention of ever getting married, it wasn't what he wanted. Charlotte wondered if perhaps, it was simply too soon for him and he wasn't ready to make the commitment, pointing out that he may feel differently in a few years time. "I'm not hanging around to find out!" he spat at her and flounced out. There were five self-catering cottages in total. At merely nineteen years old and with no experience, Charlotte knew that she would struggle without help, so in desperation she telephoned her dad's good friend Gerald to ask his advice. Marcie and her extended family moved in and organised the running of it, offering their guests boat trips around the bay, which proved very popular. The breakfasts were easy and proved no trouble at all for Beth and Peggy. Marcie and Gerald dealt with all the bookings whilst Candice took over the office, dealing with all the invoices, deliveries and paperwork. Dean and Dennis turned the extensive grounds into an allotment complete with herb garden and orchard. Eileen and Mabel tackled all the bedrooms and bathrooms. The work was easy and usually completed by lunchtime which gave them plenty of free time. Beth and Dean headed for the beach if the weather was fine, Dennis and Candice went touring around the area and the three older ladies hit the shops and cafes, indulging in afternoon teas and cakes. Marcie and Gerald did a cultural tour of the art galleries, museums and places of historical interest. After three month's Charlotte's boyfriend returned begging forgiveness and wanting to talk about their future. He knew he'd never settle to working at the barn, it just wasn't his forte. It was decided that the two of them would take over the boat trips. It suited them both very well and things quickly fell into a routine that suited them all. As the work was easy and enjoyable, nobody was complaining.

Marcie had taken to walking into the local village for provisions before serving breakfast to their guests. She took the dog with her and walked along the sea front taking in the salty air and enjoying the tranquillity before the crowds appeared. It gave her time to think and she came to love the peace and quiet, away from all the hustle and bustle. As she reached the cafe, she rang the bell on the side door, as it didn't open for another hour or so. She shouted through the letterbox, "Hi Jeannie, it's me, Marcie." There was a rattle of keys, followed by the locks being drawn back.

"Come in Marcie. The coffee's on. I'm opening early today as it's the local swimming club's day for their 'cold water' swim. The cycling club also gather for their annual charity bike ride. The two events always attract a good turnout. I've baked six batches of scones."

"Goodness, what time did you get up this morning?"

"Four o'clock."

Jeannie was seventy eight years old and Marcie didn't know

where she got all her energy from.

"You're amazing Jeannie."

"Oh, I had all the dough in the freezer. All I had to do was defrost it and whack it in the oven," she smiled, placing two mugs on the table. "All the same, I look forward to you popping in. It gives me a chance to put my feet up for a few minutes."

"Do you need an excuse for that?" laughed Marcie, enjoying the company of someone who had become a good friend over the months.

"It's getting a bit much here if I'm honest. I've thought about selling up."

"Where would you go if you did decide to sell?"

"I'm not sure, that's the problem. My brother's in a home now, he has dementia. I miss his terribly. He didn't even know who I was the last time I visited him."

"I'm so sorry. That must be tough."

"Yes, I cried all the way home on the train. The matron said he's not eating too well, often refusing his meals. I don't think it'll be long now. Take your time with your coffee. Mr Norton's not opening for another half hour. He's taking his daughter to the hospital."

Mr Norton ran the local shop together with his daughter, who had just given birth to a baby boy.

"Just a check-up I take it?"

"Yes I think so. He would have said if it was anything more serious. I'd better get on. I'll open up the cafe. Do you want to sit in your favourite spot by the window?"

"Ooh yes. I love people-watching." She took her mug into the cafe and seated herself by the window which overlooked the sea front. There were usually people walking their dogs or hurrying to work. A large group of cyclists were gathering by the pier.

"How far do they cycle?" asked Marcie.

"It's a sixty mile round trip."

"Sixty!"

"They train all year. They're super fit."

"Phew! I mean, sixty miles is a fair distance. I couldn't imagine managing half that."

Jeannie disappeared into the back kitchen after unlocking the door and turning the sign to 'open.' Marcie had just finished her coffee when a familiar face appeared in front of her at the window. He tapped on the glass and waved, his face breaking into a big grin.

"Stuart! Come in!" She ran to the door and opened it, giving him a big hug. "What are you doing in these parts?" Then she noticed his cycling shorts and realised he must be joining the race." "I didn't know you were into cycling."

"Oh Marcie, it's so good to see you. I wanted to telephone you but I knew I was being tailed by the police, so my calls might have been traced."

"Sit down I'll get some more coffee."

"Is there any toast? I missed my breakfast at the hostel."

"There are scones, I'll fetch some." When she came back he was sat with his head in his hands. "Are you alright Stuart?"

"Oh, just ignore me Marcie. I had a few beers with the lads last night. I'm not used to drinking these days."

"Here, get this down you," she said, placing the scones and coffee down. "I've got some painkillers in my bag somewhere."

"Thanks. I used to do this cycle trip every year until I went to work for Roger, after which there never seemed time."

"No there wouldn't be. They were a selfish pair those two."

Stuart laughed. "I can't believe I stuck it out for so long, but it had its advantages in the end. I wanted to thank you for helping me out the way you did. I would have lost everything if it wasn't for you." He buttered a scone and took a bite, stirring sugar into his coffee.

"Thinking about it, I was still married to Adrian, so technically I owned part of the company too. If I'd asked him for the money he would have refused but I was determined to get something out of the marriage."

"I was beside myself with worry during your trial. I didn't dare go near the courts as the police might have thought it suspicious. They were monitoring my every move and I know for sure they didn't believe my statement."

"Would your wife really have left you, or was she just..."

"Yes she would have! I had spiralling debts. The house was re-mortgaged. We had endless rows. It went on for months. In the end she told me that she wanted to end the marriage. She wanted a divorce settlement that would give her enough money to set herself up in her own beauty salon. I offered to set her up if she'd stay. She never asked me where the money came from."

"I think I would definitely have done, under the circumstances."

"Yes I know. She's always been selfish like that, puts herself first. Anyway, I was able to settle my debts and straighten things out. There was just enough left to put down a deposit on some premises in the town centre. It's in a good position right opposite the bus station. Of course, it had to be redecorated and fitted out with wash basins and such, not to mention all the equipment. By the time we'd done all that there was nothing left for me and the kids."

"Is she happy now?"

"Yes absolutely! She skips to work like a teenager."

"And where are you?"

"I'm in a one of those prefabricated cabins near the big car park at the back of the shopping mall. It's only rented of course. They're freezing cold in winter and you sweat like mad in the summer."

"How is business going?"

"It's slow to be honest but I make enough to get by. I can pay the mortgage and put food on the table but that's about it. And how are things with you?"

"We're running a B & B half a mile up the road from here. It belonged to one of Gerald's close friends who died in a boating accident. He left it to his young daughter. She couldn't handle it all on her own you see."

"Are you enjoying it?"

"Yes and no. It's not how I envisaged my life panning out if I'm honest. I'm not looking at it as a long-term project, although I haven't said anything to Gerald."

"I think you need to talk."

"Yes, you're right."

In the space of a few days after her conversation with Stuart, things changed rapidly. Charlotte and her boyfriend asked for a meeting one evening. They had no idea what it was about and received a shock when they announced they wanted out. They had decided to go travelling before settling down and had made a plan of which countries they were going to visit, starting with Vietnam and Cambodia, then Japan and China, ending up in New Zealand and Australia. They said that an American business man had made them a good offer for the boat, more than it was actually worth, considering its age. There followed a deathly silence around the dinner table whilst everyone digested the news, knowing full well that the barn belonged to Charlotte and she was entitled to do what she liked with it. It was only the boat that belonged to Gerald.

"Well I think that sounds terrific!" said Marcie. "You're both young. I approve. What about you Gerald?"

"How much did he offer you for the sale of the boat?" asked Gerald, who seemed remarkably calm. He was astounded when Charlotte told him. "Surely, it can't be worth half that amount?"

"I know," she giggled. "But he wants it badly. He's loaded."

That night, in bed, Marcie decided it was time to place all her cards on the table. If she was to spend the rest of her life with Gerald, there had to be no secrets. The fact that he might walk away once he knew what she'd done was something she'd have to live with, but one way or another she was determined to have a life, even if it was on her own. She would have a cat and a dog for company and buy a little cottage with a small garden. Things wouldn't be so bad.

"Gerald..." she whispered tentatively.

"Yes? Your cocoa's on the side table."

"Thanks. Can we talk?"

"Of course, is it about the boat?"

"Yes and something else. Something I want you to know. I don't want there to be any secrets between us."

"What's on your mind? Tell me."

"The money that went missing from the hedge fund....."

"The day the computer crashed?"

"Yes. Stuart and I took it. It wasn't planned but Stuart was in a financial mess at home. His wife was threatening to leave him. He had massive debts. He was about to lose everything, the house included. He was worried sick for the children. I wanted to help him but couldn't think of a way out for him. That is until that day the computer crashed. I had an idea and telephoned Stuart. He came down and we worked all night perfecting our plan. By morning everything was back to normal and no-one was any the wiser. Stuart was able to get back on his feet and it saved his marriage. I knew that if I'd asked Adrian and Roger for a loan they would have refused but technically, as Adrian's wife, I owned part of the company and was determined to have my share, even though it was Stuart that benefited. I took nothing for myself. If you want to disown me I'll understand."

"Marcie, don't ever think that. It's just typical of you, wanting to help a friend in their hour of need. You did what you did out of desperation."

"And got I away with it. It could so easily have gone wrong."

"But it didn't and you're here now with me. I wangled a few bob out of the company over the years, if we're being honest. I'd built up a good client base and some of them became good friends. I did deals on the side which I didn't put through the books. The money's in an overseas bank account. There's enough to see us right it things fall through here, which it's going to. We'll buy ourselves a little place somewhere..."

"Oh Gerald, I love you so much! Can we go to Biarritz in France?"

"Anywhere you like. We'll buy a chateau and do it up, grow fruit trees, keep chickens. I love you too. As long as we're together, nothing else matters."

The next few weeks changed everything once again. Peggy had a stroke and died in the ambulance on the way to the hospital. Eileen left to be near to her daughter Jasmine. She wanted to be on hand to help out with the baby. Beth and Dean, on hearing Charlotte's plan to travel, became so excited they decided to join them. Dean said he had enough funds to cover the costs, but didn't elaborate as to how he'd come by the money. He decided to save that for a future day, maybe after they'd done with all their globe-trotting, then at least if Beth decided to leave, he could say he'd lived a little. Denis and Candice also upped sticks and took off together, heading goodness knows where. They just wanted to be together. Mabel was so upset at losing Peggy but promised to keep in touch with Eileen. Within a month the boat was sold and the barn was put on the market. Jeannie sold the cafe and Marcie invited her to join them, much to Mabel's delight. Marcie assured them that their services would be needed wherever they eventually settled. The two ladies hit it off straight away and Jeannie said she'd never felt happier at the way things had turned out.

Marcie was determined to take advantage of everything that life had to offer. The days pandering to the needs of other people whilst denying herself the rich spoils of life were well and truly behind her. It was time to start living the life she was born to live and she was determined to just get on with it.

THE END

www.ingramcontent.com/pod-product-compliance
Lightning Source LLC
Chambersburg PA
CBHW030922210726
48290CB00007B/2037